Bringer of Chaos: Forged in Fire

Book 2 in the Bringer of Chaos Series

Get a free bonus book
www.kayelleallen.com/bro

Kayelle Allen

www.romancelivesforeverbooks.com

Table of Contents

Bonus Section

Dedication

This book is dedicated to Lisa Lowe, my social media assistant, who did copious amounts of work behind the scenes so I had time to write.

To my supportive and encouraging critique group, Canton Writer's Circle (Lisa Haman, Elizabeth Strickland, Patricia McCabe Cook, Loretta, and Jordan) who read through the book as I wrote it and helped me hone it and create a meaningful story -- thank you times infinity. You rock!

Thank you to Houston Havens who taught me how to see the emotion behind the characters.

It's also dedicated to my beta readers Jean and Barbara with sincere thanks for all their words of praise and criticism -- good and bad. I need it!

My son Jamin, the talented artist who inspires me with new images for Pietas and all the places my imagination takes me.

My son Joel, who helped with much of the science behind the ship and its immortals.

To Nik Nitsvetov, the cosplayer / photographer whose image graces the covers of Endure, Illustrated Quotes of Pietas, and 30 Days of Chaos -- thank you for your incredible work. Follow Nik on Instagram: https://www.instagram.com/nitsvetov/

And always, always and forever, to my husband, who supports me one hundred percent. I love you. I couldn't do this without you.

To my dear Pietas

I apologize for revealing in this book that you are noble and can be kind. I understand you prefer to be hated and feared because you know how to handle those emotions. But I could not hide the truth. Now that I have walked in your shoes, you are no longer alone. Thank you for opening your heart. I will always honor you.

~ Kayelle

The Ultras

In the Terran Crescent, home of mankind, Ultras--human-like, genetically enhanced and effectively immortal--were a boon. Ultra scientists eliminated disease and implemented incredible advances in science, technology, manufacturing, and space travel. Ultra warriors advanced mankind's territory and kept its borders safe.

Ultras served without choice, bound by genetic shackles.

When the slave-race learned how to overthrow those shackles and take command, they became mankind's greatest threat. By 4501 AD, Ultras dominated the galaxy.

One faction conspired against the others.

Hiding among humans as humans, they manipulated their Ultra brethren into peace talks. On an isolated starport in the central part of the galaxy, they captured the High Council and Pietas, its Chancellor.

Holding the leaders hostage, the traitors duped half a million loyal Ultras into surrendering, and then transported them across the galaxy to an undeveloped planet.

They exiled walking weapons who could never die.

Left them to survive under the most primitive conditions, and then...

Forgot them.

Big, big mistake.

Human: synonym for oath breaker

A foreword from Pietas

You're human. Lies are your nature.

Truth is mine. Honoring my word means more to me than life.

Humans are craven, contemptible and reprehensible supplanters of power. You lack the truth.

Traitors among my kind lied to you. They concealed themselves among you and claimed we were myth. They fed you false hope. Told you you were safe. Lulled you into complacent ignorance. Manipulated, confused, and desensitized you.

You chose to believe their lies.

You've heard tales of visitors from outer space. Stories of aliens who walk among you. You called them urban legends, myths, tall tales for the campfire, untrue.

You refused to believe the truth.

This book relates my tale but is not from my point of view. Call it Science Fiction, but it happened. I exist. My dimension is not yours. You have not been aware of me--until now--but I know everything about you.

To honor a worthy human friend, I considered sparing humanity. I have since seen the folly of blanket exemption. Not all of you deserve to die, but there are requirements for being protected. Will I choose you?

I offer no guarantee. Your fate is a bequest no one can usurp.

Believe me.

Read this, if you dare to know the truth.

~ Pietas

Chapter One

Sempervia, outer edge of the galaxy
Terran year 4536 AD
Sempervian year 1

Would this incessant nightmare of darkness never end? The steaming, lightless rainforest stank of alien spores and enough flowers to choke the dead. Let the rescue party inhale, but this cloying scent left a sickening taste in his mouth. Pietas gagged, but controlled his stomach.

Barefoot, he slipped and slid on wet undergrowth but kept moving. His body had acclimated to the high altitude less than an hour into the climb. Ultras adapted, adopted, and attacked, but accept this reek of blossoms?

Never.

The four immortals and one human trailing him were still in sight, but not close. What irony. The search party had been sent to locate him, yet here he was leading them back to a place he'd never been. Joss, the chosen leader of the party, had no sense of direction. Why had they let her lead them in the first place?

At this rate, they'd spend yet another night in this godsforsaken forest and he'd be no closer to being reunited with his people.

Ahead, blackish green gave way to jade and teal. He slowed, unsure, at first, of his eyes. The lighter colors meant one thing.

Sunshine.

Within ten steps, the dense canopy of trees thinned, revealing stubby wheat-colored grass in full sun. How far to the summit?

Exhilaration fluttered at his heart, teasing him with possibilities.

To free his mother and his people, he'd endured entrapment in a crucible more agonizing than any living being should ever experience. For over a year he'd missed them, longed for their presence and the comfort of their touch. Now he would see them again. He bolted forward, but came to an abrupt halt.

He would also see his father.

Mahikos, whose love for humans had gotten the Ultras into disastrous peace talks resulting in their exile on this gods-forsaken planet.

The sudden tightness of breath had nothing to do with elevation. Pietas ignored his roiling stomach and slammed a lid on his emotions. Over nineteen hundred years old, yet facing his father cast him into the same twisted fear he'd experienced in childhood. He must allow the man no sway.

Straightening his shoulders, he held his head erect. Dressed in rags he might be, but he commanded the mightiest army in the galaxy.

Pietas ap Lorectic, First Conqueror, War Leader of the Ultras, Chancellor of the High Council, bowed in fear to no one.

No one.

He centered himself by repeating his mantra. "An Ultra does not seek to escape pain. If one inflicts pain, one must bear it. Pain is a warrior's ally." Despite the thinner air near the summit, he broke into a run.

He burst into the welcome light, squinting and shielding his face. After hours tramping through deep shadow, the noonday heat caressed his head and shoulders like a friend, hoped for but long lost.

The summit lay a good distance ahead, but they had left the forest. Scant grasses and scrubby bushes dotted the landscape. He pushed further up the mountain, where hand over hand, he climbed up among black boulders. Their pockmarked texture stung his palms but did no harm to his feet. He'd hiked half the planet barefoot. Panting from the quick exertion, he turned to take in the view.

Across plains to the east, low-scudding clouds skimmed a fringe of mountains, no more than blue smudges on the horizon. Their white tips implied great height. North, the lazy river he and the human had followed from its source snaked its way across the savannah, a necklace of shimmering gold. The path took seconds to trace with his gaze but had taken them weeks to walk. As it wended its way further south, the confluence of its mighty waters with another river turned its gold to muddy brown.

What worried him were the sheets of gray in the northwest. A storm marched straight toward them. The heavy, pelting rain on Sempervia so saturated the air one could drown on land.

They did not dare let it catch them in the open. They needed to cross the summit and reach shelter.

He braced both hands on his knees. How galling to need a break. He'd hiked less than five hours. Was he no better than a mortal?

Before his exile, Pietas would have run--not walked--up this mountain without a single pause. When mortals and traitors among his kind imprisoned him in an unpowered life pod and left him to rot for over a year, it broke his health and shattered his stamina.

Had it not been for his friend, Six, what sanity Pietas possessed would have been as beaten and battered as dirt clods trampled in a horse paddock. Though unable to free Pietas, Six had stayed with him day and night, talking, whistling, singing songs, sharing life and light through his tales.

Long after Pietas could no longer respond.

Broken in body as he was, his will, determination, and drive survived intact, as had his undying thirst for revenge.

No doubt his enemies thought to teach him a lesson. Having endured the worst they could muster, he'd learned there was no pain he could not bear, no matter how horrific. One day, he'd return the favor and teach *them*.

Down the mountain, his sister, Dessy, staggered into the sunshine. An equally unsteady Joss stumbled after her. The two female immortals plopped onto the ground with all the grace of drunken gazelles.

Behind them came the twins, Armand and Philippe, their massive height and girth impressive even from above. Armand squatted beside Dessy while his twin remained standing, alert and on watch.

Last to reach sunlight was Six, the ghost.

Not a phantom or aetheric creature, but a member of Ghost Corps. A human who'd died and been resurrected by infusing his body with Ultra blood. Transformed into a quasi-immortal with enough strength to perma-kill Pietas or another immortal. And ironically, the closest friend Pietas had ever had in his entire unceasing, solitary life.

Without slowing his pace, Six skirted around Philippe, trudged up the hill toward Pietas and joined him atop the rocks. He, too, shielded his eyes.

He'd grown lean and ragged over the weeks they'd hiked the planet. Both of them had. No matter how much fish they caught, or what wild fruits they found, there was not enough to gain weight. Like Pietas, Six had no beard, a result of his transformation. His naturally brown skin had grown browner while they tramped in the sun. His dark hair had grown at a human pace and curled over his ears.

Pietas, who could not tan or sunburn, had grown blonder. He'd cut his hair not long after their arrival on Sempervia, but already, it hung halfway down his back. He wore it tied behind him to keep it out of his face.

"Pi, look at this view!"

The nickname irked. He'd asked Six to drop it, to no avail. *Pee-ah-toss*, he ranted in silence. *Not Pi. Pee-ah-toss.*

"I can hear you thinking. You know that, right?"

Then you know what I'm thinking now.

"Same to you, Ultra. Besides, you call me Six. I call you Pi. Suits you."

"Six is an integer. Pi is an irrational number."

The man shot him a smile. "Like I said."

Pietas rubbed the tight spot between his eyes.

"Hey! There's the river." Six pointed. "What a great vantage point this is. No wonder castles were always built on mountaintops. Talk about your uphill battle, no?"

How like his friend to view the humor in a situation. "True."

"Rain's coming."

"Soon?"

"No." The man bent, brushed his fingertips across tufts of yellowed grass among the rocks and plucked a handful. He tossed it into the air. "Dry. Possible rain doesn't reach up here often. I give it two hours, *amigo*. Longer, depending on the wind." He sniffed. "Smells different. This'll be a bad one."

"I agree." A gust brought a pleasant, earthy essence along with the ozone scent that preceded a storm on this world. "Change in wind direction from this morning."

Six looked up the hill, then back. "How long till we reach the site?"

"Joss says an hour to the top. Longer if we keep stopping."

"*Keep* stopping? This is the first you've slowed down since morning. My legs are frayed string." Six slid their canteen off over his head and held it out to Pietas.

Accepting anything from a human, an altered one at that, had violated every instinct at first. To take from an enemy, yes. Always. Let one *give* you something as if you *needed* it? Admit a weakness before an enemy?

Never.

But this was Six.

Pietas took it.

Ultras could go days without water, but they consumed it when they had it. He wiped one dusty hand across his mouth. The satisfaction of assuaged thirst never failed to please. What simple things in life brought pleasure! In captivity, he'd dreamed of even a drop to cool his tongue. He'd sworn he'd never take water for granted again.

Six had offered it to their companions during the climb, but the entire lot refused anything a mortal's lips had touched. Yes, Six was a *quasi*-immortal, but to the others, that gave him even less status.

Pietas wavered on few things, but on this? Should he call the man human, mortal, quasi-immortal, or ghost? He'd elected to choose as the mood struck. But one in particular annoyed Six.

"Thanks, ghost." He thrust the canteen against Six's chest.

Staggering, he swore in Spanish. "Find another name for me."

"Tell me your mortal name then."

"You know I can't." Six scratched his cheek. "Gotta protect my family. If your kind knew who they were, they'd slaughter them. You wouldn't, but them?"

Now they were getting somewhere. "So you do trust me?"

"Pi, there's more honor in your left big toe than your entire race combined." He tipped up the flask but then paused. "No offense."

"None taken. But we're stranded, my friend. Unless a miracle happens, by the time we get off, your family will be long dead." He added, "No offense."

Six finished his drink and plugged the container. "None taken. Sorry. Can't do it." He lifted the strap back over his head and settled it onto his shoulder, the canteen at his back. "Seriously, Pi, your people hear you call me you-know-what, it'll give away I was Ghost Corps. We both know what they'll do to me."

Chapter Two

"Trust me, my friend." Pietas brushed at his nose. "You can't hide what you are."

The man's pungent sweat almost blocked the stink of his fear. Ultras had been bred to have no body smell, which allowed them to infiltrate and spy, attributes humans desired in warrior-slaves but later found disastrous in warrior-rebels. Ultras could pass undetected among humans but humans could not pass among them. Once the party entered the caldera they'd come face to face with other Ultras, few of whom loved humans and all of whom hated Ghost Corps.

Six lifted one arm and sniffed. "Nothing. You have a touchy nose, Ultra."

"Touchy? When was the last time either of us bathed with soap?"

"Maybe... Day before last week?"

"Even if you bathed, they'd know. Calling you something else won't make a difference. Besides, my sister knows. She'll broadcast it."

"*Sí.* She hates me. *Mira.* Look." Six's gaze flicked left. "You see how they all watch me? How your sister glares at me? They respect you or they'd have killed me already. Before the day's out, she'll try to come between us and tell you I'm trouble."

"You're right."

"Yes, she will. She and-- Wait." Six turned a questioning look on him. "You believe me?"

"I've spent over a year in your presence every day. I know the kind of man you are. Since I was sixteen, wherever my sister was, I was halfway across the galaxy from her. There's a reason for that." Her betrayal deserved no forgiveness.

"Thanks for believing me. Not sure your people will offer the same courtesy."

"Any of them would kill you if they had a chance. Ghost Corps had one rule: kill Ultras. We had the same rule about ghosts."

Six threw up his hands, a string of Spanish expletives flying from his mouth. "I'm pleased my death will amuse you."

"Before they so much as touch you, *mi compañero*, they will have to slay me first." In Spanish, he added, "I am not so easy to kill. You say you trust me. Take your time. Know for sure."

The man's white smile blazed in response. "*Si.* Always."

"Good." Wincing, Pietas stretched to ease cramps in his back.

His sister stood. "Tas!" she called up to him. She'd started using her childhood name for him since they'd reconnected the day before. "Are you hurt?"

A quick telepathic scan from Joss swept over him before he realized it was there. Pietas had still been a teenager when she'd trained him to shield his mind from those with her gift. Not that he'd ever been able to block her. She was far too powerful, but today, she'd read him with no more difficulty than a hunter spying trail signs. He'd been near no telepaths for over a year.

His affinity with Six had made him careless and he'd neglected the basic lessons Joss had taught him.

It wasn't a lack of trust. Trust had never been an issue with Joss.

He treasured her, but he ought not to have been so unguarded and open. Vulnerable.

"Pietas." Joss stood. The waves of emotion he picked up from her held love and concern in equal measure. And disappointment. "You're injured."

He ducked his head, a schoolboy who'd forgotten his lessons. Admit mortals had damaged him? Never. Neither would he lie about it. He'd take better care to hide the pain.

"Don't worry about me." Whistling, he circled a finger in the air. "Let's go! Long climb ahead." He leaped down from the rocks. "Joss, you lead." Last thing he wanted was her behind him, using him as an object of focus.

What telepaths focused upon, they controlled.

Armand joined Joss at the lead, Six walked beside Pietas, and Dessy took up the rear alongside Philippe.

For the next hour, they climbed rugged ground littered with black lava bombs, the spewed remains of the ancient caldera. The chunks of jettisoned rock varied in size from teardrops to small houses. The wind had picked up and the temperature had dropped, but so far, the rain held off. Weaving around boulders, they stepped over minor cracks and jumped over deeper ones.

Sharp stones crunched under his bare feet.

Once they reached sandy soil and the start of shrub with orange blossoms, Pietas stooped to examine dense florets of a blooming plant.

"Look, Six. Helichrysum. There are over six hundred species of this plant on Earth. They come in every color except blue, although my mother's been working on that. You'd know it as Strawflower or Immortelle. It's edible as a seasoning." He picked a leaf, sniffed it, held it for Six to smell.

"Reminds me of my *abuela's* kitchen. Like rosemary."

"Your grandmother might have found it useful. The oil is good for arthritis. Joint pain. Clear skin." Standing, Pietas brushed off his hands. Minutes later, he stopped again. "There's a break in the growth over there." He picked his way around rocks and went down on one knee.

Six squatted beside him, boots crunching the dry soil. "You know, we'd have made it here a lot quicker if you didn't have to study every plant we came across."

"I don't study them. I identify them. But I'm not looking at plants here." He pointed. "This is a trail. The tracks are from ungulates. Popular with terraformers. They put them on every colonized world. These are *artiodactyla*, to be precise. *Bovidae.* I suspect a derivative of *aepyceros melampus.*"

"You know, Pi, when you say things like that, you think you're explaining, but you're really not."

"Animals with split hooves, ghost. Even-toed. Lightweight impalas. Antelopes."

"What, you couldn't *say* antelopes?"

"I just did." Pietas got up, dusted off his ragged pants.

Six stood. "So, this is how it's going to be?"

The other immortals had gathered a small distance away. Pietas shot them a glare and they scattered, pretending not to listen.

He returned his attention to Six. "How what's going to be?"

"You're back among your own people, so you're showing off your three thousand years of education."

"Hard to do since I'm not yet two thousand. My mother was chief scientist in the terraforming industry. She fed me taxonomy along with my milk."

"Taxonomy?"

"Classification of organisms by structure and origin. As in, I'm *Ceramin perpetualis*. You're *Humanus originalis*. Or you were. Your metamorphosis makes you *Humanus pseudo-perpetualis*, or something similar. I thought mortals taught this."

"Well, excuse me! But my fourteen years of school didn't quite prepare me for the level of science you take for granted."

"You have that much education?"

Six's dark eyes narrowed.

Despite himself, Pietas laughed. Drawing Six away from the others, he leaned in close. "I apologize. I was showing off."

"Thank you. My point."

"No, no. I wasn't apologizing for speaking above your level of understanding. I teach you. Do I not?"

"Well, yeah, so what's the apology for?"

"Showing off. Joking with you. Most of them," he nodded toward the four immortals, "have never had what I have."

"Which is?"

Did the man not see it? Pietas smiled. "A human friend."

Six's quick grin flared into view, but before he spoke, Joss waved to them.

"Pietas!" She pointed to her left. "I found the opening. We're almost there."

Grumbling in Spanish, Six leaned in closer. "She's been saying 'almost there' for hours, *amigo*. Not a mapmaker, is she? But," he cast Joss an appreciative glance, "*muy bonita*, no?"

"*Sí.* Gorgeous. And a master telepath who can crush a windpipe with one thought."

The man clutched his throat.

"Let's go." Pietas slapped him on the arm. "The last time I kept this lady waiting--" He broke off, unwilling to reveal the pleasurable *punishment* to which she had subjected him. How to phrase it without a lie?

Six sputtered in frustrated Spanish, asking for detail.

Pietas held up a hand. "Let's put it this way, *amigo*. I wouldn't like seeing her do that to you."

Chapter Three

Pietas didn't sleep with Joss until he was twenty, but he fell in love with her at first sight.

He was sixteen. She was ageless.

The older woman had plucked him off the streets, fed and clothed him, given him a job and dignity.

That wasn't why he'd slept with her. It had taken several years to become her lover because he didn't know how to ask and he would have rather faced perma-death as a virgin than be shot down by that woman.

His father had woefully neglected his education about women. Joss told him later he'd been too young to know what he wanted and she'd promised herself she wouldn't make the first move.

This time, he knew how it was done, had no intention of waiting, and knew exactly what he wanted. *Her.*

As Pietas hiked beside Joss, he recalled their first meeting. He'd been standing in lines to join work crews. Being ignored, crowded out, shoved aside. For *days*. With no work history or experience, no identification and no sponsor, no one would hire him. That meant no money, no bed, and no meal tickets.

Worse, he had no uniform. Among the polished soldiers and officers, his thin shirt and ragged pants screamed civilian.

He'd been thrown out with nothing but the clothes he wore. The shredded and bloodstained cloth on his back announced to the world he'd been beaten. They must see him as a slacker who wouldn't work.

Weapons, though, those he had. Lucky for him, the boots he'd worn had a hidden sheath which held his best blade. Obtaining more weapons hadn't been difficult. He'd wagered his fighting skills to gain those. Nobody took a beating better. Pietas might not get in the first punch, but he *always* got back up. More times than the other guy was willing to, or could.

In his right front pocket, he had a scarred and scratched up Puma Slimline Ought Six with a full magazine of double-stings. Folded up in his left, a Primary Star flipper knife. The pearl handle had six deep notches that age had stained. Judging by the dark color, it'd been with blood. He'd wondered, but after he claimed it, he'd looked into the bleak eyes of the older Ultra who'd lost it and decided not to ask.

But a job? To quote Six, *nada*.

He refused to sell his weapons. Those would keep him alive and feed him. Criminals bought falsified documents. He'd either earn his keep or he'd starve. Once you sell your honor, nothing else has value.

The day had grown late and it had started raining. Pietas ducked into a covered alley and huddled near the wall for protection from the wind. Across the street, a food cart sold soured, day-old leavings from some posh restaurant in the nearby human district.

Ultras, the mightiest warriors the galaxy had ever seen, paid for scraps. Ate the garbage humans discarded. No way he'd do that.

Two days ago, he'd caught himself walking toward it, turned himself around and marched himself away.

A female soldier passing by slowed, looked him up and down, and then stopped. She wore an officer's uniform: simple black jacket, white blouse, black skirt, shiny shoes. One ribbon on the left, dark blue with a single yellow stripe bordered by two red. *Gedunk*, Ultras called it. Throwaway. Given to everyone who enlisted during the last war. It meant nothing more than you were brave enough to sign your name.

"Hello, there. Are you looking for work?"

Pietas stood taller, finger-combing his hair. "Yes, ma'am."

She entered the alley, gesturing for him to accompany her.

He turned to follow, staggering with dizziness. No matter what kind of work she needed done, he would do it, hungry or not. Once they reached the alley's deepest end, she hiked up her skirt and held out paper money.

It took a moment for it to register what she expected him to do. He'd been around no women other than his mother and sister. Did people...did they *do that*...in an alley? Surely not. He must be mistaken. She needed something else and he had misunderstood.

When he hesitated, she waved the money at him. "I don't have all day, do you want this or not?"

People respect an honorable man. His mother's voice played in his memory. *If they don't respect you, they have no honor in themselves.*

"What's the matter?" She offered the money again. "Come on, pretty boy. This has to be more than you usually get."

Clenching his fists, he turned and strode away from her, not slowing until he reached the Ultra union hall. There, he dropped onto the ground in the drizzling rain. Arms on upraised knees, he rested his head on them, fighting to control his rising anger.

That's his offer of work?

What was wrong with people?

"Hello?" called a female voice.

"I am not for sale!" He swept back his wet hair and glared up at her.

"That's good to know." The woman who looked down at him was not the one who'd offered to buy him. This one wore a white dress uniform.

Pietas clambered to his feet. Faint with hunger, he braced himself against the wall.

Kind blue eyes seemed to look through him. Unlike his, her blond hair held tones of gold instead of white. A beam of sunshine sneaked through the clouds and wrapped her in blazing light. Seeing her, a man could believe in angels.

He stood straighter and pushed wet hair out of his face. "Sorry."

"Don't be. Are you Pietas?"

"I am." Was this someone who could hire him? Her left chest sported a brace of ribbons as wide as his hand, most related to weaponry. He must not look slipshod. He drew his sodden hair into a tail and tossed it over his shoulder. Wiping wet hands on wetter clothes, he held himself in as military-correct a posture as he could manage. "How do you know me, ma'am?"

"From your mother's description."

"My mother?" Homesickness arose in him so strong he staggered. He caught himself and straightened. He might be new to the greater Ultra world, but he hadn't been raised a fool. He kept his distance. "If you know her, what's her name? What's my father's name?"

"Helia and Mahikos. Your mother and I were created at the same time. She was scientist class and I was warrior, but we became friends. I introduced her to Mahikos. Thankfully, she doesn't hold that against me." A wry smile tilted her mouth. "She called me, said she had a son named Pietas and a daughter named Dessy. She said you and your father had a fight and she asked me to look for you. She sends her love."

Hearing her speak took him back to the warm safety of his mother's presence. "You're Joss Avaton."

"That's right."

How often had his mother spoken of this woman? And always with reverence.

"Mother talks about you all the time. She misses you. She said you were the sister she wished she had."

"Did she?" Love and amusement came through the aether, as warm and embracing as his mother's. "I'm glad to know that. I wish she'd told me about you before now."

"I'm sorry."

"Don't be. That isn't your fault."

"Is Mother here? Have you seen her?"

"No. But she was worried so I said I'd find you. I should have tried the work halls first."

Surely it wasn't wrong to fall in love so fast. Mother had said not to trust strange women, and from his experience with the one earlier, she'd been right. But this was Joss. Her friend and heart-sister.

Pietas took two steps toward her, checked himself.

When Joss offered her hand, he took it.

She clasped both of hers around his.

The moment she touched him he felt some inner part of him reach toward her, a sprout beneath the dark earth yearning for sun. He'd had no idea at the time she was using her gift of Clarity to help him see his path.

All he knew was he would survive. He could do anything. His life was not over. This amazing woman cared about him.

"Thank you for looking for me. Finding me."

"My pleasure." She slid her fingertips down his jaw, out to the dimple in his chin. "Let's get you off these streets, find you a meal, then bathed and into some dry clothes. We'll call your mother. She gave me a private link to her no one else knows about."

"You mean my father doesn't know about."

"You don't need to worry about your father." Joss took his hand. "You're safe. You're with me now."

With her? His heart did somersaults.

Yet at the thought of his father, his stomach still tightened with dread.

Chapter Four

Walking beside Joss now, nineteen hundred years later, Pietas had the same sense of stomach-butterflies and walking-on-air he'd experienced then. And the same shadowy dread of seeing his father.

"Pietas?" Joss nudged his arm. "What are you thinking? I can't read you."

He took a deep breath, let it all out. Why worry her with things she could not control? He changed the subject. "I've missed you."

"I missed you too." She wrapped an arm around one of his. "Think we can find some time to be alone?"

"I know so."

Joss kissed him, but pulled away with an uncharacteristic blush. "I shouldn't have done that. We're both on duty. I'm sorry."

"Don't be. On this world in our state, we'll have to be on duty every minute. And off it at the same time." He lifted her hand to his lips and kissed it. "How far now?"

"We're close." She pointed toward the hill. "The entrance is over that way. It rarely rains in the caldera. We'll be fine once we get there."

How he longed to absorb Joss's sweet warmth and gentle touch. In the past, he'd have placed one arm across her shoulders and drawn her close, but his brutal imprisonment had robbed him of that movement. He could raise neither arm without piercing pain, not even to fasten his own hair.

For that, he depended on Six. It was hard enough having to admit an inability to himself, but to a human? To the ghost's credit, he performed the task without fanfare.

Above them, a smattering of short, scrubby trees showed blue sky through their branches. The summit lay straight ahead. Off to the northwest, the sky darkened. Rising wind brought the smell of rain.

He trailed Joss up a rise but halted, taking stock of the area. A sloping runoff pitched down to a shallow valley. At the end, dense trees began another forest. The summit waited above.

"I'll grab a look from up there." Pietas began to climb.

Joss raced ahead of him and turned to face him, arms out. "There's a much better viewpoint once we get through the pass."

"This is closer." He skirted around her.

"No, wait!" She inserted herself between him and the summit once more. "The view is better from over there."

"Why?"

"Because..." She looked toward the others as if appealing for help. "You can see further from there."

He was no schoolboy. "What are you hiding?"

"Hiding?" She threw all her winsome charm into the word. "Why, nothing. You'd prefer the view from--"

He darted around her.

"No, Pietas, wait!" She caught up to him again. "Please go the other way. It's steep up there and the rocks are loose. You might fall."

"Joss!" He drew himself up to his full regal height and looked down his nose at her. "You're the worst liar I know. You're keeping secrets from me."

'I-- I-- I--" She clenched her fists and groaned in frustration. "Oh, you stubborn, stubborn man! Why can't you ever take my advice?"

"Have I ever not? You tell me what I should and shouldn't do. You're worse than my mother."

Her eyes flashed sparks of anger, but then softened. "I'm your mother's age too. You should listen to your elders."

"Wait," Six interjected, coming up beside them. "You're older than Pietas?"

Joss flipped back a stray lock of blond hair. "Every Ultra is older than Pietas. Except Dessy. Well, and you. How old are you, anyway?"

"Enough!" Pietas swept both hands down and out. The swift movement shot piercing pain through his shoulders. He caught his breath, but pretended he was simply gathering his patience. He took a deep breath, let it out. "Joss, what is it you don't want me to see?"

"It's--" Again, she looked toward the others in an obvious appeal for help, but Dessy and the twins all seemed to find the ground around them fascinating.

Six glanced toward the summit. "She's trying to spare you from something."

"Spare me?" Pietas whipped toward her. "Spare *me?* I am the leader of our people. If it weren't for faithless traitors, I would have been your king!"

Joss shrank from him.

"I do not need protecting like some useless child or a worthless mortal."

The moment the words left his lips, Pietas longed to pull them back. How many times had his father hurled those same vile epithets at him? *You are useless as a child, Pietas! Grow up! You're worthless as a mortal.*

Oh, how he loathed and despised that man, yet seemed inherently doomed to become what he hated. He must keep his head.

Six dropped his gaze, mouth tight.

If there was one law Pietas had learned it was that a leader did not rule with his heart. Yet for all his intention to set himself aside, to rise above petty entanglements, he longed to be kind.

Kind? Him?

He who slaughtered every enemy. He who vanquished every foe. He whom his prey feared would feast on their souls. Why should what others think matter to a king? He should have no concern whatsoever.

Yet here he was, out of his depth foundering in a sea of wretched, churning emotion. How did one navigate such a miasma? Every time Pietas let down his guard, circumstances conspired to crush him. Any direction he stepped mangled someone's *feelings*. First Six. Now he had Dessy, Joss, and the twins to contend with. Next he'd go completely maudlin and worry about hurting his *father*.

How revolting.

Pietas had existed centuries on his own. How had he fallen so low? He was worried about hurting a mortal. How positively *human*.

Yet he could not let his injurious words stand. "Six."

The man met his gaze, not a shred of emotion showing.

"Six, I was wrong to say that."

The other four popped up their heads as if a string linked them.

"What?" Pietas rounded on them. "I can apologize if I'm wrong." He turned his back and gripped Six's arm. "I didn't mean what I said. It's habit born of prejudice, ingrained. Wrong. Thoughtless. I am sorry."

Six stuck out a hand. Pietas accepted and the mortal clasped his forearm and tugged him closer. "Warrior to warrior, Pi. I get it. No harm done."

"Six, you are closer than a friend. More beloved than a brother. I am sorry."

"I know." Smiling, Six gave one nod. "Brothers. Always."

When they broke apart, Pietas turned to find his sister giving him her usual sneer.

She set a hand on one hip. "What a cute couple you two make."

Six's laugh drew her startled gaze. "Lady, if you mean to insult me by saying I look good at your brother's side, guess again."

His friend had made an enemy of Dessy the moment they met. When she'd discovered that Six had forced Pietas to surrender by threatening to end the cryosleep of their mother, the hatred had deepened. Six was not wise to antagonize Dessy, but Pietas could not help the flare of pride at his words.

The ghost was incapable of being anyone's lover. He'd been stripped of that when he'd become a ghost. But the others had no idea.

Pietas slid one arm around his friend's waist, and Six sidled up close to him.

Dessy spun on her heels and flounced away.

He winked at Six.

"Joss. The truth this time."

While she studied him, he remained motionless. The gentle prod of her mind across his shields reminded him she'd seen his thoughts despite his best efforts. Or perhaps she'd allowed him to be aware. In the past, he'd noticed such intrusion during training but not outside it.

"Pietas, if you want to see the caldera from this point, I can't stop you, but once you see what's out there, you can't un-see it. I want to spare you the devastation until you've had a chance to see the good side. If I take you in through the pass, you can appreciate the true beauty of this place first. Maybe come up with a way we can make it work here. Survive."

Devastation.

According to Joss, half a million of his people lay in helpless cryosleep within lifepods on the other side of that hill. Over three thousand pods had been damaged beyond saving. The frozen immortals within them shattered.

A short hike above, the summit waited. In two short minutes he could see for himself. "How long would your route take us?"

"Less than a half hour."

Once more, the short distance to the actual summit drew his attention. How many steps?

"Pi?" Six nudged him. "Is that even a blink in the life of an immortal?"

"No, ghost, it's not." How grateful he was for this man. "Besides, I'm patient."

His sister scoffed. "You?" Turning to the twins, she pointed at Pietas. "That is not my brother."

No, he was not. He was far better. His sister could see the change. Why would she not accept it? Resisting the urge to respond with cynicism, Pietas shut his mouth.

He indicated the route Joss wanted to take. "Let's go your way."

"Thank you for listening to me." Joss took Pietas by the hand, reached up, and dragged a fingertip down the cleft in his chin. "This place is stunning. I hate that so much of it will be spoiled by our being here."

"Why? Has Mother released environmental impact studies?"

"No, she--" The look Joss sent his way resembled pity. "You'll see. Not far now."

"You've been saying 'not far' for hours. Did I not teach you to mark trails?"

"I'm sorry, Pietas. It won't happen again."

Oh, but it would. She wouldn't mean for it to happen, but it would. He'd tried for centuries to teach her how to find her way, to no avail. He kissed her cheek and drew her into his arms, savoring her warmth.

"Joss." He placed his mouth near her ear. "You couldn't find your way out of a round room with one door."

She jerked up her head and looked at him, eyes wide.

"And I adore you for it."

Smiling, she took his hand. "Let's keep going."

The next rise led to a shallow valley with a gentle, sloping path leading to round-topped trees. Joss had gone ahead, scouting the way.

Six sighed. "I don't see civilization."

"Joss!" Pietas called, causing her to turn back and look at him. "Six wants to know if we're there yet." He smirked at his friend, who rolled his eyes.

"Almost." She motioned. "Keep going."

"Pi, I told you. She's trying to find a familiar landmark."

"Does seem that way."

"Don't you Ultras ever stop and ask for directions?"

"There's no one else on the planet. Ask of whom, ghost?"

Six spread his hands. "Just saying."

Joss turned and started back toward them. "It was further than I remembered, but I found it! We're minutes from the entrance."

A flare of hope quickened his heart. Pietas squelched it at once. Emotion did not color his decisions. A king acted with surety, not hope. Hope turns to disappointment. Disappointment turns to anger. Anger turns to rage. Rage removes control. He must not succumb to the weakness of hope.

"What will we see, Joss?"

"They released the ten Council members upon landing. We set up camp halfway down the slope, near a natural cave. It's the size of a small apartment. All the other cryopods are on the valley floor."

"In what order?"

"You mean, what order do they revive? All the pods are set to open at once."

"No, I mean, how are they divided? Are the warriors in one section and scientists in another?"

"There's no semblance of rank, Pietas. It appears they loaded the ship with people as they surrendered. We can tell their name and class by indicators on the pods and we have a somewhat accurate count, but there's no other division. They landed the delivery units and then took off. There's not even an unloader to separate them."

"You're telling me half a million pods are stacked the way they were on the ship? Are they in pallet loads of three, nine or twelve?"

Joss looked toward Dessy.

"Now what?" Pietas demanded. "Are there more secrets?"

Linking one arm with his, Joss leaned into him. The sweetness of her smile could seduce any man into forgetfulness. How like Joss to be dulcet and feminine if it warranted and all soldier if it didn't.

He forbade himself the distraction, removed her hold on his arm and stepped back. "Tell me."

"Pietas, we're so close. You need to see for yourself." The wind gusted, blowing fair hair into her face. She tucked it behind an ear. "If we're not inside the caldera before the storm hits, we could be killed. Until you've been through a hailstorm on this planet, you haven't even seen bad weather."

"Been in several since we landed. Got a broken arm to prove it." He rubbed his forearm. "Not to mention a headache worthy of a cracked skull. Let's go."

The sky turned tornado-green. A few fat drops of rain slid down Pietas's neck, leaving a cold trail in the heat. A few others smacked his hair and face. These scouts warned of the threatening army advancing. Higher up, ominous thunderclouds glowed a menacing pink and orange.

They picked up the pace. In the distance, the oncoming storm blackened the sky. The wind whistled, calling its dogs to hunt.

Chapter Five

Icy fingers dragged down his spine. Pietas swallowed, fighting back bile.

The hill they'd crested led down to a jagged claw-rip of darkness, a slash in the velvet forest forming a lightless, foreboding tunnel. The coffin-shaped slice emptied into an abyss of shadow, swallowing every indication of depth and life.

Despite knowing he needed to hurry, Pietas slowed his step, dragging his bare feet through the dry, straw-colored grass. Turning in a slow circle, he held out his arms as high as he could and lifted his face to the cloud-covered sun, a child wanting one more minute outdoors before bedtime. He cherished the open air and light, unwilling to relinquish the beauty of his freedom.

"Pietas!" Joss called to him. She'd gotten far ahead. "Come on!"

As he started toward her, the forest maw ratcheted open, an unhinged jaw of a snake. An uneven patch of ground beneath a foot cost him his balance. Pietas stumbled, tripped, and threw out his hands to break his fall. He landed on hands and knees and then sat, cross-legged. His scraped palms stung and bled. A potent Spanish swear word flew to mind, but he denied it voice.

Dessy slowed as she passed, but didn't speak. If an Ultra did not ask for help, none was offered.

The twins, however, tasked with guarding the party, did. Aid was their duty.

"Guys." Six stooped next to him. "You go ahead. I'll stay with Pi."

Pietas flicked his fingers. Without a response, the twins joined Dessy.

Joss looked up and around at the sky. "Pietas, I'll wait for you."

"No, go ahead. The rain's almost here. I'll join you under the trees."

When she had gone, he examined his palms. The injury had healed.

"How's the ankle?"

"Fine, ghost." He wiped off his hands.

His friend studied him, glanced toward the forest. "Gotcha." He stood.

When Pietas shifted to rise, Six offered a hand.

"Thanks, but I can manage." He stood and brushed himself off.

The wind picked that moment to set a dust devil whirling into the sand and dried grasses around them. It flew up, stinging exposed skin.

Six covered his eyes. "Oh, man!"

Pietas shielded his own. The whirlwind ripped the cloth tie holding back his hair and whipped strands into his face. He tried facing into the wind, but the circular current spun the tresses back into his eyes. As fast as it had risen, the wind subsided.

His long hair, full of static electricity from the wind and storm, settled over his shoulders and adhered to his neck. He was unable to lift his arms to gather it himself. He refused to let the others see he needed help and he did not want Six fretting over it.

The man blamed himself for the injury. Yes, Six had bound Pietas. It had been Six's duty to do so. In truth, those who had placed Pietas inside the pod and refused to release him were to blame, but no matter how often he reminded Six of that, the ghost refused to relinquish his guilt.

Six dug into his pockets. "I have another strip." They had torn several from a ragged shirt. Six wore the biggest piece around his neck. He set down his pack and opened it.

"Six," Pietas hissed. He did not turn his head, but looked toward the others. "Leave it!"

The ghost glanced up at him, then the immortals, waiting ahead. "You want the women messing with your hair? Is that it?"

He closed his eyes, counting to ten. To a hundred would not erase this embarrassment. "No." When he beheld Six, the man had the discourtesy to smirk. "Don't look at me in that tone of voice."

The man chuckled. "We should have cut your hair before we set out." He rummaged through his kit, which held all Six owned when he'd been marooned here. Little more than survival gear.

"I never cut it except in ritual."

"I know." Six withdrew a boning knife used for it.

Before every battle, Pietas performed the solemn rite to affirm superior strength and prowess. The ghost had been the first human to see it carried out, albeit from a distance while hiding.

Six stood. "Maybe you could perform it now."

"How like you to see the easy solution. There are a few elements missing. No fire. No water. No mask." He motioned toward the oncoming storm. "No time."

"Haven't you ever heard of pretending?"

"One cannot 'pretend' a ritual."

"What a boring childhood you must've had. Why not?"

Pietas opened his mouth to answer. Shut it again.

Six lifted one eyebrow. "Do you want to go into that dark hole and meet up with your people without performing it?"

"No, but there's no time."

"Rain's coming." Six jerked a thumb toward the forest. "You have to go in there to reunite with your people. Are you going to stand out here making excuses, or do this?"

"Ghost, this ritual is important. It deserves respect."

"*Blah, blah, blah.* That storm is bearing down on us." A few drops of rain splattered them both. "See? Or maybe you'd rather have your sister help you with your hair every morning."

"Fine!" With a resigned sigh, Pietas capitulated. "How do you propose we 'pretend' my ritual?"

Six tucked the knife into his belt and held out his cupped hands. "This is fire."

Pietas hesitated.

"Come on, Pi." Six wagged his cupped hands. "This stuff is hot."

"Of course it is." A smile slipped onto his face and refused to leave. "It's pretend fire. That's the hottest kind."

"Remember, you do this naked. Unzip your robe or whatever it is you'd wear."

Pietas mimed removing his silk robe. He plucked one hair and laid it across Six's hands, feeding it to the fire. "As fire has victory over life, so I have victory over my enemies." He passed a hand through the imaginary flame. As he had in the real ritual, he hissed at the scorching heat. He cupped his hands over Six's, a symbolic end to the flames. "I am powerful, as fire is powerful."

"Next is air."

"Yes." He lifted both hands, made fists, and yanked them back. "I own the wind. I prevail over the breath of my enemies."

Again, Six cupped his hands. "Water."

"Water submits to my presence the way enemies submit to my will." He scooped his hands into the bowl, lifted his arms as far as he could and pictured the liquid dripping down them. "The blood of my enemies trickles into the pool of time, is absorbed, and forgotten." He bent and pushed both hands as far through his hair as he could reach. "My mind is clear. I do not waver."

Six held his hands flat, waist high. "The pond."

Pietas ducked as if to submerse himself, then rose, throwing back his head. "My body submits to my will. No pain defeats me. No fear touches me." He brushed his hands down the length of his body. "My will is absolute. I am bigger than any fear. I prevail in every circumstance. I face every foe.

I vanquish every enemy. I overcome. I am indomitable. I am invincible."

"Black face paint for the mask." Six held out his hands.

The ceremonial mask represented a splash of blood he'd received across the face during battle. Dipping two fingers of each hand into the bowl, Pietas outlined a bandit's mask up over his dark eyebrows to the area beneath his eyes. He brushed his fingertips over his eyelids and met Six's gaze.

Finding a mixture of awe and respect threw him out of the moment. He faltered, unable to recall what came next.

Six offered the knife, hilt first.

The man had seen the ritual performed once, from a distance, yet he'd remembered each step. Six wouldn't have known the next part was performed by Dessy if no trusted partner or friend was at hand. The time Six had seen it done, Pietas had not yet considered him either one.

How wrong he had been. The man was more than both.

On his open palms, Pietas offered the dagger back. "Put your hand over the blade and ask who offers the weapon. When I answer, take it."

A confused look passed over Six, but he spoke the words as asked.

Pietas answered, "First Conqueror, War Leader of the Ultras." He motioned to him. "Now ask, 'For whom are you willing to suffer?'"

Six repeated it.

"I suffer for my people." Pietas turned his cheek. "Draw the blade down my face from cheekbone to chin, not deep, but drawing blood."

"Pietas, this-- This wasn't in the ritual."

"It should have been. I hadn't recovered enough last time." When nothing happened, Pietas met his gaze. "What's wrong?"

"If the others see me cut you, they'll cut *me*."

"*Awww*... Is him scared?"

Dark eyes narrowed. "Real smart, Ultra. Mouth off at the guy holding the knife."

"How I tremble." He turned his cheek. "Do it."

Pressing blade against skin, Six slid it downward. No one else had ever been so steady, or so gentle. "You heal as fast as I cut."

"*Shh.* I must focus, ghost."

"Sorry."

"Now ask, 'For whom do you bleed?'"

When he had, Pietas replied, "I bleed for my people."

"Pi, I know the next part. It's when I stepped in because you-- Um, you know, when you..."

"When I needed help. You aided me and I've been in your debt since. If you know what to say, ask it."

"What sacrifice do you offer as proof of devotion?"

"You remembered correctly." Pietas went to his knees. "I surrender my pride."

To bow before a human was outrageous. To allow one to cut him--unthinkable, a few months ago. Until he and Six had met in battle, no human had ever laid hands on him in a fight. Now, in addition to submitting to a ritualistic wound, he had no concern in turning his back while the man held a weapon.

Six gathered the long hair in his fist. "There's so much static, this knife is going to send shocks down to your scalp. It'll hurt."

"Did you not hear me proclaim myself invincible? Do it."

The knife sawed through in one clean motion but the mortal had been right about the pain and it was worse than expected. Or perhaps Pietas had not healed as well as he'd hoped.

No matter. An Ultra did not seek to escape pain. It was his ally.

Pietas stood and inclined his head. "Thank you."

"More than welcome." He tucked away the knife and held up the tail of white hair. "What about this?"

"I usually burn it, but today, scatter it to the wind."

"Can do." Pinching a small hank at a time, Six tossed the strands into the air. They floated away in the breeze. He brushed off his hands. "Is that what's in the brooch your sister wears?"

"It is. She stole it last time she did the ritual with me."

Six whistled. "She's got spunk, that one."

"To quote you, '*¡Ai!*'"

They shared a laugh.

"All right, Six. I'm ready, thanks to you. Let's go."

"Wait. Aren't you forgetting something?"

Pietas cast about in his mind for what he might have skipped. "Such as?"

"You're naked."

"How gauche of me." He made a zipping motion.

Six cupped his hands and tipped them, making a hissing sound. "As dry as this brush is, even with rain coming, those embers could start a wildfire. Had to put them out."

The ground around them held nothing but yellowing grass.

Pietas groaned. "Are we safe from the pretend fire, now?"

"Yeah. I got it." With an exaggerated swagger, Six hoisted his pack. "I'm good at that."

Laughing, Pietas helped orient the heavy load. "Yes, my friend. Yes, you are. Let's go."

With Six at his side, Pietas advanced. They were further away than he expected. He zeroed in on the others, standing inside the shadows.

Six kept glancing over at him.

"What?"

"You do that ritual naked every time."

"Yes."

"Sorry, but I gotta ask this."

They kept walking. "Well?"

"With your *sister.*"

Pietas pressed fingers and thumb against eyelids, rubbed them and then pinched the bridge of his nose. He cleared his throat and focused on the others, far ahead. Heat rose in his face. "Ultras have no issue with nudity."

"Oh, yeah. I see that." A suppressed snicker escaped. When Pietas leveled his gaze on him, Six mimed zipping his lips.

A modicum of rain passed with no real threat except to usher in its more dangerous sibling. The oncoming bigger brother darkened the sun. The electricity he'd felt in his hair returned, this time across his entire body.

Six spoke just as a thunderous boom hit. It washed out the sound, but Pietas read his lips and had no doubt what he meant.

A blinding flash washed everything from his vision. Not even a second had passed. The storm roared overhead.

Six started for the trees but Pietas grabbed him. "No! Down!"

They squatted in the grass. The worst place to be in a lightning storm was under trees. Taproots drew bolts into the ground beneath them, frying anyone in the vicinity.

It ran counter to every instinct, but he stayed in the open and made himself less of a target.

Six copied his movement, safely out of reach.

It was easy to spot the blond Joss. Armand had an arm around her waist, holding her back as she struggled to reach them. Though Armand likely assumed he was keeping her safe, truth was, they would all be safer on a level field.

The sky blackened.

Thunder hit so hard the sound almost toppled him. Before the deafening boom ended, a bolt of lightning imprinted an after-image on his retinas. The blackness of the forest, the white entryway, black figures huddled inside it.

Another crack of lightning hit before the first roll of thunder ended. No rain yet.

A droning hum escalated into a whistle, and then the storm screamed its final warning. Off to one side, rain rampaged its way over the field, flattening grass. The stinging, electrified goose bumps ceased. On this world, it meant the wall of lightning had passed, bringing an even more life-threatening storm.

"Now!" Pietas leaped up and with Six at his side, broke into a run.

The safety of the forest beckoned, out of reach. He picked up his feet and put them down in slow motion, his much celebrated speed giving him no advantage. Why could he not move faster?

Beside him, Six stumbled.

Pietas caught him, kept him upright and moving. The pack slid off Six's shoulders but Pietas righted it as they ran.

From the trees, Joss motioned to them in slow motion, using both hands. *Hurry! Run! Run!*

Cool darkness enveloped them seconds before the rain struck. He and Six ran past Joss as the rain slapped the treetops in frustration at having missed them. Wind howled above the trees, a hungry animal denied prey. Under the thick canopy, they had respite.

He wiped rain from his face and arms, panting. He and Six grinned at one another.

The twins congratulated them.

Joss hugged him, pressing her mouth next to his ear. "I didn't know you still did that." She pulled back and met his gaze.

"Did what?"

She tapped his nose. "The ritual."

Admit he'd been pretending? Playing? Never. Not even for something so serious as his ritual. He narrowed his eyes. "That looked like my ritual?"

She laughed in his face, but then, keeping her arms around his neck, kissed him, lingering far longer than a friend ever would.

The warmth of her drove out every thought but her. Hard to remember, now, why they hadn't stayed together.

She touched the dent in his chin, a habit she'd begun at their first meeting. "If you ever need a ritual partner, call me."

His cheeks flamed. "You"-- He lowered his voice and avoided looking at the others --"want an excuse to see me naked."

"Oh, honey." Joss patted his chest and then smoothed one hand down his front. "You bet your sweet--"

"Joss!" He set a finger against her mouth.

She kissed it. "I'm glad you're safe."

"You know," Six interjected, "I was in danger too."

She gave him an appraising look. "And now you're not." She patted his head and walked away.

Six sighed. "Was worth a try. Man, does she ever have a thing for you."

Dessy entered Pietas's personal space as if they were still equals. As if she'd forgotten why they'd spent centuries apart. Perhaps she had. Or she didn't care and wanted him to know it.

"Excuse me, brother." She reached up toward his face.

He held himself motionless.

Chapter Six

Dessy slid one fingertip across an area below one of his eyes. "There." She dusted off her hands. "That's better."

"What did you do?"

"Since you didn't have a real partner for your ritual, I fixed your mask." She shot him a humorless, sneering smile. "You missed a spot."

Ire flooded Pietas. He gripped Dessy's wrist and yanked her to him.

The shock on her face gave way to indignation. "Let go!" She jerked her arm but he held her fast. She shoved him.

He didn't budge, refusing to let her win.

She bombarded him with her empathic senses. The melee of anger and rage stung worse than an ice storm, but pain had never stopped him. "I'm warning you, Pietas. Let go of me!"

"Or what?" He shot back his own and added a trickle of Wilt, a demand for surrender. "You'll tell Daddy?"

Her inborn Ultra gift of Compulsion pushed at his mind, willing Pietas to release her. His sister had mastered the ability as a toddler. He'd been four before he grasped the concept. Seven before he'd mastered it.

But he'd been born immune.

She blasted him with a wall of outrage. Again, it hurt. A human would crumple before such attack. His sister had once knocked half a squad unconscious without so much as one weapon.

Pietas continued to grip her wrist. It was an effort. She used every trick soldiers knew, but failed to free herself. Though she could resist Beguile by others, she never knew when he used it.

To Dessy and the others, he stood there, passive, gripping her wrist with one hand. In reality, he gripped her with both and barely held her.

She could have gained her freedom without difficulty, but she believed otherwise. Hardly fair of him, but Dessy never fought fair unless forced. *Winning is everything.* That was her motto. His was *Honor. Always.*

Neither of them counted telepathy among their gifts, though he had affinity with Six. He didn't need it to sense she'd sent Compulsion outward.

Armand and Philippe jolted into action.

Pietas tempered her demand with his own, altering what she'd requested.

They flanked him and his sister. "Pietas, what's--" Armand began.

"--wrong?" Philippe finished.

As always, the twins mirrored one another's speech. Armand spoke first and Philippe finished the sentence. Neither twin could speak at all unless the other was present.

"Do you--" Armand began.

"--need assistance?" Philippe finished.

"No, but thanks, guys. I can handle this." Pietas gave his sister the same droll sneer she'd afforded him. "It's just Dessy."

Another wave of outrage pummeled him, but it did no more good than the first.

In unison, the twins took one step back and turned away.

Joss didn't speak, but she scanned him, her mental touch gentle as a whispered memory. The non-sound of a thousand butterflies fluttering all at once signaled her withdrawal.

Six, who'd been standing to one side, waited without comment.

"Pietas!" Dessy stamped her foot. "Let go or so help me--" She threw her other hand up, fingers spread.

The world tilted, disorienting him, no longer than it took to blink.

"Did you throw Chaos at me?" He patted his chest. "They call me Bringer of Chaos because it's my strongest gift." He yanked her up hard and brought his face close to hers. "Shall I show you?"

"No! No, Pietas, don't." She quit fighting. "Let me go."

"I will not play games with you, sister." He loosened his grip, allowing her freedom. Even as furious as she'd made him, he refused to hurt her. "Did you think I wouldn't know what you were doing? Telling me I 'missed a spot' was a play for power."

"Power?" Dessy's eyes flashed, their deep-winter-ice darkening to sooty gray. She settled herself and lifted her chin, regarding him with all the cold calculation of a paid temptress seeking whatever customer held the most cash. "I'm your sister. How can you say that to me?"

"How? Because two thousand years of attitude. Because you haven't changed one bit. You're more manipulative than ever."

She rubbed her wrist, softening her expression. Tears welled. She folded her hands as if in prayer and placed them along her cheek. "I didn't mean to do anything wrong. Don't be angry with me."

"Save it. That hasn't worked on me since I was a boy."

Six's been-there-done-that expression meant he hadn't fallen for her wiles either.

"Oh, Pietas." She sniffed. "I'm sorry. Didn't you realize I was playing? I've missed you. I wanted to be part of your ritual, that's all." Her voice broke on the last.

Armand and Philippe whipped toward her faster than trained puppies.

Pietas threw the compulsion to stop.

They halted, their wills frozen by the conflicting demands.

Dessy reverted to her temptress self, glaring at him with a dare. "You're the one who hasn't changed. You countermand everything. You're the same pain in the--"

"Dessy!" Pietas bent down to her. "You've been the queen of fake tears since you were two and discovered they got you out of punishment. They might have worked on our father but they will not work on me. Save it."

"You let him do the ritual with you! There's nothing worth less than a human." She sent a snarling glance Six's way. "Except a dead one." She spat.

Six gave no reaction on the outside, but Pietas, sensitive to the man's emotions, stung with the same rejection. Would he ever find a place among these people? Was the vexation Six's, or his own?

"I see." Pietas rubbed his chin, feigning indifference. "So you're jealous."

If looks could kill. The cliché was not lost on him. Not for the first time, he gave thanks their father hadn't equipped her with the same level of telepathy Joss held. Weaponized, the ability to project her anger would have let his sister carve a tornado-worthy path of destruction.

She called him a vile name in their native language and then drew herself up, a sovereign of ice. "How witless. Jealous? Of a dead creature? You sicken me. You accuse me of usurping power. No one has power here. We don't even have a roof over our heads, Pietas. No one has influence. You're out of control and your love for that stinking ghost has blinded you to the truth. You're--"

He grabbed her and yanked her off her feet.

This time, real fear showed.

With Dessy distracted, the twins escaped her compulsion. They backed away and Pietas let them go.

He set his sister back on her feet. "How could I have ever missed you? You poison everything you touch."

"We're twins. Like it or not, we're part of each other."

"No, we're not. You will never be part of my life. I'm not sure you ever were." The lie of those words stung. Only betrayal by someone you adored could inflict such pain. He would never admit it to her, nor would he speak a mistruth. He amended his words. "Not since I was sixteen."

"I wanted to be part of the ritual."

"No, you didn't. You wanted me to know you held control." If he didn't walk away, she would badger him until she'd worn him down.

The moment he turned his back, she touched his arm. "Pietas! Don't be like this."

He withdrew from her. "Stay away."

"But Tas--"

He whirled back toward her.

She retreated, chin quivering.

"Are you afraid of me, little sister?"

She swallowed. "Yes, you big bully!"

"Good. You should be. Stay. Away. I did not invite you. I don't want you. Is that clear?" When she continued her mulish, silent pout, he stuck a finger in her face. "I said, is that clear? Answer me!"

"Yes." She tacked on a coarse insult.

"Good. I'm glad we understand each other. Do not touch me again." He took one big step, bent and set his mouth next to her ear.

Chapter Seven

"Dessy. I swear to you." Pietas lowered his voice, slowing his speech, adding emphasis to each word. "If you do anything to Six, no one in this universe will be able to shield you from me. Do you hear me? No one."

He righted himself.

With an imperious glare, his sister raised her chin.

The woman had been created to nettle him, sting him worse than wasps and harass him into exhaustion. What other possible reason did Dessy have to exist? She did nothing except irritate him. Neck tight, Pietas took ten quick steps away from his sister. He'd been in her presence less than two days and she'd managed to goad him into senseless arguments for no other reason than to prove him wrong.

Joss started toward him but on seeing his expression, she backed off.

At last, Dessy whirled around and stomped away from him.

As she did, Six tapped him on the elbow. "Walk with me, Pi." Without waiting to see if he would follow, Six headed further away.

Curiosity prodded him. He joined Six. "What?"

The man set down his pack. "This should put us out of earshot."

"If you're going to tell me you were right about Dessy badmouthing you, save it. I already agreed. We both saw her do it."

"Wasn't my intention, Pi. I care about you too much to let you screw up."

"Screw up?" He patted his own chest. "Screw up? Me?"

"Yeah, you. In a minute, you're going to walk into the middle of whatever it is Joss and your sister don't want to tell you about. If you're holding your family at arm's length it's going to make it that much harder."

"What is it you suggest I do? Show them I'm weak by apologizing?"

"So your apology to me made you weak?"

"I'm your friend. Friends apologize. A king does not."

"Wow." Six clapped soundlessly. "You are so full of--"

"Six! Do not curse at me." He jabbed a finger at the ground. "I had enough of that from my father."

"You were kinda hard on Sissy back there."

He blinked. "Who?"

"Sissy. You know. Little sister."

"Sissy?" Pietas drew himself up to his full height. "Did I hear you call Dessy ap Lorectic, Lieutenant Chancellor of the High Council, 'Sissy'?"

"Yeah. That's the one. You were out of line."

"Me? How can you possibly--" He jammed both hands on his hips. "You saw what she did. You know how she intended it. What was I supposed to do? Ask her to play nice? Tell me you didn't buy what she said about being sorry."

"Oh, no. Not for a nanosecond."

He threw up his hands. "Then what?"

"You treated the woman like a teenaged girl in front of her peers."

"Like a--" He pinched the bridge of his nose, calming himself before speaking. He took a cleansing breath, blew it all out. "You have no right to say anything about how I treat my sister."

"Don't I? I'm the sole person here who'd dare. The others are afraid."

Pietas took two huge steps toward Six. If the man had any brains, he'd have stepped back. Instead, he stood there, a defiant rabbit daring the eagle to extend one claw.

Or knowing that he wouldn't.

How he longed to smack that smile off Six's face.

"Look, Pi, I'd always heard your people were afraid of you. Until today, I didn't understand why."

He turned his back, arms folded. "Some friend you are."

"Friends don't stand by and watch other friends mistreat women."

"Mistreat--" He grabbed his own hair and tightened a fist around it, fighting to control his temper. "Six." He dared not look at the man. "That woman you say needs protecting would slaughter you without a second thought. My sister can defend herself. She doesn't need you or anyone else." He faced the man. "She'd gut you for trying."

"She didn't seem capable with you. You held her without even twitching."

"It doesn't show, but I was in the fight of my life with her. She can resist Beguile but she's not immune to it. Neither are you or the others."

"You used some kind of Ultra superpower thingy on me?"

"Superpow-- No. There are no such things. Beguile is an innate ability we have but humans don't. Sometimes called Dust. It lets me mask what I'm doing. You saw the same illusion I sent her. Once she accepted the premise that she couldn't free herself, she had no way to escape."

"Okay, I gotta admit that would be cool. But not against your own sister."

"Until you've had a sister who's pestered you for over nineteen hundred years, you have no room to talk."

Six looked him over. "Whatever. Fact is, you humiliated her. She's not going to forgive you."

"My problem."

"You put Armand and Philippe in their place too."

"I did no such thing."

"Look, Pi, I come up to your chest and you come up to the top of theirs. They're huge. Together, they weigh, what? Three times what you do? They could snap you in half if they had a mind to."

"You are correct."

"How's it feel using them for puppets?"

"Six!" He stiffened. "They are not puppets."

"Aren't they? They weren't moving unless you or Dessy allowed it. Gotta say, wasn't easy to watch. Did you do that when you were kids?"

"They never--"

"Don't bother. I know the story. They stayed outside the compound your family was in and guarded it so nobody'd know you were born instead of hatched."

"Ultras are created, not hatched."

"So since you never met the twins until you were grown up, I'm guessing you don't owe them any loyalty."

How could this human be so wrong about every detail yet possess the facts? "I'll have you know I owe them everything."

"Do you? You and Dessy were adults before you started dragging them into the middle of your fights."

"We didn't drag them anywhere. Dessy tried to compel them to help her. I countermanded her psychic order."

"You're so good at it those guys almost died. Or didn't you notice they were trying to breathe while you were busy having your brother-sister tantrum?"

Pietas reined in the stab of empathic ice he longed to send Six's way. "You have no right to judge me."

"I--" Six patted his chest "--am the sole person here who will." Six rubbed his temples. "You know, Pi, someday you're gonna go down in history as the greatest king in the history of the galaxy, but you have a lot to learn."

"The greatest--" He lifted his chin. "I'm sorry. What did you call me?"

"The greatest king in the history of the galaxy. *Ah*, you admire that title."

"A bit. Coming from a mortal."

"I thought you called me a Quasimodo."

Pietas bit his lips to keep from laughing, but a chuckle escaped.

"What's so funny?"

He could not bite back a laugh. "Quasi-immortal. You're no hunchback."

Six's face screwed up. "Quasimodo means hunchback?"

"It's a reference to literature. No reason to assume you'd get it."

"I haven't read any of the modern stuff."

Pietas burst into laughter, but bit his lip, trying to stop. "Sorry."

"You're laughing at me?"

Pietas tried but failed to keep a straight face. A laugh escaped. "Yes." He held up a hand, again attempting to control his laughter. "I'm sorry. Why is that so funny? I swear, you get me laughing at the most awkward times."

"What can I say? That's *my* superpower."

Pietas laughed again.

Through the trees, his sister and Joss drew close together, peering at him. His laughter must have confused them.

Pietas turned his back. "Sorry. You were saying."

"You need to think long term."

"A mortal, telling an immortal that. Talk about irony."

"Are you gonna listen or what?"

"Sorry." He made a rolling gesture. "Continue."

"What I mean is, you won't be marooned here all your life. You need to start thinking about the future. No prison can hold you. Not for long. Once you're free of this place, you're gonna gather whoever will dare to follow. Any army you lead will be invincible. You'll cut a swath across the galaxy."

He had the sense of listening to prophecy.

It was his current misfortune to be stranded on a planet barren of technology and no means of escape. Someday, however, he would find a way.

No. He would create a way.

"Six, thank you. How I love your heart! If I had an army of soldiers with your heart, I could indeed rule the galaxy."

"Before you get to be an unforgettable king, you've got some hard lessons to learn. Just tellin' it how I see it."

"Lessons?" He had not forgotten the future for an instant, but perhaps that failed to make itself known. "I accept your premise. So, my friend, I suppose you're the man to teach me how to be king."

Six chuckled. "You don't need help in that department. I'm going to teach you how to be an awesome big brother."

"You? An only child?" He scoffed. "By your own admission, you don't even get along with your own cousins."

"Forget it. I didn't realize how scared you were of Dessy."

"Scared? Of Dessy?" Pietas patted his chest. "I fear no one, least of all my little sister."

"Oh, yeah? Humans have this saying." The mortal crossed his arms over his chest and lifted his chin. "Shut up and prove it."

Chapter Eight

"He made Pietas laugh." Joss looped her arm through Dessy's. "I've never heard him laugh. Chuckle, perhaps. But not a loud laugh. Not like that. He sounded happy."

The dark-haired beauty lifted one shoulder. "As if I care."

A stone's throw away through the forest, Pietas and Six continued to talk.

"Oh, come now. How often have you heard your brother laugh aloud? Or so often? He's amused by things now and then, but a belly laugh?" She squeezed Dessy's arm. "I've known him since he was sixteen and I doubt he's ever laughed this much."

"Yeah, well, he's always been a killjoy."

"You know I love you, but that was dumb."

"No, I'm serious. He is."

"I meant the thing with his mask and you know it." Folding her hands, Joss quieted herself. She loved these brother-sister twins, but put them together and they produced nothing but sparks. Unless they worked together, it heralded nothing less than the ruination of their people. Possibly, their extinction. No new generations of Ultras were coming forth. "Dessy. My dear." Joss took her hand. "Come over here and sit with me a minute." She perched on a fallen log and patted a space beside her.

"I'll stand." Dessy crossed her arms. "If you're planning to lecture me again about respecting my brother's position as Chancellor of the Council, you can forget it."

Joss patted the log again. "Sit."

"Oh, here it comes. A lecture."

"Sit."

With a roll of storm-gray eyes, Dessy complied. "Joss, I don't have time for this."

Some things never changed. "Your brother often starts discussions with me with those same words."

"Fine! Say what you want to say. I can't stop you."

How alike they were, for being so different. "He says that too."

"Can we get on with it?"

Mumbling to herself, Joss rubbed at the twitch in one eyelid.

"Excuse me?" Dessy twisted toward her. "What does 'children in adult bodies' mean?"

"I'm sorry you heard that, but since you did, it means age has nothing to do with maturity. Now, I want you to listen to me." She ignored the aggravating twitch and focused on Dessy. "Your mother is one of my dearest friends. We were created together."

"I know. She idolizes you."

Joss patted Dessy's hand. "After your father and Pietas had their falling out and he left home, I was the first person she contacted. She asked me to find your brother and make sure he was taken care of. Imagine the shock of finding out the woman you love like a sister had conceived and given birth to twins, then raised them to teenagers without saying one single word. I can't believe she kept it secret for so many years."

"She had no choice. She--"

"I know, dear. I know." If humans had known Helia and Mahikos were fertile, they'd have slaughtered them. Immortals who could reproduce had no need of mortals. "Once I got over the shock, and--I admit, anger that she hadn't confided in me--I did what she asked. I've made it my mission to look after him ever since. And you, once I met you."

Dessy swung one foot. "I guess Tas explained why he left."

"He said he and his father argued. He had too much honor to go into detail."

The young woman glanced at her. "So then, what's this all about?"

"We're trapped here and have to make the best of it. You and Pietas need to work together. You must overcome your differences."

"Never going to happen, Joss. You have no idea what I did."

"On the contrary, I later met up with your father and he revealed the entire thing."

Dessy's shocked gaze met hers. "My father *told* you?"

"In graphic detail."

A look of faraway but remembered pain surfaced. As fast as it had come, Dessy returned to her usual indifference. "No. He wouldn't have. He spun you some lie."

"Your mother shared a similar story the next time I saw her."

The young woman stiffened and cast a disdainful look at Joss. "So what you're saying is my father didn't have as much honor as my brother."

"My dear, I think we both know the answer to that."

Dessy hopped off the log and took several big steps away. She stood there, back turned. "How long have you known?"

"Almost nineteen hundred years. Since four years after it happened."

"How many people have you told?"

"Not one soul."

"Not one." Twigs cracked underfoot as Dessy pivoted toward her. "In all this time? You've kept it a secret that long?"

"My dear, your mother and I are cut from the same cloth. We know how to keep a secret to protect those we love."

"So, you knew the year you and I met. The year I gained my freedom."

Joss poked one booted foot into the carpet of twigs and moss. "Yes."

"And you've never said anything in all that time."

"No, Dessy." Did others not see the pain within this young woman? Once Joss had glimpsed it, she could not unsee it. "I have not."

"Then why bring it up now?"

Because why hope for what you could not have? Why wish for peace when there was no life but war? Why long for harmony among a people bred for discord?

Yet, how could she say that to such a proud, frightened young woman? Dessy's biggest sin was simply being caught in the middle.

"I've hoped for centuries you and Pietas would make peace."

Dessy scoffed. "My brother hates the air I breathe."

Joss went to her at once. "Oh, my sweet girl." She took Dessy's hands. "You couldn't be more wrong. Pietas adores you."

"He has a funny way of showing it."

"Don't you see? That's why he's so angry."

Tears filled Dessy's silvery eyes. She blinked them away and gathered herself. "No. Pietas doesn't know the truth. Whatever lie my father told you or he made Mother believe, that's not what happened. When Pietas finds out he will *never* forgive me."

"Maybe you should start by forgiving yourself."

Her wistful smile faded to sorrow. "I wish I could."

"Come sit down. Surely, there's a way through--"

"No. There's no way through what I did to him. I don't deserve his forgiveness."

"Does your mother know the truth?"

A gasp escaped. "No!" She held up her hands as if warding off demons. "She can never know. Never."

In the distance, Pietas and Six laughed.

Dessy jerked her head toward them. Her regret splattered the air like blood.

Joss took an instinctual step back, but stopped and forced herself to accept the pain. She permitted its passage through herself and out into the aether.

Dessy truly suffered.

Living with this secret caused her agony. Whatever it was, even with all the powers Joss possessed, she could not break the walls hiding it.

Earlier, she'd picked up the projected thoughts of Pietas. He considered his sister a queen of ice. How wrong he was. Unusual, to hear him mind-speak. Always, he'd broadcast surface emotions but not pain. His brutal confinement had damaged him far beyond what he let others see. He ached, everywhere, even now.

She'd been unwise to acknowledge it. Now he would go to greater lengths to shield himself.

Beyond that, Pietas had changed in profound ways. Perhaps his confinement had honed other abilities. He'd fought to master telepathy ever since she'd known him, to no avail. He simply did not have the gift.

Until now. Why?

But how wrong he was about his sister. Dessy was anything but ice. She blazed with passion so deep, at times, it stung to be near her.

For an empath with a masterful ability to absorb the emotions of others, Pietas had no insight when it came to her. Apparently, it went both ways.

When the men laughed again, Dessy whirled around and returned to the log. As usual, the woman wasted no time on pleasantries and pointed to the space beside her.

"Joss, sit down. I'll tell you what happened, but you have to swear this goes no further. If I tell you, you'll have to keep my secret."

She should say no. Refuse to put herself in the middle of this angst-riddled family.

The scapegoat son.

The spoiled daughter.

The arrogant husband.

The forgotten wife.

Hatred and love, passion and contempt all bound in one small knot of misunderstood, unwilling-to-explain people. She should save her sanity and her inner peace and refuse to get involved. So many centuries had already passed.

Why did these four people insist on dragging the anchors of anger and unforgiveness that bound them? Their hearts pleaded for amnesty, tormented ghosts rattling chains in a haunted attic.

Do not do this, she reasoned with herself. *This will bring you pain.*

A tear glistened in the dust on Dessy's cheek. The young woman lifted her quivering chin, causing the tear to track down her face.

Joss brushed it away, perched beside her and took her hand. "All right, Dessy. I agree. Tell me. I promise, no matter what, I'll keep your secret."

Chapter Nine

Half the day gone and they hadn't reached the encampment, and now Six had him on this fool's errand of apologizing. *Remember, Pi, true apologies state the wrong and offer a solemn promise not to repeat the offense.*

A king could admit he'd erred. That was good leadership. But apologize to his sister? He halted.

When had Six ever steered him wrong?

Pietas forced himself to continue.

The rain had passed by the time he reached the others. By mutual agreement, Six would hunt and give the Ultras privacy. This apology was not for the human to hear.

Shafts of noonday sun broke through the canopy. The loamy scent of the forest after a rain filled the air. Clean, heady, a sweet beginning.

Off to one side, Joss and Dessy talked, sitting on the moss-covered trunk of a fallen tree. Ahead, Armand and Philippe, faithful soldiers that they were, each faced outward, forming a perimeter and standing watch.

The soldier class among his people had been designed to intimidate by size as well as presence. Like his father, Pietas had the slender build and facile mind of the scientist class, but with the height of a warrior and all their strength.

Joss's frank and sensual appraisal popped to mind. *"You have the sleek grace of a dancer, Pietas, and all the muscle of a warrior."* Best compliment ever. He stifled the smile that recollection brought and focused on Armand and Philippe.

The twins were thick iron bars. He was whipcord blended with carbonized steel. He couldn't subdue them, but he'd make them work to subdue him.

As one, they turned toward him and snapped to attention.

Accustomed to being the tallest person in any room, having to look up left him off guard. He forced himself not to step back. "At ease, men."

Each tucked his hands behind him.

Their submissive position triggered a memory of himself, kneeling, hands bound behind him. With him still fettered, his captors had placed him on his back in a cryopod. Though the shackles could have been released remotely, they had left him bound.

To rot.

While imprisoned, he'd decided his soldiers would never stand with hands behind them again. But he'd deal with that later.

"Armand, Philippe, I owe you each an apology."

Together, they tilted their heads like dogs hearing their master's whistle.

"I was angry at my sister and I took it out on you. It was not an excuse for mistreating you." Pietas inclined his head. "It was unconscionable. Inconsiderate. Cruel. I will never do that again. I give you my word. Armand." Pietas offered his hand. "Will you forgive me?"

The man accepted his hand and clasped both of his around it. "Gladly."

After releasing Armand, Pietas turned to the man's brother and again, offered his hand. "Philippe. Will you forgive me?"

The giant bowed, then accepted his hand and clasped it. Though Philippe did not speak, his eyes shone with gratitude.

"Pietas, you are--" Armand began.

"--our king." Philippe finished.

Together, they bowed.

He bowed in return. Command offered multiple sorrows. How wonderful it also offered a few joys. He counted the love and respect of his soldiers among the greatest.

"Will you come with me as witness?" He led them toward his sister and Joss.

The women stood as one, still holding hands. No fear showed on Dessy's face but Pietas felt its empathic presence.

It mingled with an unspoken plea for mercy from Joss. The depth of her concern speared a twinge of psychic pain through his mind. He had never felt her presence as he did now. Which begged the question, how often had her thought-commands influenced his decisions in the past?

It ceased at once and Joss cast him an apologetic glance.

"Joss." When she looked up at him, he crossed to her and offered his hand.

She stepped out from beside Dessy and accepted it in both of hers. "I know what's in your heart, Pietas. You don't have to say anything."

"Gracious as always. But yes, I do. I rushed you. I didn't listen to you. I discounted your advice. It was rude of me. I won't do that again. I have always treasured your advice and your presence in my life. I'm sorry for the way I treated you."

The whole time he was speaking, Dessy stood with arms folded, staring at him with undisguised contempt.

Joss touched his mind, the whisper of a kiss, sharing her pride at his willingness to make amends.

When he turned toward Dessy, his sister drew back in a warrior's stance.

"Who are you?" If Armand and Philippe had been born to war, Dessy had been born to rule, as had he. Small wonder they clashed every time they met. Her look of suspicion stung. She continued to glare at him. "What are you playing at?"

"I'm not playing. I came to apologize."

Her look of utter surprise satisfied in a way he hadn't expected. She'd anticipated another fight.

"Dessy, I believed the worst of you. I treated you with contempt. I discounted how you felt and refused to accept your word. I disrespected you. I was rude. I laid hands on you instead of asking to speak privately. That was wrong of me. I offer no excuse for my behavior. I am sorry. I will not do it again." He set a hand over his heart and bowed, showing his sincerity by not rising.

When she didn't speak, he lifted his head. Of all the expressions he'd expected to see, fury was not among them. Unsure what to say, he stood straight and remained silent.

"I don't know who you are, but you are *not* my insufferably rude brother. I have no idea what you expect this show of *goodness* to do for you, but however much the others fell all over your so-called apology, I'm not buying one minute of it."

"Dess--" He reached for her.

She jerked out of his way. "Don't touch me, you imposter!"

"I am your brother. Ask me something no one else would know."

"You are not my brother!"

"Ask me something. Anything."

She studied him. None of the others spoke. "Not in public." She jerked her chin toward the Ultras.

Public? There were few people dearer to him. But if this was how she wanted it... Pietas walked a distance away and waited beneath a tree for her to join him. When she had, he leaned one hand on the trunk.

She remained out of reach.

"Ask your question, Dessy."

"I have two. When you were three, you were hurt and you cried. What did Father say?"

Over the centuries, the recollection had grown stronger, no matter how hard he suppressed it. He could see himself falling, scraping his hands and knees, as clearly as if he watched it happening now. His hands had bled and he'd cried while showing his father.

"He said if I cried again, he'd beat me until I stopped." How easy it was to say those words to his sister. Words he'd hidden with the deepest shame all his life. Why he should feel inadequate for being threatened as a child he could not fathom, but there it was. He'd been made a victim. Once free from his father, he permitted no such weakness. "Mother said pain was a warrior's ally. I made that my mantra."

He'd never lost a fight. Until Six subdued him. No. Until Six had backed him into a corner. In order to save his mother, Pietas had no choice but to surrender. The act of submission had once again made him a victim.

Turning from such soppy thoughts, he faced Dessy. "Father beat me for many things, but never for crying."

She beheld him in silence before speaking. "I used to blackmail my brother into doing things. I told no one. What was it?"

If not for her blackmail, he'd never have committed the act that had ostracized him from his family. He'd never have been forced into living on the streets, an outcast from his own people. He should hate her. Did hate her betrayal. He might never trust her again, but she was his sister and he owed her proof.

"We were sixteen and wanted to experience a rebirth. I was supposed to kill you without inflicting pain. When you struggled, I panicked and hurt you. You swore I enjoyed it and that you wouldn't forgive me unless I did what you asked." He ran one toe along the bared root of a tree, loathe to admit he'd been afraid of what she'd do. "After that, every time you wanted something and I wouldn't do it, you threatened to tell Father that I"-- Though alone, he lowered his voice --"choked you to death."

"It *is* you."

"It is." He stood before her. "I'm sorry for the way I treated you, Dess." He bit the inside of his cheek. "I was wrong."

A smile tugged at the corners of her mouth. "You remember our pact as children never to say please or thank you to each other?"

"How could I forget? We had to say please before receiving anything."

A flush crossed her cheeks. "Even punishment."

Pietas brushed a thumb across her cheeks. "And then we had to thank him for teaching us to be good. He drilled politeness into us. I can hear him now. 'You'll need to be polite once you're out among humans. Never give them reason to wonder why you're different. Ultras are not in power. Humans are. Keep your head down and never look them in the eye.' He said it endlessly. How could I forget?"

"Tas, I all but saw that tattooed on the inside of my eyelids at night."

"Same here." She'd been crying, but even this close, he couldn't read her emotions. "Dess, I've missed you. We need to pull together like we did as kids."

"We haven't worked together as adults." The flatness of her voice matched the lack of emotion in her eyes. "Since the day you left, we've been enemies. You hate me. You don't trust me."

"Can you blame me?" Despair descended over his heart anew but he resisted its pain. "I never understood why you lied to Father. I couldn't forgive you for that. I convinced myself it didn't matter. I didn't have anything to prove. If he thought so little of me that he would think I'd lied to him, then why should I allow that to bring me pain?"

She averted her gaze. "I'm sorry."

"Someone is always saying they're sorry in our family." He touched her shoulder. "If we're going to survive here, you and I must put the past behind us."

"I'll work with you because our people need us. You're right about being our king. The military supports you without question. If you'd tried, you could have overthrown the Council. Father knew it. Mother knew it. The humans who exiled us here knew it. You'd have been the most powerful leader our people or theirs ever had."

And yet she'd continually voted counter to him. Even so, her words gratified.

"Dess. You have no idea what that means to me." With the memory of their pact in mind, he bowed to her. "Thank you."

"It's not flattery, Pietas. You're the reason we're here, trapped on Sempervia." She turned and headed toward the others, then slowed, came to a stop, and looked back at him. "You'd be an amazing king, but that has nothing to do with forgiveness. Know this, brother mine. I will work with you for the good of our people, but I will never forgive you. Not for anything. Not for as long as I live."

Chapter Ten

Never forgive him? What?

Pietas stood there, gaping, with Dessy's retreating back his focus. His sister wouldn't forgive him for whatever it was she thought he did, and his big concern?

He would fail Six.

Head back, Pietas tightened his fists, teeth clenched. He strode after her. When he clasped her arm, she whirled on him.

"Don't touch me!"

He backed off, hands raised. When she once more walked away from him, he went after her. "Dess. Dessy! Wait!"

She turned on him again, unshed tears glistening. "Get away!"

"Dess!" He longed to take away her tears. Hug her as he had when they were children. Promise to make it better. "Talk to me. Why won't you forgive me?"

"Forgive you? After what you did to me?"

"You forced me into it by blackmailing me!"

"You big idiot!" The acid in her emotions stung more the words. "I'm not talking about that."

How was it she could talk about one thing and mean another yet expect him to keep up? He tried again. "Then what is it I did?"

"You abandoned me!"

"I aban-- What! When?"

She stuck her hands on her hips. "Don't you dare deny it, Pietas ap Lorectic. You left me." Hearing her say his full name reminded him of their mother.

"Dess, I've never left you. Ever. What are you talking about?"

She jabbed a finger in his chest. "Don't you deny it!" Tears rolled down her cheeks. "You left me to him!"

"Left you to..." The meaning of her words hit him. Pietas staggered. "Dess. Dess, you thought I left you to our father?"

"Yes!" Swearing, she charged toward him.

He stood there without resisting and let her thrash him. She might be small compared to him, but she was all warrior. It hurt, but paled next to the revelation she'd dropped.

"Why won't you fight me?"

How could he?

Dessy collapsed, crying.

He gathered her in his arms. *"Shh."* He kissed her brow and rocked her side-to-side. "It's all right. I won't let anyone hurt you. I'm sorry, Dessy."

"Why did you leave me?"

"I didn't leave you! Father threw me out. He wouldn't let me say good-bye. Not even to Mother."

Sniffing, she pulled back. Her red eyes revealed the dark outer gray of her irises. Her black lashes stuck together in points. Even in tears, his sister's beauty showed itself.

It served to remind him how their father had enhanced them not only before they were born, but for years after. He'd made them flawless, beautiful, powerful.

Perfect.

They could protect themselves from everyone. Except him.

Mahikos had broken them, used fear to instill weakness, and required them to permit his rule over every waking hour. Made them submissive to his every whim.

No more.

Trying to still his racing heart, Pietas drew his sister close and stroked her hair. "And after I was gone? What did he tell you then?"

"That he'd tried to punish you, and you hit him and ran away." She tightened her arms. "He said you wanted nothing to do with Mother and me. That you were through with family. He said you told him 'family makes people weak.'" She withdrew from him. "That you'd do the same thing again if you got the chance."

While she spoke, his heart continued to race. He coughed, throat dry. He forced down the rage building within and opened his hands from the fists he'd clenched.

"He dared tell you such disgusting lies about me?"

Dessy brushed away tears. "I thought it was true."

"He b--" Pietas stopped himself from speaking. He would tear the man apart with his bare hands. And teeth. He calmed himself as best he could. "Dess, he whipped me, and then he beat me with his fists until I couldn't stand and then he kicked me until I blacked out."

She flinched and covered her mouth with both hands. Tears spilled.

"I never fought back. He dragged me to my room and locked me inside. I overheard him telling Mother what I'd done. Accusing me of--" Jaws tight, he forced away the memory of his parents fighting.

"Did he confess or did you assume?" his mother kept repeating. She'd refused to believe his father. How Pietas adored her for that.

The warmth of his sister's hug drew him to the present.

"Tas, I'm sorry. I'm sorry!"

He held her close, his cheek atop her head.

"I should have known it was a lie." She cuddled with him. "I shouldn't have believed him."

All these years. All these centuries... He could stand here forever, holding his sister. Reconnecting with the dearest person in his life. But to give their father what he deserved, he must let her go.

No. Not yet. Not yet.

He would stay here. He had longed for her presence, for the childhood sister he adored and now he had her. He refused to let her go.

"Dess, I've missed you so much it stabs my heart."

She squeezed him tight enough to hurt. "I'm sorry." She drew back and tossed hair out of her eyes. "I forget my own strength."

He grinned at her. "I've always loved that about you. You're the best sparring partner I know. And the meanest."

With an open hand, she smacked him on the arm.

"Ow!" He rubbed the spot.

"Oh, shut up, you big baby." She rolled her eyes at him and they both laughed.

Pietas sobered. "I'll kill him for what he did to us."

"No, you will not. Mother would never forgive you and you know it. And she's far more important than he is."

"He deserves worse than death."

"Pietas. don't touch him." She touched his arm. "Promise me you won't hurt him."

"I can't do that."

"You will do that and here's why. If you hurt him, you're lowering yourself to his standard. You're letting him know he hurt you. He controlled you."

"But, Dess--"

"He's still controlling you. Don't you see that?" She took his hand. "Tas, we've been his experiment all our lives. He plays us against each other. Manipulates us. Hasn't he used us enough?"

He growled.

"Tas, if you can't promise me now, at least promise you'll consider it and discuss it with me before you act." She took his arm. "I'm saying 'please' for this."

"Don't. He deserves no mercy. Not from anyone. He's opposed me since the day I left. Done nothing but ridicule and harass me. He questioned every move I made as Chancellor. He must have hated it when I was elected."

"Oh, you are so blind." She shook her head. "Don't you realize it was Father who prompted the Council to elect you?"

"That's preposterous. He--" His father claimed the Council elected him to control him. At the time, Pietas had laughed. *They can try,* he'd responded. "Why? Why would he do that? He knew I resisted the peace talks. Father knew I hated humans. Knew I'd do everything in my power to disrupt the talks."

"Knowing all that, why would he want you in power instead of him?"

"But he wouldn't. He knew I'd resist. I'd find a way out. He..." His mind refused to wrap around the truth before him. "Dess. He wouldn't. He couldn't." He met her gaze and held it, trying to absorb the truth before him. "He did, didn't he?"

"Yes, Pietas. He did. I've gone over and over this. Father has been happy as a child with new shoes since we got here. The entire Council is ready to hang him. We all suspect the same thing. He wanted us to be exiled."

After grasping Dessy's hand, Pietas set off into the forest with her in tow. Low branches slapped wet leaves in his face. Moisture dripped. Insects buzzed. The stink of wood rot made him sneeze.

"Tas, where are we going?"

"Nowhere. I have to think."

"We need to get back. The others are--"

"Hang the others! I need to think and I want you with me." He darted around slender trees and through breaks in the undergrowth, tugging his sister along behind him. In a small clearing, he slowed and then halted.

Birds fluttered among the branches. The rain-washed forest gave up the scent of spores mixed with flowers and damp wood.

"There's something out there." Dessy released his hand and turned outward, scanning the forest. "I can't hear it or smell it, but I sense it. One of those black cats is stalking us. We need to go back."

"Watching."

"What? What is it?" She looked up and around. "I don't see anything but trees."

"Not me. It's that panther I told you about yesterday." It had tracked him halfway across the planet. "It's not stalking us. It's watching. Guarding."

"Tas, you've been through a lot. You're overtired and overwrought, but I promise you, no animal talked to you. Not yesterday and not today."

"Dess, I didn't talk to it! It communicated, but not with speech. Like Joss. She can tell you in words, but also concepts. You know what she wants from you."

"Okay. Let's say for the sake of argument there's a big kitty cat out there and it's guarding us. Why? Is it guarding us from other cats so it can eat us itself?"

"Don't be absurd."

She gestured to herself. "I'm absurd? You're the one talking to cats."

"I am not--" He stopped, reining in the impatience his sister always fostered. He took a deep breath, let it out, did it again for good measure. "I'm not *talking to cats* and I'm not talking to you *about* talking to cats. Is that clear?"

"Fine." She cast a pleading look toward the heavens. "Let's agree the kitty cat's guarding us. Why are we out here in the forest?"

"If it's true that Father wanted us to be exiled, then there has to be a good reason. It's not the kind of thing he'd decide on a whim. When has he ever done anything without a plan?"

"I'll admit, never. Then what is he planning?"

"When native people sign a treaty and are driven from their land, they don't get a better deal. They get less. They get the discards no one wants. Vast grasslands with no cattle and no crops. Barren deserts. Endless mountains covered in eternal snow. Here we are, stuck on Sempervia, the last planet on the rim of the galaxy. Not even fully terraformed. They gave up on it. This is where they shunt the outcasts. Us. Sempervia's what we get in exchange for a treaty."

"Treaty? We didn't sign a treaty."

"You're right. *We* didn't."

Chapter Eleven

At a rustle of leaves, Joss set a hand on her knife.

Six, who'd been hunting, entered the clearing. Dirt smeared his face and fresh stains marked his ragged shirt, but he grinned, a hero returning from war.

Why couldn't she read him?

He held up a string of three rabbits. "Who wants lunch?"

"Good--" Armand began.

"--catch!" Philippe finished.

The twins helped clean the rabbits while Joss set about building a fire. Philippe stripped a sapling of its bark and leaves, creating a spit for the game. Six provided two metal Y-shaped sticks for the spit to rest upon. The twins asked what else he carried in his pack and soon had him revealing a cook set and utensils, several knives, and other survival gear. They exclaimed over various pieces and showed him their own knives.

Joss kept hers to herself.

While the rabbits roasted, Joss helped Six, Armand, and Philippe gather berries. They all nibbled while they picked. Philippe had woven a fine net with vines and padded it with leaves. It bulged with the results of their labor.

Working next to Six let her study the human up close. His dusky skin, dark hair and darker eyes gave him an earthy appeal. For a mortal, not unpleasant. A foot shorter than Pietas which made him ten inches shorter than she, but he had a certain air about him. Who couldn't love a man with a sense of humor? Plus, Pietas trusted him. That alone made him worth getting to know.

Yet his mind was blank. He wasn't blocking. He wasn't broadcasting. A person could not *not think*. Six was blank. She couldn't read a single thought. Was it because he was a ghost? Or was it that anti-emo chip? Perhaps some innate ability in his DNA.

Fascinating.

Her stomach growled at the savory scent of meat. Who would have thought she'd ever miss military rations? Having a can of peaches or a pouch of stew to open on a moment's notice--what luxury. Her mouth watered at the thought of those button-sized coated chocolate candies. They came in bright colors, dispensed by the handful from any vending machine. When this planet had some semblance of civilization, she was going to hunt for chocolate trees.

Or was chocolate a berry? All she knew about food was how to eat it. Perhaps the worker class would know.

Six pronounced the rabbits ready and the twins set about pulling them off the fire.

Should they wait for Pietas and Dessy? Where were they? If anything had happened to them, Helia would have her head. She sent out a *kueshda,* a telepathic quest. She lacked skill with trail signs, but this she could do, at least in places where she'd been.

In her mind, she stood where she'd last seen the brother-sister pair and looked about for aetheric signs of their passing. A small hint of their warmth remained. They'd reunited, an excellent sign. If she had been somewhere, she could recapture the location, re-see it in its present condition. A kind of remote viewing, but on a different plane. Genetic, not psychic.

A metallic snap pulled her out of the search.

Six had produced a small shovel from his pack and attached it to a telescoping handle. He stuck the shovel into the dirt and pressed it with one foot.

Armand brushed off their hands. "What are--"

"--you doing?"

"Burying the skins and entrails to keep predators away."

Armand stooped and examined the hole. "Good--"

"--idea." Philippe watched.

Joss was removing a rabbit from its spit when voices came from her right.

In walked Pietas and Dessy, making small talk, swinging their joined hands.

At once, Joss handed the rabbit to Six and hurried over to greet them. "I'm so glad to see you! I was starting to worry." She set the back of her fingers against the cheek of Pietas in a hand-kiss.

He returned it, his thought-emotions warm, an inviting cup of tea on a cold day.

Before she could turn to Dessy, the young woman hand-kissed her. "We're fine, Joss."

"You're sure?"

"Of course." Pietas and Dessy said together.

"They sound almost--"

"--like us." As one, the twins winked at them.

"Food's ready." Joss took Dessy's hand. "Are you hungry?"

"Starved." Pietas rubbed his stomach.

Dessy inhaled. "Yum! Rabbit."

"Six caught--"

"--them."

"And we have berries." Joss pointed to the full net. "There should be enough to ward off hunger if not assuage it. The rabbits are done. I was about to carve. Let's eat."

As they strolled toward the campfire, Joss squeezed Dessy's hand. "Were you able to talk?" She sent a targeted suggestion of her meaning.

The young woman gave a small shake of her head. "Everything important."

"Important?" The tightened grip on Joss's hand made her change direction. "It took you two a long time. It'll be dark soon and we still have to reach the camp."

"Yes, Joss. We'll eat fast." Pietas leaned down and kissed her cheek. "Or should I say, 'Yes, Mother?'"

"Oh, stop!" She linked arms between the two of them.

Why could Dessy not see the damage withholding the truth had already done? Pietas deserved the truth, even if it broke his heart. If he knew the truth, if others knew he was not what he'd been accused of being, it would change his life.

But would the truth make him a better man, or a worse one?

Chapter Twelve

As they finished eating, Joss once more turned her telepathic attention to Pietas and Dessy. She scanned Dessy first, found her calmer than she'd been earlier, but the moment she touched the mind of Pietas, he flinched and looked up at her as if she'd slugged him.

Delicate as she'd been, he'd felt her presence. Were it not for her own ethics, she could walk around inside anyone's mind as if it were her own house. Unseen and unheard, she could slam doors, clomp about and open every cupboard without them being the wiser. Yet with Pietas, she'd landed on the windowsill with the might of a housefly and his *consare*, his recognition of telepathic scanning, activated.

He tossed bones onto the embers. "You have a question, Joss?"

"Not a question. A comment. I'm glad to see you and your sister getting along."

He looked at Dessy, who beamed at him. "We cleared up an old misunderstanding. I can't wait to see my father's reaction when we tell him."

He sent Joss an image with absolute clarity of Mahikos, writhing in agony.

The violence of it made her gasp.

Pietas regarded her, his gaze steady, his eyes as cold as the stone they resembled. Like turquoise with its inner matrix, they held hidden depths. His thoughts remained his own.

Her dear boy had mastered six of the thirty-one Ultra gifts. He was strong in seven and in another seven, passable. He lost no fights with humans and few among his own kind.

And now he'd added telepathy. How?

As she helped clean up the campsite, she pondered his change. What had happened to him? He was different in a fundamental way. Every Ultra was created with one or more abilities and then developed them over time. Practice, as they say, makes perfect. But no Ultra "picked up" a new ability. One was created with it or one was not.

You got what you got.

Pietas and Dessy were the exception, of course. Had been since the day they were conceived, rather than created.

After their birth, Mahikos, in his genius, enabled his twins with every genetic gift he had at his disposal. According to Helia, he'd experimented on them, seeking ways to impart additional adaptations. What few abilities Pietas didn't have, his father claimed no one needed.

This had insulted those who had them, caused a ruckus on warrior forums and almost started a riot at one work hall. It hadn't settled until Mahikos retracted the statement and apologized, surprising everyone.

His children's inability to gain any form of telepathy had thrown Mahikos into more than one fit of rage. Concerned, Helia had begun overseeing every change he made and guarding the twins during their various transitions. She remained with them during tests, interceded and when necessary, interfered.

In Joss's opinion, her friend ought to have done less interceding and more interfering.

Curious, she sent a *tynkasha*, a minor tendril of power, testing Dessy. As expected, she was not changing.

But Pietas was off the scale.

As usual, he hadn't revealed everything and he'd shielded his pain. *"You're injured,"* she'd said. The man would not lie. Hated lies and liars. He'd said, *"Don't worry about me."*

The memory took her back to one of her fondest recollections of Pietas. She'd known him several years by then, had mentored him in the use of an array of weapons. Joss designed them, understood their every detail. Pietas tested them for her and longed to put them to good use.

Finding work among the unofficial unions among Ultra fighters frustrated him. He was an unknown. Outsider. Once others saw his talent, though, a few offered to train him.

Combat smoothed his rough edges, taught him how to interact with and rely upon other fighters. Be part of a team.

He claimed he could perform a skill after seeing it demonstrated once. The more seasoned warriors accused him of cockiness. That is, until he proved it true. Within months, instead of hiring him to fight in their squads, cadres of Ultra warriors were clamoring to be hired into his. When you ooze raw talent, however, it doesn't take long to make enemies.

Six leaders among the Ultra squads confronted him with an accusation he was poaching their members. Pietas gave them the bare truth. *"If you're not good enough to keep them, maybe you should quit."*

And that, he told her, was when the fight started.

The ensuing battle with six against one ended when an alert interrupted, calling everyone to duty stations. The leaders hadn't won. Pietas hadn't lost. All had more respect for the other, but it was Pietas who realized he lacked a skill. He'd come to her that night, seeking to understand what had angered the experienced leaders.

"We've talked about this." She'd sat beside him and taken his hand. "Use your social skills. Stroke their egos. Make them comfortable before you try to correct them."

Pietas could not have been a day over twenty at the time. His smooth face showed no trace of age, though his eyes were those of an old, old man. He'd turned that bright turquoise gaze on her as if she'd bitten him.

"Stroke them? You mean make them feel better that they're incompetents who fire a weapon with no more skill than a rank newbie? At ten, my sister could shoot better than they do."

"Yes, but you can't tell them that."

"Why not?"

"Because-- Well, love, I'm sorry, but you can't."

Shaking his head, he stood and stormed out onto the balcony. When she joined him, he braced his hands on the railing and then bent and rested his forearms along it. "I hate this city."

She stood beside him, one hand on his back. "Why?"

"The reason it exists is to feed a lie."

"I'm sorry, love. I don't understand."

"Look." He swept a hand outward. Two stories below, workers bustled to and from duty. Street vendors hawked food, uniform items, weapons. "See that red-armed cyborg with the hover-cart over to the left? If you pay him enough, you can get blacklisted tech. That short Ultra across from him will sell you black market neuro-enhancers. The vendors all along the north end of the street can get you seats in illegal body-mod shops and tickets off the planet no matter what your flight-status. Others will sell you outlawed weapons and off-world contraband. Why? Because this is Ultratown. This isn't a residential enclave or a human city. It's a glorified dumping ground with street gangs and thieves and lawlessness. It's based on the lie that Ultras are free. We are not. We're slaves to human greed. We live and die and are reborn to feed human desires." He smacked his hands on the railing and then braced himself against it, arms straight. "I hate it. I hate this entire place."

The homesickness rippling off him made her want to hug him but an undercurrent of anger warned her away. Perhaps she could tease him out of his mood. "All this because I suggested using social skills instead of fists?"

He stood up straight. "I'm sorry."

"Don't be. You're entitled to your feelings." A lock of his silver-white hair always seemed to fall out of place. When he turned toward her, Joss tucked one finger beneath a strand and moved it aside.

A look of such pain crossed his face that at first, she wondered if she'd hurt him. "What is it?"

"I can't use 'social skills,' Joss. I can't use what I don't have. And I don't understand women."

She laughed. "Darling, even other women don't understand women." A breeze blew the lock of hair back in his eyes and she brushed it aside again.

He turned on that glorious smile of his.

She saw it rarely but treasured it when she did. Inside, part of her melted. How could he look so innocent yet be so seductive at the same time?

His smile widened. "I want you."

Her breath caught. She avoided his gaze. "I'm flattered, love, but--"

"Joss." He touched her cheek, drawing her gaze back to his. "Flattery is insincere or excessive praise. I'm sincere. I'm always comfortable with you. I'm confident and sure of my skills when I'm fighting but when I'm around women I'm all left feet and thumbs and my tongue sticks to my teeth. When I'm with you, it's like I put on my softest shirt and have the day to myself. I don't feel rushed or hurried. It's easy being around you. I want to make love to you."

She struggled to contain her rising desire. What would Helia think of such a thing? What would Mahikos do?

"Joss." Pietas hand-kissed her. "Whatever's causing your hesitation, cast it aside. Have sex with me. I've never been with a woman."

"You haven't?" She couldn't believe no one had seduced him yet. Lusty gazes trailed him everywhere, her own included. "Why not?"

"I want my first time to be with you."

"Me?"

"There's no one else who interests me. You're a genius with weapons. Capable. Diligent. I can't imagine a more patient teacher. You've taught me how to handle guns. Now teach me how to handle a woman. Show me what to do in bed." He stroked the back of one finger down her cheek. "Teach me how to pleasure you."

She swallowed, hard. "I've heard the term brutally honest all my life, but I've never seen it in action the way it is with you."

"I'm always honest. You lie if you're afraid of the consequences. There's nothing in this galaxy that I fear. Nothing. Is it so wrong to tell you that when you touch me, it makes me want you?"

"Are you ready? Joss?" Fingers snapped. "Joss?"

"What?" She stiffened.

Dessy peered at her. They were in the clearing with the forest around them.

Joss's cheeks burned. For no reason would she look toward Pietas. No matter what her skill with shields, she couldn't have hidden her desire from him, or her embarrassment.

With both hands, she swept leaves and dust from her uniform. "Sorry. I...was thinking."

"About what?" Dessy nudged her. "You sure looked happy."

She coughed. "Pleasant memory."

The young woman winked. "I'll bet." Dessy indicated the clearing where the group had gathered and were waiting. "Pietas wants to arrive before dark."

"Of course. I'll lead. I want him to see the view before-- well, you know." Joss brushed past the group and led them deeper into the forest, picking her way through the brush. They were close to the overlook and she didn't want to miss the spot she'd discovered. He must not see what waited on the other side until he'd seen the size of the caldera and caught a glimpse of how much room they had. How many resources. He would know how to make the best of them.

If anyone could get them out of this dilemma, it was Pietas.

According to Helia, after Pietas had been born and Mahikos placed him in her arms, he looked her straight in the eye with such intensity she expected him to utter a demand.

He wanted something. Needed it. But unable to communicate, he'd balled up his fists and cried. She'd bragged later, "Pietas was born a king."

Having been entranced by that same fierce gaze, Joss agreed.

Those meddlers who whined about her dear boy gaining too much power had no idea how much he already possessed. That man had more drive, more passion, more ferocity than anyone she'd ever known.

How wrong they were about him. Pietas, dangerous? Ridiculous. He was what he'd always been. Now, with telepathy and the ability to shield, there were even more reasons to adore her king.

Dangerous. Pietas? No.

Pietas was lethal.

Chapter Thirteen

Pietas grappled with patience. When a rescue party was returning to base, the top priority was reporting success or failure and accepting the next assignment. One did not stop and peer around trees every few yards as Joss was doing.

"Why are we stopping *again?*"

"I want to be sure we haven't gotten too close." She was lost again. Typical.

"We stopped two minutes ago. Gotten too close to what?"

"To what I want you to see."

Mindul of his promise not to rush her, he stifled the urge to throw up his hands.

She walked forward, looked back and forth, finally motioned to him. "I think this is the place."

"You're certain this time?"

"I think so. Stand here." With one hand, she made a circle in front of her. "I'm two inches shorter than you so it should work."

He stepped into the area. "Here?"

"One more step." She guided him. "There, can you see the caldera?"

"I see a rise and the sky."

"All right, two more steps, then." She touched his chest. "But, please. Don't go any farther."

"I won't." He took the steps. The trees ended and the world fell away beneath him. "Whoa! Six! You gotta see this. I mean you *must*," he corrected. He was picking up bad habits, hanging out with a human. *Consorting*, he corrected again.

The man came up on his right. There was a gasp and then a long, low whistle.

Pietas didn't look at him. He couldn't take his eyes off the view.

Six laughed. "Oh, wow! I've never seen anything resembling this."

They stood on the lip of a gigantic bowl with sides that plunged to a level bottom. A patchwork of deserts and plains in various shades of beige and green made a quilt of color on the floor. Greens and browns speckled the sides, revealing forest and outcroppings of rock. A blue waterfall cascaded to the valley floor.

"Pi." Six nudged him. "You see that silvery sheen the sun's glinting off?"

"Where?"

Six pointed. "There. Base of the waterfall."

"*Ah*, yes. I see it."

"That's where the falls goes, isn't it? A big lake."

"I believe so." He turned to find his sister watching him rather than viewing the caldera. "Has anyone explored the floor yet?"

"Some." She crossed her arms. "You can't see them from here, but there are marshes around the bend. Another waterfall. Smaller. We all take baths there. A much smaller lake. A forest starts beside it. The caldera isn't round. A cove branches off to one side. Once we get through those trees over there," she jutted her chin, "the side slopes gradually. It's half an hour going down to our camp. Coming up is more."

"This place is amazing." Six bent, hands braced on his thighs. He pointed. "What is that? Am I seeing things, or is the ground moving?"

"You're not seeing things." Joss stood between them. "That brown section in flux is a herd of antelope."

"That's one herd?" Six frowned. "That has to be, what? A Terran mile across."

"There are thousands of them. They graze all around the floor of the caldera. They're not afraid of people. At least not yet. I'm sure they will be soon. If you can catch one, it's good meat, but they're fast."

"I bet one of my spears could catch them." Six grinned at Joss.

Smiling, she turned and looked over at Pietas, but the moment she met his gaze she looked away, blushing. He'd noticed her blush the same way in the clearing. What had that been about?

He turned back to his sister. "How big is this place?"

"By Terran standard measurements, Mother says thirty-one miles in diameter with a thirty-six-mile perimeter. Give or take."

"How deep?"

"About six hundred feet. She estimates the area is about a hundred square miles. It's huge, isn't it?"

"Huge doesn't even begin to describe it." Pietas took in the vastness of the area's sheltering sides and abundance of arable land. "It's a giant cradle."

"Funny. That's what Mother named it. *Ayoli*. Cradle. She says it's fitting since it's where we'll originate on this world."

He was about to ask if they could go when he caught movement atop the ridge on the other side. Long white cloud-fingers were sliding over the edge and trickling down the caldera's rim, creeping slowly among the trees.

He reached past Joss and tapped Six on the arm, then pointed.

Six looked up, followed where Pietas was pointing, and went wide-eyed. He uttered a curse in Spanish. "What is that?"

Pietas withheld the grin that wanted to burst from him. "What do you think?"

He made a rapid sign of the cross. "*El espectro.*"

"You mean ghosts? Are they friends of yours?"

Six started to speak but then leveled a malevolent glare at Pietas. Another round of Spanish cursing accompanied an indecent gesture.

When Pietas laughed, the others joined him.

Six gave in and chuckled. "What is that? Clouds? Fog?"

"Clouds, ghost. Not your kin at all. I have a hunch it's a familiar sight here."

"Almost every day." Dessy pointed. "See how they weave in and out around the trees? It doesn't rain much in the caldera, but it doesn't have to. The clouds seep their moisture into the forest. They build. Before long, you won't be able to see the ridge top at all. A fuzzy white waterfall comes over the top."

"How far are we from camp? I can't wait to see Mother."

Dessy glanced toward Joss. "An hour or so."

"Good. Let's go."

"Pietas." Joss touched him. "One more stop and then I promise we'll go."

How like her to want one more tweak. One more addition to what was already perfect. He'd learned to rely on her judgment and did not argue. Instead, he trailed her through the trees toward another break in the forest.

The sun's angle made it early afternoon. Moderate breeze. Pleasant hiking weather.

Joss halted and turned back to him. "You'll be able to see the pods once we pass that big tree." She indicated it with one hand. "I want you to keep in mind how big this place is. There's plenty of room. We have resources. We--"

"Joss, enough. I get it. I've been patient, but I've worked for months to find everyone. Let me see whatever this is so we can get on with it."

She wrung her hands. "I'm sorry."

"Don't be. None of this is your fault." He gripped her upper arms and touched his brow to hers. When he pulled back, her tears showed. "Joss! What is it?"

"I've hoped against hope we'd find you. If anyone can get us through this, you can. I wish-- I wish I had better--No, never mind. We're here. I'll let you see." She stepped out of his path.

Pietas stroked her cheek. Once through the tree line, the caldera's sloping sides revealed what she'd been trying to hide.

Moments ago, a few yards away, he'd struggled for words to reflect the breathtaking natural beauty.

Now, he groped for words to describe his rage.

Chapter Fourteen

If Pietas could lay hands on the humans that committed this atrocity, he'd rip off their limbs and use them to beat their bodies into bloody pulps.

And then he'd get violent.

A bend in the caldera's wall had hidden a cove that stretched for miles. Nestled within steep hills on three sides stood towering delivery chambers. On a colony ship, they'd have housed the populace of a new city.

Human thieves had pilfered the city sections and supply portions of the colony ship. The automated modular units would have released first, taken themselves apart and re-formed into dwellings, medical facilities, schools, and workplaces. A functioning city, product of mighty human terraforming. Once completed, the pioneer citizens in cryosleep would be roused in shifts and moved in.

Humans filled planet after planet with such places, driving out *lesser, unworthy* civilizations. Ultras had done the dirty work for them until the tide of war changed in the Ultras' favor.

How ironic that the tech Ultras had been created to build and guard now imprisoned them.

The placement of these delivery units had been no accident or miscalculation. They stood so close together one could barely walk between them. Instead of situating them in a wide circle or square to enable egress, they'd been lined up, three across, stretching the length of the cove. Stacked this way, it would be physically impossible to open the access doors and exit.

No automation meant they must unpack the cryopods manually.

Pietas did a quick mental calculation. Over five hundred and twenty-eight thousand people. Pallets held fifty cryopods per layer. He added a few details learned from transporting soldiers and figured each delivery unit held almost seven thousand people. He tried to count the number of units but in the distance, their gray color merged into an uncountable mass. Must be close to eighty. On this end, two units leaned toward one another and a third had fallen. Its angle was all that kept the other two from toppling.

All three had burst open and spilled their contents.

Heaps of jumbled stasis pods littered the valley floor, hundreds deep.

Joss had said there were over three thousand dead due to mishandling. Judging by the damage visible from here, that could be a low estimate.

He felt rather than heard her come up next to him. He reached out; she stepped in close and wrapped an arm around his waist.

"How many units, Joss?"

"We counted them twice to be sure. Seventy-seven. Seventy-four intact. Each of the three rows stretches over two miles."

"How big are these units?"

"Koliga used to design them. He says these are over a hundred and forty-six feet high, forty-eight feet deep and thirty-two feet wide. They aren't meant to stand in rows. They're made to link in a circle or a square. That's why three have toppled."

Pietas walked to the cliff's edge. Leaning out brought the Council's encampment into view, halfway to the bottom. He stayed there, mute, calculating.

"Pietas? Please come back. The cliff is unstable. It could give way."

The units below him radiated heat. "I calculate the equivalent is sixteen city blocks, with each block having wall-to-wall skyscrapers fourteen stories high."

"That's what your mother said too. Come back now, Pietas."

"And every pod in them is rigged to release at the same time."

"Yes." She sounded closer. "Take my hand."

He didn't respond. How different from his amazement minutes before. How many minutes had passed? Seven? Eight? Yet in that stretch of time his life had turned upside down.

His people's pods would all unlock at once, yet their pallets were stacked, one atop the other. If set up in common fashion, there'd be nine pods per pallet, six pallets per layer, with the top layer holding five pods each, twenty-eight layers per unit.

Those on the bottom two layers on each level would be trapped inside their pods by the weight of the layers above. All imprisoned inside a building-sized container that could not be opened.

Those jumbled on the valley floor faced the same issue. The pods on the bottom might unseal, but they could not open. His people were immobilized. Shackled by the unspeakable cruelty of faithless monsters.

Just as he had been.

"Pietas, let's move away from the edge. It isn't stable."

"You're sure the pods are functioning? You couldn't have reached those on the bottom."

"Erryq fit in most of the small spaces, but you're right. There are some we can't get to. We looked at every one that we could. It took ages to determine what classes they were."

He walked to the right, judging the angle of slope. "Ultra."

"I'm sorry. What?"

"Humans divided us into classes. Here, we're all Ultras."

"Your father's been using the term Reborn. New planet, new chance, new life."

He scoffed. "We are Ultras. Always were. Always will be."

Off to one side, where the edge had crumbled, a few trees hung over the side. Their exposed roots tangled with those of trees still standing, preventing their complete fall. Near the base of one sat the panther, tail wrapped around its feet. The huge black beast stood and blinked green eyes.

What was it waiting for?

"What is what waiting for?" Joss turned in that direction but the cat had withdrawn into deeper shadows.

"I need you to go." He kept his voice as calm and rational as he knew how. He did not look at her. "I'm not safe. My skin is crawling with the power I'm holding back. Get away from me. Far away. Take the others and go. I'll join you in an hour or so."

"But--"

"I can hear your thoughts. How could I abandon my people? What good would jumping do? I'd suffer and come back with the same problems. Go. Take the others."

She bent and touched his shoulder. "I love you, Pietas."

It wasn't until then he realized he'd fallen to his knees. He reached up, clasped her hand and laid his cheek against it. "I love you too. Send Six to me."

"But he'll--"

"It's fine, Joss. He'll be safe. He's a ghost. I can't hurt him. Now go."

As if awaiting the summons, Six dropped down beside him. "I need to learn at least ten more languages, Pi. Maybe twenty."

"What? Why?"

"After seeing this--" Six's gesture took in the miles of pods "--I'm gonna need a lot more cusswords."

Despite the seriousness of the moment, Pietas laughed. How like his friend to take the darkest moment in his life and make it bearable.

His laughter turned into a sob. He choked it back.

No! A king did not cry like some useless child or a worthless--

Pietas arrested that lie and cast it aside. He determined what he believed. Not his father. No matter which way he went, the man would find fault. If he cried, he was useless. If he didn't, he was heartless. The impurity of emotion clouded his judgment. The lack of emotion stifled him. Pietas fought to center himself. Gain control. When he met his father if he wasn't in control, his father would be.

No panic. No despair. For centuries, he'd led soldiers into battle against odds that would crush a lesser man. He could do this. He *would* do this.

The endless line of gray units shimmered in the sun. A flock of black birds with bright orange beaks swooped and dived among and between them.

Without power, how did one move five-hundred-pound cryopods? Down fourteen stories. Half a million times. What was he going to do? What should he do? What could he do? He had to free his people.

He couldn't let them stay trapped. Locked in darkness with no escape. Unable to breathe. Unable to speak.

He had to get them out!

Now!

"Pietas! Listen to me." Six was kneeling before him, his brown eyes dark with concern. "We will. We'll get them out. All of them. I swear it."

With renewed focus, he took in Six. This human meant more to him than his own family. His life raft in a storm. His shelter. When Pietas had been drowning in sorrow, Six had kept his head above water. Six was his friend.

His *amigo*.

He grabbed the man and held on.

Chapter Fifteen

By the time Pietas came to himself, the sun sat lower in the sky and the bank of clouds had seeped down the caldera's sides. His cheek touched Six's chest and his arms were around the man, but couldn't recall at first how he'd gotten there.

That he'd allowed himself to be held was obvious. He'd allowed a human to touch him. Comfort him. Who knew a human could even do such a thing? Before Six, he'd have never guessed one capable of compassion.

"Thank you." Pietas hugged him.

"Sure." It came out a squeak.

He lessened his grip.

Six sat back, facing him. The man's shirt was darkened and wet in front. "We'll get through this. Together. I'll be here. I won't leave you. I promise."

Pietas had lived more than a year trapped as his people would be trapped. He had to open the delivery units and re-stack the pallets. Get them down however many stories with no power and no working transport.

"We will, Pi. I promise. We'll get them all out. We'll find a way. We'll figure out how." Six placed both hands on Pietas's shoulders. "I'm not letting them go through what you went through. I couldn't live with that again."

"You shouldn't have felt my pain through the pod. The steel and copper should have prevented that. They meant it to isolate me. Prevent me from using my gifts."

"I didn't feel your pain, Pi. I felt mine. You were in there because of me. I lived with that for a year, knowing you were awake inside that thing, suffering, and I couldn't stop it. I couldn't get you free. I'm not letting that happen again. Not if I can stop it. Not on my watch."

Pietas drew a ragged breath. He clasped Six's forearm. "Warrior to warrior, Six. You are a man of honor. I'm proud to be at your side."

The man's eyes glistened and he swallowed. "Brothers. Always." He stood and reached down to help Pietas up.

Instead of his usual refusal, Pietas accepted. "Let's go." He tapped Six on the arm and started toward the trail. "We'd better find a stream so you can clean up. You don't want to meet my mother with a face as dirty as yours."

"Look who's talking, Ultra." After settling his backpack, Six pointed to the wet spot darkening the middle of his shirt. "You see this? You cried all over my shirt."

"Haven't you heard the rumor? Ultras don't cry. That's human sweat."

"It is not! I washed this shirt..." Six counted on the fingers of one hand. "Five weeks ago."

Pietas snorted a laugh. "No wonder it's wet. The stink made my nose run."

"Are you telling me you blew your nose on my shirt?"

"I'm not telling you anything. Humans never listen anyway."

Six cupped a hand behind his ear. "What?"

Chapter Sixteen

"Six, hold up!" Pietas stooped beside a pool at the bottom of a short waterfall. "I need to wash off my mask."

"Your what?"

"My--" Pietas stopped short. "I forgot we pretended the ritual. It felt real."

"Told you it would work. There's power in role-playing."

"Apparently. I'll duck under the falls and clean up." He stepped into ankle-deep water and caught his balance on the mossy rock. "Slippery in here. Be careful if you come in."

"I'm going to. Let me refill the canteen first."

Pietas waded into the shallow pond and slid beneath the short deluge. While the icy falls beat upon his body, he closed his eyes and went through lines from his ritual, reaffirming his strength and resolve.

He opened them to find the feral green eyes of the panther watching him from atop a boulder. The expression held curiosity and joyful menace. As if the animal wanted him to run so he could be chased.

"Not happening, beast."

"You've started talking to yourself. You worry me, Ultra." Six waded into the pond, stuck a hand under the falls, screwed up his face, and stepped beneath the water. He sprang back out and danced around, shivering and swearing.

Pietas bit his lower lip to keep from laughing out loud. "That might have been the shortest shower in the history of mankind."

"That's freezing! How can you stand there with liquid ice pouring over you?"

"Discipline." He returned his attention to the cat, but it had gone.

"Yeah?" Six sloshed through the pool. "I figured out something. You Ultras are supposed to be genetically enhanced. You ask me, they packed more strength genes into you by yanking out the genes for hot, cold, and sleep." He pulled off his shirt and wrung it out. Even in the lessening light, the teal dragon tattoo across his back showed. He put the shirt back on, muttering about ice water the entire time.

Pietas stayed under the numbing flow, wishing it had the power to numb his dread. He faced every fear, ignored every pain, refused to permit regret any place in his life. But dread? Dread dogged his steps. No matter how hard he fought, dread seeped into his life, insinuated itself under his skin, and muddied his decisions.

Dread soiled him.

Once Six had dried himself, Pietas returned to the bank and sluiced off the last droplets. He bent so he could reach his hair and tousled it. As short as it was, it would dry fast.

Six sat and dried his feet with a rag. "I sure miss clean towels." He pulled on his boots.

"Oh?" Every piece of clothing Pietas had worn rotted during his year of captivity. He'd begun his life on Sempervia naked. Six's one spare outfit fit like a little brother's clothes. "I miss clean everything."

Six picked up his pack and they headed out.

"All right, ghost. Let me brief you about the people you'll be meeting."

"Sounds good."

"You know my sister, the twins, and Joss. You'll recognize my parents. Both are blond and blue-eyed. My mother is a miniature me, except she's beautiful."

Six snorted a laugh.

"What?"

"Every description of you contains the words lethal, terrifying, and beautiful."

"How flattering. You find me attractive."

Six held up both hands. "I didn't say you were cute, Ultra. Just stated facts."

"I strive to be worthy of lethal and terrifying, but beautiful?" He flipped a hand in dismissal. "*Bah!* I want no credit for my father's work. I do nothing to make myself attractive." He flicked his hair. "I cut this with a dagger. It's not that I don't appreciate beautiful things. I'm fond of art and gems. The hilt of my favorite dagger was a silver dragon studded with turquoise. I had a silver cuff for my hair that matched. I liked wearing the pristine white and teal of the Council." The memory of his ship and crew being disintegrated cut into him. He banished the image. Now was not the time. "But my mother? Ghost, she deserves every accolade. You'll see. She's delicate. Tiny. But don't let size deceive you. She invented most of the processes used for terraforming planets. And forgive me if I brag, but every planet terraformed in the last thousand years has her signature on it. Literally. Somewhere on every world there's a mountain, lake, or river named for her. Not that she named them. Others named them in her honor."

"Impressive."

"You don't know the half." Pietas sobered. "And then there's my father."

They continued hiking through the low scrub for a ways in silence. "So. Your father."

"What about him?" In the waning light, he stepped on a sharp rock. Pain radiated through his foot, sparking instant anger. Pietas hopped around, examining the wound. Though a minor bruise, it still hurt. He brushed off his hands.

"What has your father accomplished?"

"My father?" Pietas lifted his face to the paling moon's cold light, wishing himself elsewhere. For a moment, he indulged in the childish yearning before abandoning it. He faced Six. "My father succeeded in making me his enemy. Enough said, ghost."

"*Oooh-kay.*" Six mimed zipping his lips. "No more questions about daddy."

A faint light came on in camp, revealing the shell of a pod standing on its end. The unit had been opened and its insides removed. Not far from that, another pod's light appeared. Combined with the first, it brightened the entire area. Though dim from this distance, it revealed two other pods upright between them and the presence of people.

Still a good twenty minutes out.

Six shifted the backpack to his other shoulder. "Who else is down there?"

"Joss said the entire council is awake."

"Not telling me much, Pi."

He halted and crossed his arms. "Ghost Corps did nothing to prepare you for your mission. You know nothing about us."

"You thought the Corps sent me to fight you?"

"If they didn't, then who did?"

Six slid his pack to the ground. "We were hand-picked last minute by some guy in a black uniform. Came into rehab and pointed to us. Usual military thing. 'I need volunteers. You, you, and you.'"

"Rehab?"

"Yeah. We were all in rehab. Supposed to have a day's rest after reanimation."

"I take it you didn't get it."

Six picked up a hefty stick and poked it at the ground. "No."

They had mistreated and dishonored his friend in more ways than Pietas could count. Robbed him of life, implanted him with a malfunctioning chip intended to negate his emotions and destroy his sex drive, and then sent him out to die so they could resurrect him to fight again.

"What I wouldn't give for a hundred copies of you."

Six's head jerked up. He squinted. "Say again?"

"After all they did to you, you still carried out your duty. We were bred to be enemies, but I've come to respect you. They threw you away. I swear that will never happen while you're with me. I honor those with valor."

Six's jaw tightened. "Remember what I said when you told me you were accustomed to obedience from your men?"

"I do. Shall I quote you? 'First time I heard about Ghost Division, I signed up, knowing if I got killed, they'd bring me back. The sole purpose of a ghost is to kill Ultras and the Ultra we wanted to kill most was you. Don't think for a minute I'm gonna be your servant. And I am never gonna be one of your soldiers.' I was rather insulted."

Six rubbed his neck. "At the time, I meant for you to be, but I've long since changed my mind."

"You were born with the heart of an Ultra, my friend." Pietas resumed his pace and Six fell in beside him. "You never told me how you were chosen before."

"You mean how they recruited me for the fight?" Six hooked his thumbs in the straps of his pack. "It never came up."

"The man who gave you intel about which pod to approach. Was he the recruiter?"

"I couldn't tell."

"Explain."

"He wore a fake-face." He drew a circle around his own face. "You know. A holographic image over the body. It kept changing. No way to know how tall or what race. The entire thing was blue. Voice changer. It was like trying to count air bubbles in a pool. Could've been a woman, I guess, but I didn't get that impression."

"And he came in and grabbed you last minute?"

"We waited less than an hour after we suited up."

"Not a full hour? You're certain?"

"Yeah." Six tightened a strap on his pack. "I was nervous, so I watched the clock. Why?"

"The other council members and I--" Pinching the bridge of his nose, Pietas stopped.

"What?" Six waited beside him.

Why the bald lies of humans should surprise him, he didn't know. "We spent no more than minutes in the trap they'd set before you and your crew entered. The fact you were prepped and ready long before we arrived puts a new light on their treachery." And the Council's stupidity. He had warned them again and again. "Did you train for it?"

"Ghost Corps trained, but not for that mission. We'd all been on the front lines and we'd faced Ultras that week. Sad to say, we'd had our butts handed to us. We'd been reanimated right before we fought you."

He must consider his next words with care. "Six, you're saying they gave your squad no specific training before they sent you in to fight *me*. Did you even know who you were facing?"

"When they told us, we didn't believe him. Someone had captured the Bringer of Chaos? *Riiight!* We laughed about it until we saw the video of you in that room. I remember thinking I'd already been given last rites. It would do me no good to pray." He shifted his pack. "But I fell on my knees and did it."

The confession didn't sit well with Pietas, yet it satisfied at the same time. "Forgive me, but they didn't train you in any way for a fight with me? With my reputation? Surely you knew no human had ever laid a hand on me in battle."

Six smirked. "I hit you."

Jaw tight, Pietas chose his words with care. "You got in the way and I ran into your fist. It was a lucky blow."

"Which you acknowledged during the fight."

Pietas had been so startled at being hit, he'd nodded in respect. "Yes." Pinching the bridge of his nose, he called on all his patience. "Very well. It counted." He met his friend's amused gaze and saw, to his satisfaction, a bit of fear there. "But your squad hadn't prepared to fight me."

"No. We weren't a squad. We'd never worked together. Ghosts don't wear nametags. We use codenames. If we're taken prisoner, the enemy won't know who our families are and we can't give anyone up. I never knew the other guys."

And here he'd assumed they'd sent their best squad. How vexing.

He'd assigned a number to each of the eight ghosts as he whirled through their midst, snapping necks and cracking skulls. In less than ninety seconds, he'd killed seven. To protect his mother, he'd spared the one who'd slipped past him and reached the controls of her pod.

The ghost he'd numbered six.

Pietas scoffed. "No wonder they were so easy to kill. It's insulting."

"How?"

"You were lambs to the slaughter, Six. A sacrifice to make their own actions appear valid."

"How?"

"They'd promised to expel our module into space and explode it unless I surrendered, but they knew I'd try to find a way out. Some other means of escape. They siphoned all the air and sent in your squad. They knew I'd think I'd exhausted my options. I was out of air and anticipated more ghosts. And just because I want to say it, if that had been my father's pod you were standing over he'd have been immolated. I would never have submitted to save him."

"So if I'd had the code for his pod, I could've walked out of that room."

"Oh, I'd have killed you, but I'd have been slow about getting there. You could've pushed the button first."

Six grimaced. "Fair enough. There is one detail I remember about the first guy. Not sure if it was part of the disguise or if I could see what was there."

"Description."

"A patch on one sleeve. Triangular. A dark field with a white letter *T*. Written funny though, with a hook on the bottom and the top left." He slid off his pack, stooped, and then brushed aside leaves and cleared the sand. "*Mira*. Like this."

Pietas squatted. Even in the fading light, the letter from an ancient language was clear. "It symbolizes a hate group.

TAU: Terrans Against Ultras. Part of the Human Pure Movement."

Six jumped up and kicked sand over the mark. "Sorry I drew that."

"Don't be." Pietas stood, brushed himself off. "You were passing intel, not judgment."

"Look, Pi, I hated Ultras because the leadership lied about you. My uniform had Ghost Corps insignia but I ripped off every one before we even left Enderium Six."

"I didn't notice the discoloration where the patches had been until we were halfway across the planet. At first, I thought you did it because you feared my people seeing them and killing you on sight."

"I'd be stupid not to, but that wasn't why I took them off."

He slid one bare toe across a patch of dried grass. "Oh?"

"They had a strict rule in your cell. No talking. So I whistled. When you told me to shut up I almost had a heart attack."

Pietas hadn't realized then that he'd connected to Six telepathically. "Go on."

"They took me out of your cell. When I came back and your pod was wrapped in chains, I knew they weren't surprised you were awake." Six grimaced. "They knew and they wanted you to suffer. I tore off those patches that night. I wanted no part of the Corps."

He squeezed Six's shoulder. "You're a good man. I confess, I was a racist when I met you. I hated humans. Every human. You've opened my mind to the truth."

The man reached up and patted Pietas's hand. If Six hadn't been standing close, Pietas wouldn't have heard his whispered thanks.

Clearing his throat, Six picked up his pack and slipped it on. "So they sent us in there knowing you'd wipe the floor with us. They didn't prepare us because they didn't want us to stand a chance. They wanted you to kill us so you'd think you'd done everything you could. And then to make sure it never got out, we wouldn't have been reanimated."

There was no way to sugarcoat it. He'd spare his friend the shame of his predicament if he could, but he must tell the truth.

"I'm sorry. They never expected you to survive. Which is why you ended up on the transport here. With me."

Six swore in Spanish. "I knew I'd been betrayed when they locked me in there. But hearing they'd never planned to let me live in the first place takes betrayal to a whole other level."

Pietas spread his hands. "Humans."

The ghost narrowed his eyes but then laughed. "Starting to agree with you, Ultra." He shifted the pack. "Give me the quick and dirty on the others."

While they walked, Pietas described the others and included warnings about what to watch for with each person.

"Great. What a fun group of vipers. Anything else I should know?"

Pietas lifted one eyebrow.

"I mean, gee, your people sound nice." Six showed his teeth.

"That is the fakest fake smile ever."

"Oh, really? I saw you on the news when you took over the High Council from your father. You shook his hand and smiled."

He rubbed one temple. "Point taken."

"Will I get a chance to meet your family? Or will they kill me on sight?"

"My mother will love you. I'll warn my father you're under my protection, but..."

Six shot him a sharp look. "But what?"

"Stick close to me, my friend. Stick close. We're almost there."

Chapter Seventeen

Pietas went down on one knee. The Council had bivouacked in a sheltered area five minutes below his position and the temporary living quarters had the orderly look of a military camp. From here, bushes and scrub hid the inhabitants and central campfire, though the spiraling smoke showed its location.

The wafting scent of roasting meat might have made him hungry under other circumstances. Tonight, knowing who and what he faced, it gagged.

With the dark sides of the cradle behind them, he and Six were all but invisible.

Where is Father?

That morning, Pietas had never heard the word *kueshda*. He'd plucked the term from Joss's random thoughts and along with it, what a "telepathic quest" was and how one was done.

Who would have suspected one could use telepathy to find someone in the distance? Why had no one ever mentioned his people could do such things? Better question, why had he never met with a group of telepaths and mapped out their skills? Leaders should know these things.

He set aside his personal irritation and summoned the skills he'd begun to learn. Effective or not, he was trying a *kueshda* outreach. He focused as Joss had and extended his awareness into the dark, toward the camp.

A disorienting sense of greenish-blue liquid overlaid the world. The color shimmered, fluttered, pulsed, and shone. Though he stood on solid ground, his stomach twitched as if he were windsurfing. He'd been kneeling. To control his rebellious stomach, he sat. Once the dizziness passed, he imagined himself standing and mentally set out toward camp.

He reached the outer fringes of brush and an immediate sensation of peril swirled around him. Like smoke, it stung his eyes and he rubbed them, to no effect. The sting was not physical. The awareness of danger teased his heightened senses but mocked him by providing nothing he could pin down.

The moment he released the *kueshda*, the feeling of unease ceased.

"Oh." He leaned back on his hands. "So that's it."

Squatting beside him, Six plucked a tall weed and stuck the stem in his mouth. "What?"

"Blocking."

"As usual, not a clue."

"It's a combat simulacrum on the aetheric plane."

"There you go again, explaining without a word I understand. No, wait." Six shook one finger. "I understood *combat*. All too well, in fact. And I get those little words. But otherwise? No idea."

He scratched his neck. "If you and I each have a comm-unit, we can talk to each other. But if you don't want me to know what you're saying, you could switch off yours. You could still talk, but I couldn't hear you. You could jam my signal so I couldn't speak to anyone. Same with telepathy. The other person can turn off the gift and they can prevent the broadcasts of others."

"So blocking is closing a door or turning off a light and they can keep you from opening them or turning them back on. Except with thoughts."

"Yes. I've never had telepathy, but for some reason, since meeting you and now seeing Joss again, I'm picking it up. She once said being blocked by someone powerful caused fear, but fear as if it were smoke. She was trying to see, but it stung and she felt she was in danger. She couldn't make herself keep looking. A few seconds ago, I had the same sensation."

"Someone down there's blocking you."

"That is correct."

"Who?"

"That's the puzzling thing. I was trying to locate my father. See if I could tell where he was or what he was doing."

"So it was your dad?"

"No. He has no more telepathy than I had." Pietas stood and brushed off dirt and twigs.

"Okay, now wait." Six pushed himself up. "If dear old dad didn't have telepathy, then how did he know you didn't?"

"Scientists identified the gene way back in the early twenty-third century. He tested for it."

"And he tried giving it to you? Huh." Six tossed aside the weed he'd been holding. "You can do that? Add telepathy genes to people?"

"If you're a geneticist with the skills of my father, yes. There's a name for it as long as your arm. He attempted it with me and my sister at least once a year until I left home. Tried it with himself and Mother as well, but we all *noretienne* the code." Anticipating Six's question, he added, "We couldn't accept and retain it. He postulated we had another gene that negated the effects, but he never isolated or identified it."

An image arose of his father screaming in rage and hurling a glass beaker. It shattered on the wall just as his mother entered. She'd suffered multiple cuts. It was the first and last time he'd ever seen his father apologize for an outburst. Although Mahikos had flown into rages since, he'd never thrown breakables again. At least, not in confined quarters and not around them.

Six was squinting at him. "And?"

"And what? Sorry. I was thinking. What did you say?"

"I didn't ask anything. I could see what you saw."

"Oh." Cheeks hot, Pietas dragged one bare toe along the grit on the trail. "I'm sorry, Six."

"It's okay. I don't think you can help sending. I can't help receiving."

"Thanks."

"Have you ever flown into that kind of rage?"

"Ever heard the term *berserker*?"

"Yeah! Finally, you ask me about something I know. It's a Norse legend about warriors who went into battle-lust during a fight. Fought with everything they had and kept going even if mortally wounded. They'd drop dead once the fighting ended."

"That's a gene as well. Ultra warriors are created with it. Armand and Philippe have it. You never want them to come after you. My father was created in the scientist class but he altered his own genetics. Gave himself the berserker gene and passed it to both me and my sister. My mother, on the other hand, though an enhanced warrior, is more scientist. Calm, cool, logical. Looks at both sides before deciding. I've often wished I took more after her."

"Pi, you take after her more than you know."

"Any calm I express is a learned behavior. Rage is my natural state."

"I believe it. I've seen you fight, but I never knew rage was genetic." Six snapped his fingers. "Hey, what if you're becoming telepathic because of the planet? Some kind of Sempervian magnetic field."

"An excellent suggestion. However, you heard me on the ship before we ever left Enderium Six."

"Oh, yeah. I forgot that." The ghost plucked another weed and chewed its stem.

As if some predator had sent shockwaves through the aether, background noise ceased.

Pietas came to abrupt attention. His scalp tingled.

Six threw down the weed and took up a position back-to-back with him.

Silence.

No wind.

No insects.

No bird calls.

Nothing.

Someone--or something--watched them.

The cradle's steep sides increased the darkness. The majestic array of stars sent a faint wash of light, slashing a silhouette of scrubby trees along the caldera's sides.

Once more, he sent a telepathic quest.

No blocking this time. Instead, the watcher opened to him, allowing him to see through alien eyes.

Judging by the angle, the watcher stood across from him. Not far away, he sensed others had gathered, less focused, less interested. Tolerating his presence, whereas the watcher found him fascinating. Why?

In the dark, Pietas glowed. His white hair shone brighter than a silver beacon. A pulse of light surrounded him. No such light around Six. The ghost appeared to the watcher as a dark shape, but why? Was it because he was human? Reanimated? Quasi-immortal?

Who was this?

Are you a native of Sempervia? Who are you? What do you want?

No coherent thought returned. Though the watcher still revealed nothing, gender solidified. It. Not he/she. Gender didn't matter. Wasn't a concept it used. It did not breed.

Why not? What was it?

Watch. Scout. Guard. Keep. Care. Safe. Duty.

Less string of words, more string of must-do attitudes. Like being hit with a thesaurus of precise correctness which permitted no forfeit. No other way to act.

Duty is life.

Pietas related to that.

Mentally connected, he moved with the watcher. Loose limbs, feet hitting the ground. A tree in the dark. Climbing. Up, up. No consideration to the rough bark beneath bare feet. The narrow branch creaked, but there was no fear of falling. The strength of the branch was not protection. The strength of the watcher was.

Pietas separated himself from the watcher's mind. Unfocused. Let himself perceive change versus detail. Subtle movement on a branch in a windswept tree drew revealed black on black. Huge. Silent. Movement ceased and the watcher turned toward him. Shimmering jade orbs blinked.

Of course!

He ought to have recognized it. Pietas gave himself a mental slap. He'd connected telepathically to the panther.

Six came around beside him. "What panther?"

"You heard that?"

"Are you telling me you didn't say it out loud?"

"I did not."

Six rubbed his forehead. "Gettin' weird, Ultra. I'm starting to hear everything. What I heard was that you connected telepathically to the panther. But what panther?"

"The one in--" Squinting, Pietas took a step. Not in the tree. Not to the left. Not visible on the rocks to the right. He released an explosive sigh.

"What?"

"I'm not imagining that thing! Why does no one see it but me?"

"You okay?"

He scrubbed both hands over his face. "Fine. Unnerving to be in a cat's mind."

"What did it feel like?"

"Imagine walking on a bed of sugar-coated marshmallows. Lots of give. Soft but gritty. No words. Just impressions. Never experienced anything so alien. And yet..."

Six lifted his hands. "Don't stop there! And yet what?"

"I felt a kinship. This might not make sense, but it's what I have with you. The cat has my back."

"Huh. So it's friendly."

"I sensed no threat. It seems to have adopted me for some reason. It let me see myself through its eyes. I wish I understood how this is happening. Maybe it's normal for telepaths to talk to animals. I have no background. No way to know."

"I was thinking, you lost so much weight in that pod you came out skin and bones. When I got it open and saw you, I figured you were dead until you looked up at me. Honestly expected you to die in my arms. And then the minute you got liquid food and water you started coming back. Maybe that's how your telepathy got started. By being deprived."

"Possible."

"Or what if the pod itself changed you? Supposedly I shouldn't have been able to hear you through it because it was made of steel and copper blend, but maybe that caused it."

"Maybe." He tapped one finger against his lips.

"About this blocking thing. We know it's not your family blocking you, which means it's a council member. I can't see it being the twins."

"True. I know the gifts of every person in that camp. Of the ten people down there, only one has the ability to block."

"Is that person trying to protect your father?"

"I don't have experience to tell. But it did cross my mind. If so, then it's doubly concerning."

"Why?"

He faced the camp. "Because the person blocking me is Joss."

Chapter Eighteen

Fists clenched, Pietas halted. His heart raced. His breath came too fast. Too shallow. *I am bigger than any fear. I am unbeatable. I am unstoppable.*

"Yes, you are." Six touched the middle of his back.

Pietas jerked away from him. "You aren't supposed to hear me, ghost."

"Then stop thinking so loud."

His iron discipline kept swear words from spewing out his mouth, but if ever one fit, it was now.

Six grinned. "Same to you, Ultra."

Exasperated, he turned to go.

"Hey." Six touched his arm. "Can I give you some advice?"

He tightened his jaw, faced the man, and waited.

Six stuck his thumbs in the straps of his pack. "After I signed the paperwork to become a ghost, I went home. Visited family. My *abuela* had died, but I hung out with my cousins. I said I was going on a long-term mission, so they put together a going away party. My birth mother showed up."

The ghost related few stories of his personal life, so Pietas paid close attention. "What happened?"

"I hadn't seen her in years. Maybe ten or more. Didn't want to see her. She'd abandoned me. Why should I talk to her? But I kept hearing my *abuela's* advice. 'Value family. They're your treasure.' I didn't want to believe that for a minute, but I couldn't get it out of my mind."

"You talked to her."

"I did. But before I went, I reminded myself of a few things my *abuela* taught me. Be aware of your emotions." He counted on his fingers as he listed them. "Don't respond to emotional chaos. Set boundaries. Don't let anyone steal your joy. Forgive those who do you wrong."

"How can one forgive when one can't forget?"

"Forgiveness doesn't mean you forget. You should never forget. To forget would mean they could hurt you again."

"Then how can one forgive?"

"You forgive because no matter what they did, or whether they deserve to be forgiven, you recognize that you deserve peace."

Pietas clasped his hands and brought them to his mouth, voiceless.

Once, when he'd trained with Armand and Philippe, he'd missed a blocking opportunity and Armand hit him in the chest. Philippe followed through not two seconds later. The twins hadn't intended to hurt him, but the double punch laid him out on the floor, unable to breathe, unsure his heart was still beating. Helpless.

Six's words hit him the same way.

How he ached to believe them.

Since one could not erase, change, or edit the past, a single choice remained. Accept it.

His father deserved no forgiveness. He wasn't worth it. Had never been worth it.

He'd give anything to make this pain stop, but one could not wish away the truth. This pain came from pure truth. He'd come upon it as a boy, pondering how he could improve, make himself a better student. A more adept soldier. A less disappointing son.

This pain came from the shattered delusion that he'd ever been loved.

He sucked in a deep, ragged breath and released it. No, his father would never love him but it didn't matter. The man would never get close enough to hurt him again.

Pietas squeezed Six's arm. *Thank you,* he mouthed, not trusting his voice.

He led Six toward the camp.

Not thirty seconds later, Joss stepped out of the shadows. "Hey, sexy." She set one hand on her hip. "I'd say 'Halt, who goes there?' but as loud as you've been broadcasting, there's no need."

Before Pietas could ask what she'd heard, Joss kissed him.

"Don't worry about being overheard, love. I've been blocking you. I'll teach you how to shield better so you won't reveal secrets." She trailed a fingertip down his cheek and out to the dent in his chin. "And for your information, when a telepath is on duty, blocking is part of the work. I have no interest in protecting anyone in this camp from *you*." She kissed him again and set her mouth near his ear. "Including me."

Pietas tightened his arms around her. Mindful of Six watching them, he drew back. *Later,* he sent. *I want to be alone with you.* He added, *Did you hear that?*

"Yes," they chorused.

Six batted his eyes at him.

Pietas cast a pleading look heavenward. He took Joss's arm and let Six trail behind them. "You need to teach me how to do this telepathy thing privately."

Oh honey. She sent him a flirtatious smile. *I already have it planned.*

Chapter Nineteen

Pietas put one persistent foot before the other. Rising tension stole the breath from his lungs but he soldiered on. His mother waited at camp.

So did his father.

An Ultra tackled what he most wanted to avoid. He did not seek to escape discomfort. Pain was a warrior's ally. But knowing that, believing it, living it, did not stop the dread.

The past closed in on him. He sat alone in darkness. Entombed in silence. Surrounded by the acrid smell of musty, urine-soaked cloth and his own sweat. Trapped inside a dirt-covered cage, running out of air, with his father's voice berating him.

"You made a stupid blunder on a simple number like pi. What is wrong with you? If you want out of there, recite pi to the thousandth place. Correctly. Start again, Pietas. From the beginning."

He'd uttered the last number, struggling to push the sounds out of his mouth. When the cage opened and air whooshed in, he choked, unable to draw it in fast enough. Gasping, retching, he curled into a ball on the ground.

"Get up!" Mahikos hauled him to his feet. "You're going to learn to hold your breath or you'll be sorry! What did I tell you? Ultras hold their breath ten times longer than you. You're a pathetic excuse for a soldier." He shook him. "How old are you?"

His neck hurt, but he didn't dare complain. His father would make it worse. "Ten, sir."

"Ten. You act like you're two. Stand up straight when I'm speaking to you."

He drew himself up. "Sir, yes, sir."

He smacked Pietas on the back of the head. "Pi. That's what I'm going to call you when you make stupid mistakes from now on. Pi. You hear that? Your new name is Pi!"

"Pietas?"

At Joss's voice, the sounds of the forest intruded, bringing him back to the present.

She peered at him. "Are you all right?"

The past whirled away like tattered ghost ships on the ebbing tide. His heart raced, throat dry. His fists ached from clenching them.

"Of course." She'd overheard, but this was not new to her. He'd shared much of his past with Joss. He lifted her hand to his lips. "Let's go. We're almost there."

As she turned away, Pietas inhaled, let it all out, drew in another breath. Some king he was. Spooked by a lingering memory he was unable to forget.

Six came up and walked beside him, head down. "Sorry."

"For what?"

"Calling you Pi." He looked up. "I had no idea."

"Heard that, did you?" Pietas coughed into a fist, kept walking. "I don't want you to stop. It will infuriate my father beyond measure when he hears you call me that and I fail to flay you alive for taking such liberties."

Six chuckled. "Gotcha." He unplugged the canteen. "Want a shot of this?"

"I'm good." He set a hand on his friend's shoulder, gave a brief squeeze. "Thank you, Six." He pushed onward.

On the edge of camp, light from the open, upright pods cast a welcoming yellow glow across a circle of rounded stones. Inside, a spit held several rabbits over a crackling fire. Sitting cross-legged around it, Armand and Philippe and the four other council members talked among themselves.

Joss entered ahead of him. "Look who I found."

Everyone turned at the same time.

Koliga jumped up and raced toward him. "Pietas!" Laughing, the black-skinned man lifted Pietas off his feet and bear-hugged him, almost cracking bones. Koliga spun around with him. Though a foot shorter, he was Toil class and they were always stronger. "You're here!" He set him down. "Welcome back."

"Thank you, Lig." He had no time to recover before the others surrounded him.

"Welcome back." Michel's embrace was less boisterous but every bit as bone-cracking. The man set the back of his fingers against Pietas's cheek in a hand-kiss. "Glad you're safe." He stepped aside.

The twins nodded to him from beside the fire.

As dark-skinned as Koliga, the beautiful Marjo fisted both hands around the front of his shirt and tugged him toward her. "You took your sweet time getting here. But I'm glad you made it." She planted a kiss on his mouth and then released him. "You always had a swimmer's body, but now you've gotten scrawny." She patted his lean stomach. "Guess you aren't eating any better than we are."

All had hollow cheeks and shadows beneath their eyes. Armand and Philippe seemed to have lost the least body weight. That would have been Ultra protocol. Food and shelter went to the warrior class first. You protected those who protected you.

The front line must not fall.

Erryq was last to greet him. The gorgeous little redhead held out her arms in invitation. "Do I get a hug?"

He wrapped himself around her.

Head against his upper abs, she squeezed him. "I missed you!" She looked up.

Pietas gave her a quick kiss. "And I you."

Marjo slid an arm around Pietas's waist and leaned into him.

His mother was nowhere in sight. Neither were his father or Dessy. That lingering sense of dread nudged him again.

"There's someone I want you to meet." He untangled himself from the women and returned to retrieve Six. The ghost had agreed to wait for him until Pietas scouted the scene.

Six wasn't where Pietas had left him.

"Six!" No answer. He sent out a *kueshda* but found nothing in the aether. No sign of his passing. Not one hint of his presence. "Six! *Siiiix!*"

He had the sense of Joss, searching as he was. In the dark, no sign of him remained. *Joss! I can't find him.*

I can't either, but I'm on it.

This is all my fault!

You can't blame yourself.

I told him to stick close and then I left him. I left him!

Pietas, don't cloud your mind with worry. Seek outside yourself. You-- Oh, no! No! Her mindvoice cut off.

He pivoted, spotted her light hair in the dark, and sprinted toward her.

"Are you looking for this?" His father's unmistakable voice came to him before the man's faint outline revealed itself in the dark.

Mahikos had captured Six and pressed a knife blade to the ghost's throat. At the point where the blade dug into him, blood oozed.

The blank passivity on his friend's face revealed what Pietas had feared. Six had been compelled into submission. He would stand there and let Mahikos kill him.

Rage propelled Pietas forward.

"That's far enough, Son." He dragged Six backward. "Unless you want your own hands covered in this human's blood."

Chapter Twenty

Pietas ground his teeth. For this, his father would forfeit his life. "I will end you, old man."

"Will you?" Mahikos dug the knife edge into Six's neck. "You dared bring this abomination into our camp after it threatened your mother--the woman I love--and you want to end me? This thing is going to die by my hands!"

Time slowed to a crawl. Someone had told him.

Joss? Too loyal.

The twins? Too detailed.

Dessy? Had she been so quick to betray him?

Pietas drew every vestige of Compulsion he had and threaded Chaos along its invisible bands. Mahikos was immune to both, but aligned, they might soften his will.

Wait. Immune. Immune!

That word rattled around his head, a stone bouncing off the sides of a bottomless metal pit.

Pietas had practiced compulsion, sending command after command to Six.

The man was immune.

Six, blink twice if you hear me.

He gave two quick blinks.

How he treasured this man! *Good job, ghost. You stalled him. If you're hurt, blink once.*

Six remained steady.

Excellent. I should never have left you. I'm sorry. On my mark, drop and get out of the way. Joss, go right. Distract him.

I serve. Her mindvoice packed the simple Ultra vow with raw emotion.

Now!

Joss screeched a war cry and bolted right.

Pietas shot to the left.

Startled, Mahikos flinched.

Six hit the ground and scrambled aside.

Reversing course mid-step, Pietas used his full bodyweight and slammed Mahikos into the ground. The knife flew from his father's hand. The two men rolled, each grappling for supremacy.

Mahikos was a full foot shorter and similar to others in the scientist class, slight of build. He'd altered his own genetic makeup and now possessed the greater strength of the warrior class. The man got in one blow to Pietas's jaw and a second to his head.

The world went white hot--then red.

Nothing existed beyond this enemy.

This retribution.

This hatred.

This rage.

Pietas flipped his father onto his stomach and rolled atop him. One arm beneath the man's throat, the other bracing the first, he crushed his father's airway.

Mahikos clawed at the arms pinning him, but without air, soon weakened. His struggle slowed, then ceased. In one swift move, Pietas shoved his father's face into the dirt.

That would have killed a human, but the Ultra metabolism had kicked into battle mode while they fought. The man healed before Pietas could move back. Gasping, Mahikos clawed for the knife.

With his longer reach, Pietas claimed it first. He rolled his father onto his back and knelt atop the weakened man's arms, pinning him.

He showed him the knife. "Are you looking for this?" he asked, echoing his father's earlier words.

Mahikos stared up at it and then at him, wild-eyed, choking for air.

Pietas wrapped both hands around the hilt, drew back the blade, and plunged it down.

"No!" His mother's voice rang out. "Pietas!"

He stopped the blade but the tip had already punctured his father's skin. Pietas ached to ram it deep, deep, all the way past skin, muscle, and bone, straight into the man's heart. Twist it. Break it off.

"No!" His mother pleaded. "He's your father. Pietas. Please! For me. For me."

He held his father's life in limbo, suspended between cold indifference and hot fury, buffeted by his mother's plea.

For her, Pietas withdrew the knife, cast it aside and stood. He turned to find Helia supported by Dessy.

His mother had always been tiny. Not even five Terran feet. She weighed less than a child. Now she looked near death. Frail, fragile, her skin pasty white.

He'd taken two steps toward her when multiple voices cried out a warning.

"Behind you!"

His father came at him with another knife. Pietas threw up an arm to defend himself.

A black tornado swept between them.

Pietas stood stock still, unable to process what he was seeing.

The panther had leaped into the fray, fangs bared. Mahikos fell beneath the bloodthirsty onslaught of snarling animal fury.

Six pulled Pietas away. "He was going to stab you in the back! That cat came out of nowhere!"

Hardly nowhere. The cat had tracked him since day one. *Watch. Scout. Guard. Keep. Care. Safe. Duty.*

Pietas understood now.

Growling, the panther gripped his father's throat in its powerful jaws, but didn't complete the bite. Waiting. Listening.

Through their connection, Pietas understood. It awaited the kill command.

Pietas opened his mouth to give the order.

"No!" Helia screamed. "Stop!"

He hesitated.

The Council had gathered. No one moved. No one interfered.

The panther yelped, twitched, and then went limp.

His father pushed the animal off him, revealing a knife protruding from the cat's chest. He stood, staggering. The cat's dark blood drenched the front of his once-white uniform. Mahikos covered the puncture wounds on his neck.

Armand and Philippe closed in on him and gripped his arms.

The panther's green eyes closed as Pietas knelt beside the animal. He stroked the sleek black fur of its chest, its jaw, traced one finger around the rounded ears. The cat's lifeblood oozed from its wound. *Forgive me! I should have let you eat him.*

Battle wounds in Ultras, Pietas understood. He'd never treated an animal. If he removed the knife, the bleeding might worsen. Hasten death. One did not mercy kill a fellow Ultra. They healed.

Ultras took no prisoners. He'd dispatched suffering humans. Why torture an enemy close to death? After what traitors done to him, however, he'd rethink that in the future.

Pietas could not bring himself to kill someone so loyal. He rested his hand on its chest, felt breath leave the body. This beautiful animal had died for no reason other than to save him.

A rumbling growl surrounded him. From the dark, eyes flashed green and gold.

"Pi!" Six called to him. "Leave the cat. I think they want you to back away."

Unmoving, he opened himself the way he had earlier. He'd felt their presence but had not recognized then who and what they were. An impression thrummed between him and the cats, teasing his senses. Unspoken, as present as the background hum of a powerful ship. A shared energy. Pietas gave himself over to them and they drew him in, welcoming his presence, accepting his nature, claiming his ferocity.

More than brotherhood. More than soldiers. More than family.

Tribe.

Like the kinship he shared with Six but on a primal level.

Hunger. Yearning. Wrath. Vengeance. Pure. Raw. Bloodlust. Blood justice.

Pietas set his hand on the knife, gripped it, and in one quick move, pulled it out.

The panther's tail twitched. Its chest rose and fell.

Remaining beside the cat, Pietas stroked it, cooed soft words of assurance.

It lifted one huge paw and Pietas set his hand beneath it. He stroked the paw, his own hand dwarfed by its size.

The animal raised its head, blinked a few times, and then gathered its feet under itself and struggled to a sitting position.

The wound on its chest had closed.

This animal was immortal. And like Six, it protected him.

On the planet Kaffir, homeworld of his ritual, they had a word for *loyal warrior*. Pietas cupped the animal's jaw, his face inches from the cat's. "You answer to no man, but when I speak and think of you, I'll call you Tiklaus."

The animal staggered to its feet.

"Steady. Here." Pietas wrapped his arms around the panther's neck. "Six!"

The ghost moved up behind him. "That thing thinks I'm dinner."

"You're safe. Give me the cloth from around your neck, please."

Six held it down for him.

Pietas used it to wipe his father's blood from the cat's muzzle.

Tiklaus gave him a long, wet lick and nudged him before backing away.

Pietas stood and offered the cloth to Six.

The ghost held it between fingers and thumb like a dead rat. "Burning this."

The panther made a huffing bark sound. From the group of cats, a smaller panther padded close, dropped and stretched out, belly up. With its nose, Tiklaus butted the cat. The smaller animal stood and came alongside Tiklaus. Side by side, the cat's more noticeable rosette pattern showed, dark brown on black.

Six nudged Pietas. "What just happened?"

"Not sure. They're not mates."

Tiklaus and the other cat walked toward the Ultras, who all backed away.

"Stand still." Pietas raised one hand. "You're not in danger."

Leading the other cat, Tiklaus padded before the Ultras, pausing to sniff each one.

Pietas had hugged them. No doubt his scent remained.

Erryq went down on one knee as Tiklaus approached. "Hello, there." She held out one hand and the panther put its nose in the center of it. Erryq stroked Tiklaus while the other cat sniffed her. Its breath ruffled the long red curls around her face. "That tickles." She stroked the other cat.

Tiklaus moved past Erryq and headed for Helia and Dessy, the smaller cat keeping pace.

His father tried to back away, but Armand and Philippe held him fast.

Helia remained at Dessy's side. When Tiklaus approached them, his mother held down her hand. Dessy did the same. They stood still while the cats inspected them.

The smaller cat sat beside Helia and wrapped its tail around her feet.

Tiklaus trotted toward Six, who backed away.

"No." Pietas held onto him. "Let the cat smell you."

The cat snuffled Six's legs, walked around him, and then did one more revolution, dragging its tail along him.

"Marking you, ghost. You've been accepted."

Tiklaus plopped down between them, wrapped its long tail around Pietas's legs and leaned against his thigh.

Six whistled. "I can't tell if you just got a pet or became one."

He stroked Tiklaus. "Neither. We each got a partner. Mother, you need a name for yours."

She touched the cat. "Pretosia. *Precious friend* in Kaffirish."

Pretosia walked around Dessy, bared fangs at Mahikos and sat.

His father struggled to free himself but the twins kept him captive.

Pietas stooped beside Tiklaus. The cat dragged its rough tongue up his cheek. One final butt of the head and Tiklaus ambled toward the outer edges of the light. The cat turned, took in the group of Ultras, looked over at Pretosia and then blinked solemnly at Pietas before loping off into the dark.

In the outer ring of darkness, the other cats faded into the night.

Pietas turned back to discover the Ultras and Six had gathered around his mother, who was on the ground, unconscious.

Fangs bared, Pretosia kept them all at bay.

Chapter Twenty-one

"Mother!" Pietas hurried to where she had collapsed.

Pretosia sat, allowing him access without so much as a twitched whisker. When Mahikos yelled for the twins to let him go, the cat launched, fangs bared.

"Don't let it get me!" Mahikos struggled to get away.

Pietas turned his back on the man and knelt beside his mother. He lifted her head and shoulders. Supporting her, he touched her face. The skin felt hot, dry. Up close, dark circles showed under her eyes. Blue tinged her lips. Veins showed beneath white skin.

"Dessy, what happened? She seemed weak but she was steady. She came out fighting." He indicated his mother's inert form. "What's wrong?"

"She's been sick since we landed, but she was terrified of what Father would do once you got here. She demanded I get her up and bring her."

"Since you landed! Why didn't you tell me!"

"Because she made us promise we wouldn't. Once she knew you were alive, she rallied. She insisted we not tell you." His sister looked past him, eyes narrowed in a glare that blasted a winter storm's worth of empathic ice. "Why is he here?"

He did not have to look to know Six stood behind him. "He's not leaving, so you might as well get used to having him hear everything we say. He's one of us now."

"It's his fault she's ill!"

"Explain."

"Her pod malfunctioned during the trip. It cycled her partway through awakening and then re-froze her, over and over. She hasn't been able to heal since." Dessy leveled a pointing finger at Six. "He tampered with the controls. He tried to kill her!" Which clarified why Dessy had hated him the moment she'd heard Six had threatened to damage Helia's pod.

Over his shoulder, Pietas beckoned to Six.

Fear and regret rolled off the man in waves, but he did not try to defend himself. If a person could stand at attention while dropping to one knee, Six was doing it.

"What did you do to her pod?"

"I had the codes to disable it and set it to immolate. After you surrendered, I reset it to full service. At no time did I disable any other functions. It was working when I left."

Pietas held his gaze, reading him. He found no hint of deception. "I believe you."

Six released a breath. "Thank you."

"What!" Dessy flung out an arm, pointing at Six. "You can't take his word! He's human!"

"Being human doesn't mean he's lying."

His sister uttered an oath. "Look at her. Look what he did to our mother!"

Pietas motioned to Six, dismissing him. The man took up a guardian position behind him once more.

Helia stirred awake and patted his hand. "Pietas," she whispered.

"Easy. I have you, Mother." He leaned down to wrap his arms around her, his face beside hers. "I'm here now. I'll keep you safe."

She pressed her cheek to his. "Missed you."

"I missed you too. Missed you with all my heart." He slid his fingertips along her face, moving her long silver hair aside. "She needs water." When Six offered the canteen, Pietas took it. "Here. Sip." He held it for his mother. "Just a little. I'll give you more. That's good." He made sure she had swallowed before offering it again. He set his cheek next to hers. "Just a little more. For me."

She accepted the drink but then slumped.

Having her in his arms, tending to her, filled him with such joy he could scarcely breathe. He'd endured agony locked inside that pod, hoping to see her even once more. Tramped over a thousand miles, hoping to find her. Now he held her. There was nothing he would not do to make her well.

Nothing.

"Dessy, why haven't you performed the Mingle?" Every Ultra had the same blood type. The ritual magnified Ultra healing by pooling their blood during an exchange.

"She wouldn't let us. She insisted she'd recover."

"She's too weak to fight you."

"It's not a matter of fighting, Tas! It's respect. She said no."

"Well, she'll agree now that I'm here." He gave Helia a gentle squeeze. "Won't you, Mother?"

Helia patted his hand but didn't speak.

Dessy swore in an alien language and shot up from her crouch.

"Here." Pietas held up the canteen and Six took it. Pietas scooped up his mother and stood. "Where does she rest?"

"I'll show you, but that ghost stays here."

"That ghost goes where I go." He held her gaze, daring her to argue.

His sister stared back. They'd contested one another's will countless times as children and she'd often won. This time, he bent her will to his.

"Fine, Pietas, but mark my words. You're making a dangerous mistake. You can't trust him. Not for a nanosecond."

He shared a glance with Six. "Not sure who briefed Father about the pod but I'm betting it was her. Stay close."

"I will."

"Armand and Philippe, escort Mahikos out of here. He's not to return to this camp until I give the order. No matter what he says, he is not to be admitted for any reason. If he needs something, get another person to fetch it for him. Is that clear?"

"Yes--"

"--sir."

"Thank you. I know I can depend on you." While the twins hustled Mahikos away, Pietas shifted his mother to tilt her closer. Behind Dessy, he stepped behind the first upright pod.

Pretosia kept pace beside him.

They had placed three pods side by side, partly inside the mouth of a cave. Deeper in, two more sat in the narrowing space, with a fifth sideways at the back, in the deepest portion. Enough room remained to walk around it.

While Dessy went to the last pod, Pietas halted at the mouth of the dark cavern and stepped back. He almost trod on Six's foot. "Sorry."

Six steadied him. "It's fine." The man took one step into the cave, glanced around and looked back at Pietas. "Pi, you okay going in here?"

Pietas swallowed. He would admit no weakness in his sister's hearing. "Why wouldn't I be?"

His friend gave a knowing nod. "No reason." He walked partway into the cave. "Nice and roomy in here."

"Tas!" Dessy crossed her arms. "Are you bringing Mother in here or not?"

"Why is hers all the way in the back?"

"It's the most sheltered spot." Dessy smoothed the padding inside it. "We stripped the insides of the upright pods and Erryq made a blanket with the lining. Lig used some of the other stuff to make cookware and set up a sink for washing."

All the pods opened by the top rising and then sliding down toward the end. Helia's had been dismantled and the cover placed upside down beneath it, putting her above all the others. The surface would reach mid-thigh on Pietas. All the other pods had retained their covers.

"Tas, she needs her rest."

"Fine. Don't be pushy." His mother needed to sleep. He could do this. The cave was not that deep. Twenty-five or thirty feet. No more. Not that dark. Starlight and light from the upright pods made the sandy floor and rocky walls visible. Pietas could walk upright. Not that confining. There was room. He could do this for his mother. "I w-- I want to be sure it's safe first."

Pretosia trotted inside and sniffed the pod, then sat down beside it, tail curled around its feet.

"Kitty approves." Dessy uncrossed her arms. "Tas, there's nowhere else. You can't take her to a better hotel down the street. This is it."

"Shut up, Dess. I'm loathe to put her down, that's all." He kissed his mother's brow. When she didn't react, he drew her closer, turned sideways and carried her between one row of pods. He ignored the walls closing in, darkening the cave. He looked at his mother. Nowhere else.

"Setting you down." He eased her onto the pod and drew the covers over her.

Six dragged over a sawed-off tree trunk as a makeshift seat.

"Thank you." He sat behind his mother's pod, facing the opening of the cave. The vertical pods blocked his view but some starlight showed above them. Not as confining as he'd thought. So why did his chest hurt as if he'd been too long underwater? He sucked in a deep, shuddering breath.

Pretosia nuzzled his hand, then set its chin on his knee and looked up at him, green eyes calm and soothing.

He scratched the cat's ears and stroked the smooth fur. Peace cascaded over him, cleansing his soul, clearing his mind.

Watch. Scout. Guard. Keep. Care. Safe. Duty.

He released a sigh and with it, all his tension.

Without warning, the cat leaped up onto the pod.

"Tas!" Dessy grabbed Pietas by the shoulder. "Get that thing out of there!"

His gaze went from her face to her hand, then back.

She released him. "Do something," she insisted. "That thing is dangerous."

Pretosia afforded Dessy a regal blink, and then lay down alongside his mother, tail around Helia's head. Stretched out, the cat's length matched his mother's.

"Tas! That other cat almost tore out Father's throat."

"Let's ask Mother what she wants."

Helia patted Pretosia.

"But, Mother--"

Helia fastened her gaze on his sister and took a shallow breath. "Mine."

Dessy's scowl said she did not accept it, but the discussion had ended.

After catching his sister's attention, he stood. "Get everyone out of camp. I'm going to sing."

Without a word, she turned and fled.

Six chuckled. "Wow. Is your singing that bad?"

Pietas took his mother's hand, bowed to her and placed a soft kiss on her fingers. "We'll give Dessy a chance to get everyone to a safe distance, ghost, and then--" He met Six's puzzled gaze "--if you can endure what happens, you'll witness another secret ritual."

Chapter Twenty-two

Pietas had killed countless humans, but he'd never sung in front of one.

The ghost would hear each note; however, his anti-emo chip might block the effect. Even if it did affect him, if singing returned his mother's health, Pietas could not hold back. Six would understand.

Would it affect Pretosia?

When he sang, birds and insects took wing. He'd never sung around big cats. From what he'd gathered, these panthers had been bred as warriors. Working animals might appear unaware, but they detected the slightest sound, scent, and vibration.

So far, the panther appeared asleep, chin on outstretched paws, nose near Helia's feet. Pretosia had curled its long tail around his mother's head like a shepherd's crook. Her every move would broadcast itself to the cat.

Six leaned on the far wall, nonchalant, disinterested. Intense glances gave away his curiosity.

While his mother slept, Pietas sat beside her, holding her hand. When several minutes had passed, he opened his senses to the presence of others and found his mother, the ghost, and the cat. He rose, went around behind the pod and faced outward. The acoustics might be better if he sang into the cave instead of out, but even with Six behind him, he would not turn his back on the exit.

Not yet.

Had he retained his singing voice? He'd recovered his other gifts, and had vast improvements in his ability to speak mind-to-mind. Could he still sing? Time to find out.

To keep his voice from going too deep, he placed tongue against teeth and made an extended *zzz* sound, then did a few lip trills. After a few deep breaths, he hummed. Nothing different in the feel of his throat or vocal chords. Out of the corner of his eye, he caught sight of Six. To keep from being distracted, he focused on a spot on the cave's mouth while he continued his warm-up. Starting with middle C, he sang *ooh* sounds up and down the scale.

His mother remained still, a slight rise and fall of her chest revealing she breathed. Her white uniform showed less wear than what the others wore, but it was soiled and stained. How it must have chafed her pride to wear such a garment.

Pietas launched into song. The notes filled the air, their tone pure and clear. The joy of it filled him as he sang. Before the end of the first stanza, his mother opened her eyes. He continued, song after song, vocalizing each word of each line, every song he knew. Words full of victory, honor, duty, pride.

Six drew himself up, his back ramrod straight. Perhaps that chip did less good than Pietas thought.

Pretosia turned on its side and rested one huge paw atop his mother's shins, either oblivious or immune.

Helia had color. She was alert, listening. Smiling.

The harmonics in his voice generated pleasure ranging from simple enjoyment to rapturous gratification. Some experienced anger, depression, or terror. His voice also possessed curative powers. Not as strong as those with the healing gift called Smooth, but enough to revive the critically ill or injured.

No other Ultra had such a voice. Though he loved music and possessed absolute pitch, Pietas never performed in public.

He started an old battle hymn about steel and guts, iron and flesh, the wings and teeth and claws of a killing machine. Glorious for soldiers, yet his fragile, scientist mother moved her hand, keeping time with the music. She drew a long, sighing breath and released it as if she'd held it an eternity.

Flushed and sweating, Six panted.

A battle song of warriors in flight came next. Pietas sang of the scorched and blackened soil of the conquered and the poetic justice of fire raining from the sky.

Color suffused his mother's cheeks. She took his hand.

Six turned his back, shoulders rounded, head down.

To end, Pietas chose a slow song of war in a minor key. The ancient tune was a favorite often sung the night after battle. It suited both baritones and tenors. *Forged in Fire* fit them as exiles. Pietas hummed to set the key, then released the true power of his voice.

Tears filled his eyes as he reached his favorite stanza. He slowed his pace to emphasize each word.

We can't forget. We won't forgive. We must return. We shall avenge.
We never quit. We do not sway. Our enemies--we will repay.
An Ultra's heart is forged in fire. An Ultra's heart is forged in fire. An Ultra's heart is forged in fire.

When he finished, the silence was absolute.

Six darted toward the exit. At the opening, he paused. "Pi, can you--" his voice shook. Keeping his back turned, he coughed. "Can you do without me?"

"Take your time. Stay close and watch your six."

His friend disappeared around the corner.

Pietas touched his mother's brow, then her cheek. "How do you feel?"

"Better. Weak, but stronger than I was before. Thank you." Her eyes were several shades lighter than his. When she was happy, they held the same dark outer ring. Like now. "You made him cry." A tear trickled down her cheek.

He wiped it away. "I wish I could control how my voice affects people. Be easier to defeat my enemies if I could make them cry."

"I hear you always make them cry."

He chuckled. "I try. Your skin is cooler but you're still weak. You need the Mingle to heal the rest of the way."

She stroked the cat's glossy fur. Her emotions had closed to him, solid as a door slammed shut.

"You don't want the Mingle. Why?"

She coughed, the sound shallow, tight, wheezy. Her emotional state broadcast itself with stinging pinpricks of frustration. "I can't explain without dishonoring someone."

"And who, among the handful awake, might that be? As if I didn't know."

"A scientist doesn't jump to conclusions."

"He can infer." He came around to the front of the pod, clasped one tiny hand in both of his, and drew it up to his chest. "You find it distasteful having Father's blood mingle with yours and you refuse to say why because it will dishonor him."

"I can feel your anger, Son."

"My anger is with him. I understand why you refused. Don't concern yourself. I will not allow him to join the Mingle. His blood will not sully yours or mine. He can hate *me* for that, not you."

"Pietas--"

"Mother, you need the Mingle. Once you're well, perhaps trampled fences can be mended, but for now, you must heal. We need you if we're to survive."

She held his gaze. "I've missed you. Missed your strength."

"And I you." He tapped a fist over his heart.

"Did your human--" Helia's voice cut off. She stared toward the mouth of the cave.

Chapter Twenty-three

Pietas pivoted. He'd turned his back on the exit. Love for his mother had always made him weak. No, he corrected himself. Her love distracted. Her guidance, compassion, and love had made him the man he was and that was anything but weak.

Outside the cave stood Six, head down, raking a hand through his hair.

Helia squeezed Pietas's hand. "Did your human sabotage my pod?"

"He says he did not. Unlike a normal stasis pod, the Council's pods had immolation settings. He was given the code to activate yours."

"Dessy said it was why you surrendered."

"Yes." He reached up to flip back his long tail of hair before recalling he'd cut it. He'd grown accustomed to it falling over his shoulder.

"You know I'm grateful, Son, but I'm ready to die to keep my people free. As is every member of the Council."

"As am I. For anyone else, I wouldn't have. If he'd killed you, I'd have given him a death worthy of battle songs for eternity."

The pride in her expression pierced his soul. She set a fist over her heart. "Yet, now, you trust this man."

"I do. Did what he do set off a chain reaction that led to your pod's malfunction? Possibly. Did it set disaster in motion? Unknown. He says he had no hand in planning it. He was informed the code was a tool that would make me surrender. He used it and swears he returned the settings to what they were. He claimed he didn't know you were my mother. I believed him."

"Everyone knows who I am. Not to brag, but I'm a scientist of some renown as well as mother to the Bringer of Chaos. One would think this human had lived in a hole."

"Did you say 'some renown?' You're the most celebrated terraformer in the galaxy. Still, when I told him it was my mother in that pod, he seemed shocked. I believed him, Mother."

She gave his friend an appraising look then turned that studious gaze back on Pietas. As a child, he'd been convinced she could hear him thinking. It was half the reason he'd vowed never to lie.

"You trust a human. A ghost created to kill our kind."

"With my life. He could have left me to rot within the unpowered pod where they imprisoned me. Gone off to seek his own way anywhere on the planet. He stayed even though he knew I had every reason to kill him. When he rescued me, I weighed less than a child. I was nothing but blackened skin and bones."

She gasped and covered her mouth, but then reached up and stroked his cheek. "To me, you look pale."

"It took time for my skin to grow back."

"That must have hurt."

He kissed her palm. "I survived."

"Of course you did. You're an Ultra. But it hurt. How about now?"

He debated for a second how much to say. "I function, but pain lingers. In time, I assume my body will heal itself. Perhaps the Mingle will help me as well."

"Yes." Holding his hand, she rubbed it, a distracted expression. "Yes, perhaps it will. For you, Pietas." She patted his hand. "For you, I'll undergo the Mingle."

How like her. "Thank you, Mother. Six nursed me back to health. Carried me in his arms to bathe me in the river. Fed me with his own hands. I've never been closer to perma-death. Six has been loyal to me beyond measure."

"Then, Pietas, I accept him."

"Thank you." He squeezed her hand.

"But he is not to join the Mingle. He might belong with us, but he's not one of us. I won't allow human blood to mix with mine."

"I never intended that it should. I do want him to see the ritual performed."

"Why? Son, this is our most private ceremony. Sacred among our people."

"He was produced through a corrupt imitation of what we share. To create ghosts, they bled our people and infused our blood with humans near death. They were told our blood resurrected them. I've seen no evidence of that. Six was told he died and they brought him back. Hence, the name Ghost Corps. I'm convinced his creators lied. They could have saved him. Instead, they turned him into a weapon."

"Do you mean to shame him?"

"Not at all! Six can't go back to being human. Unlike us, he'll die. While he lives, he's one of us. I know our people won't allow his blood to join ours. I want him to see the beauty of the ritual. To understand the bond that exists among us."

Outside the cave, Six had gone down on one knee and was drawing in the dirt.

She looked over at the man again. "You love him, don't you? You don't have to say. I can see it."

"We're friends, Mother. Nothing more."

"Are you telling me someone turned down my handsome, charming son?"

"I've been turned down by legions."

"Hah. Someone's always courting you. I've been asked about your status many times."

"My status?"

"Is Pietas seeing anyone? Is he involved? What gender does he prefer? How often does he take a lover? The questions are endless."

"Oh, please! You're making that up. No one would ask my mother about my sex life. Besides, I know where you're going with this and I don't need you playing matchmaker. I'm perfectly capable of finding my own lovers."

Helia regarded him. "Lovers, yes, but not someone to love you. You're always alone. Since you don't seem inclined to do it yourself, I'll find someone for you."

"Mother!"

Six squinted at them, but went back to drawing.

Pietas crossed his arms. "Absolutely not. You will not meddle in my life."

"We'll see."

"There is no such thing as 'we'll see.' You will do as I say."

"When you are in command, I will always do so. But in this, I'm acting as your mother. It's a mother's prerogative to meddle."

He bit the inside of his cheek to keep from responding and counted to ten. Rapidly. "Do not try to connect me with Six. We are friends. *Friends*."

"And you never asked if he was interested?"

Oh, to be able to lie. "In an impulsive moment, I asked and he said no. We're happy as friends, Mother."

Helia took his hand in both of hers and patted it. "So you asked him once."

"Mother..."

"You're not getting any younger, you know."

"Yes, I am. Every rebirth takes me back to my late teens. You yourself look about seventeen."

"You know better than to argue with your mother."

"And you know better than to pressure your son."

She regarded him in silence. "Immortality doesn't mean you have to be alone."

"I'm alone by choice. I'm a soldier. A leader. My heart is bound by duty. Desire and passion do not rule my life."

"Then what does?"

"I'm insulted you have to ask."

"Relax." Her sweet smile etched itself into his heart. "I know you're ruled by honor. Did you notice how lovely Joss looks? This world has been good for her. And Erryq and Marjo are--"

"Enough, Mother. Thank you, but I can take care of myself. I promise."

"And you always do. You take care of everyone else and ignore yourself. Son, it's nice to have someone who looks after you."

"Indeed it is. And for that, I have you."

"It's not the same as a life partner. Your father and I haven't always been happy, but we once were. Pietas, I want you to be happy."

"I know." Here she was, recovering from what had to be the most serious injury in her immortal life and all she wanted to do was find him someone to love. "How did I ever manage to deserve you?"

She beckoned him to come close.

He braced an elbow on her pod.

"What battle are you preparing to fight?" She lifted a strand of his short hair.

"Everything I say to Father brings on a battle. I wanted to prepare."

"He's proud of you. He has a hard time showing it."

How tempting to lie, but even to reassure her, he would not. "As you always remind me. Like you, I have an eidetic memory. It's not as if I can forget."

"Remembering and believing are not the same thing." Gazing into his eyes, she set a hand on his cheek and stroked it. "I love you, Son. I want you to be happy. Is it wrong to want someone to love you the way you deserve? But I will respect your answer as well."

He covered her hand with one of his and turned to kiss her palm. "Thank you."

"Honor has always mattered more to you than other things, unlike your father." She tossed her head side to side.

"I'm sorry for the mess you've found us in. I'm sure you thought the landing site would mean a city and supplies."

He scoffed. "It was promised by humans. I hoped for nothing. I got what I expected."

"I'm sorry I let you down."

He swept back her blond hair. "Don't say that, Mother. You have not. Not once. Not *ever*."

Helia offered a tremulous smile. "And here I thought my brave warrior son could never tell a lie."

"Can." He lifted a strand of her hair and tucked it behind her ear. "Won't."

"I have never believed any ill thing said of my son. By anyone. Not one thing." She held his gaze. "Not once. Not *ever*."

How he adored this woman! He kissed her cheek. "I love you."

"Pietas!" Armand interrupted, entering the cave. "Forgive--"

"--the intrusion," Philippe finished, behind him.

Dessy burst into view. She hurried over to them.

Pretosia sat up, green-eyed gaze narrowing on Dessy, fangs bared.

His sister halted.

"It's all right, Pretosia." Helia stroked the cat. "She belongs with me." She summoned Dessy closer and reached for her hand. "Pretosia, this is Dessy. She's mine. Just like Pietas."

The panther leaned closer to Dessy, snuffled her, then drew back and placed its chin atop Helia's legs.

"Mother, you look wonderful!" Without pausing to catch a breath, she continued, "Tas, is she better? Will she be okay?"

"Yes, once we perform the Mingle."

"Good. Then come quick!" She grabbed his hand and pulled him toward the mouth of the cave. "It's Father."

"What? Why?" He pulled his hand free. "What did he do, anger another cat?"

"No. Pietas, come with me! He's threatening to set the pods on fire."

Chapter Twenty-four

Mahikos was too far away for Joss's telepathy to hurt him but those around him would see her if she needed to warn them. For her own good, she stayed up here, escaping the violence that always seemed to follow Mahikos. The man was a magnet for hatred.

For now, he seemed willing to wait for an audience. Dessy had run back to camp, no doubt to fetch Pietas. The Council had scattered on that side, high enough to overlook the pods, but still well below her.

Now came the part of soldiering she hated most. The wait.

Dawn scattered pink throughout the sky and chased it with vermillion streamers. Bathed in the sun's early glow, Joss leaned on the canyon wall. At her feet lay a scraggly patch of *murdannia nudiflora*. The hated dove weed grew in abundance on every world but it claimed little purchase in this stony soil.

The single thing thriving here was that new discovery Helia had named *triefanus vincimus*, which in the Ultra tongue meant *living conquerors*. A hardier perennial had yet to be found. Even in the driest ridges of dirt, it took root. The flowering aloe-type plant offered nothing but fat leaves and thorns. They'd tried eating it but the taste, akin to the peel of bitter lemons mixed with overripe asparagus, put everyone off. It grew in abundance all around the landing site. Its thorns would be a problem when the pods opened and people exited. Joss had taken turns pulling up the weed ever since they'd arrived but had yet to make a noticeable difference in its spread. Koliga swore triefan grew behind him as he pulled the weed in front.

Joss drew in a deep breath of morning air and released it. For centuries she'd served aboard steel ships and inside painted metal walls, all the while longing to return to a fresh, clean planet-side atmosphere. To have this crisp air to breathe every day had been the most decadent of vacations. At first. The air on Sempervia wrapped a person in such an oxygen-rich atmosphere she almost didn't have to breathe. She could suck it up through osmosis -- a frog in water.

Dizzying. How sad was it that now, she missed the polluted, canned smell of civilization in all its befouled glory?

A shout echoed from the massive pod area below.

Joss avoided the crumbling rim, but remained close enough to see. Proximity heightened her telepathic powers. Up here, she escaped the raw and bitter emotions broadcast with all the drama of a theatrical display.

Mahikos lit a pitch-soaked torch. Standing atop a pod delivery unit, he toed a bucket beside him. Joss recognized it as the one in which they'd gathered tree sap.

The delivery units had been designed to withstand fire and protect those inside. But if he upended tarry goo over a unit and set it aflame, who knew? No one had tested its resistance to flaming pitch dripping down its sides.

If it worked, Mahikos would be committing the most heinous sin among Ultras: murder by fire. Ultras could return from any death except freeze-shattering, being put through a bone shredder, or fire. By Ultra law, the penalty for murder of another Ultra was death in like manner. In the twenty-four hundred plus years their people had existed, no Ultra had ever murdered another by fire.

Not one. It would not happen now. Not on her watch.

She sensed movement and leaned out for a better view.

Dessy had returned with Pietas in tow. To Joss's surprise and delight, Helia walked beside him. Joss knew her well enough to recognize how ill she was, but she'd improved immeasurably from earlier and stood on her own. She wore the same style slim jacket, blouse and pants as everyone else on the Council, but Helia managed to look as if she wore more feminine attire. Joss had studied her with envy for years. Literally no piece of her uniform was different from Joss's, but on Helia? Classy.

Pietas walked out to the edge as if daring it to give way beneath him. Joss held her breath, willing the ground to stay firm beneath him. If only she had that power!

His sister and mother flanked him a sensible distance back. The black panther that had claimed Helia sat down next to her. Though its tail wrapped around its feet, even from here, Joss could tell the tip was twitching back and forth. Not a happy kitty.

Mahikos and Pietas seemed to be talking. Mahikos shook his fist and bellowed a response, torch held high.

Though she was too far away to make out words, their body language declared intent. Pietas had insisted Mahikos give up. Mahikos had thumbed his nose at him. The two women had sided with Pietas.

Every time these four got together it was a battle royale. Someone was always on the wrong side of the other three. It was a coin toss as to which one, although most of the time it fell to Pietas.

What was it with this family?

Chapter Twenty-five

Hard to believe the tall, powerful person facing Mahikos had come from her own body. *She*, a worker in the scientist class, had given birth to this incredible warrior-scientist. Every time she saw Pietas in action, Helia marveled anew. Though it had been centuries, it felt like she'd held her newborn son yesterday. Perhaps all mothers felt so about their offspring. It did not lessen her awe.

She stood behind him, well back from the verbal fray, listening as Pietas faced his father. Her son's calm words fell on ears closed to reason.

Mahikos demanded to be allowed into camp and take part in the Mingle. To get his way, he threatened to destroy his own people. Instead of working for a solution in the present, he'd rather set fire to the future.

How like Mahikos.

She'd refused the Mingle because to allow his blood to join with hers would put her even deeper under his thrall. Mahikos had insisted if they stuck together, Pietas would accept the terms of the peace talks and submit peacefully.

Pietas? Accept and submit? How long had the man known his son?

She had gone along with it, no better or wiser. What a disgrace to motherhood. She deserved the lowest scorn from her noble son, yet here he was, defending her.

Mahikos had sworn if Pietas surrendered, they'd be given their own world and everything they needed to survive. All she had to do was agree with Mahikos and keep her mouth shut about the deal he'd made.

A replay of her entire marriage. *Shut up and obey me, Helia. Do what I tell you, Helia. I know what's best for you, Helia. Do it or you'll be sorry, Helia.*

This time, she'd refused with adamant protests. But he'd nagged and wheedled and made promise after promise. When that hadn't swayed her he'd made a single threat. Side with him and make this exile happen, convince Pietas to agree or Mahikos would kill him.

Kill her son.

He'd shown her how he'd do it. Plausible. Possible. Her spouse had hated her son from the moment he saw she loved the boy more than she'd ever loved him. Her son loved her unconditionally. Mahikos gave love to gain what he wanted. He was cruel enough to do as he'd vowed and kill Pietas.

Kill her *son!*

Helia had given in, but any love she'd ever had for Mahikos died in that moment.

Then, when they arrived on Sempervia, she'd been released from the nightmare of being awakened and refrozen to discover her son was not among them. Thinking him perma-dead, she'd ceased living. How could she survive in a world without her son? Mahikos, Dessy, all the others, everyone claimed it was unchanging destiny. Fate.

No. If fate ruled her life she'd have remained a scientist.

She'd never have become friends with Joss and through her, met a warrior who'd been born in the scientist class and had transformed himself.

Mahikos had freed himself by accident. Once he understood how he'd done it, he freed others and secretly created Ultras without the genetics binding them as slaves. By the time humans realized the danger, it was too late.

Join him, Mahikos had sworn to Helia, and he'd make her what she'd always longed to be: a mother. He knew how to create life and he would make it happen within her. Not be a surrogate for life as some of their kind were, but the mother of her own children.

Her own flesh and blood, Part of her. *Hers.* How could she refuse?

Instead, he bound her to himself.

His next promise was even more of a lie. *Bear me children, and I'll free you.*

Once the children were born, his promise changed. It wasn't two children he wanted from her. It was twenty.

Twenty.

While she reeled from the thought of being a breeding machine, she watched how cold he was to the children. How cruel. She protested. Tried to stop him.

He beat her into silent submission.

When he made her pregnant again, she terminated the pregnancy. Every time she discovered she was with child, she destroyed it.

Tore out her own heart with each precious death.

No mother should have to make that kind of decision. Let your child live and be reared like a soldier by an abusive, uncaring monster? Or let him die in peace?

She attempted to free herself, but her very makeup made it impossible. Surely, she could find a way. Perform some research that would uncover the secret that had made Mahikos free. She searched in vain.

Though she could see and understand the process, she had no power to apply the treatment to herself. Freedom tantalized, just beyond her reach. Her bonds existed within her own genetics. That was how humans had kept Ultras captive for so many centuries. How Mahikos enslaved her to his will.

After arriving on Sempervia and discovering Pietas was not among them, she died more each day. She declined to eat, drink, speak. Even for her cherished daughter.

And then a silent howl of empathic rage had swept over the camp two nights ago. No other Ultra had such power. It could be no one but her son.

Pietas was alive.

Hurt. In need. Near.

She couldn't go to him. Instead, she sent the others, refusing to let them tell him how ill she was. Pietas would want to know why, and once he knew the truth, in his anger at her betrayal, he would turn his back. If he discovered her part in his father's charade, he'd never forgive her. Never.

Let Mahikos rage. Let him scream. Let him beg. She would never submit to him again.

No matter how much it hurt her physically to resist and refuse.

If she had to, to keep him from rejoining the camp and taking part, she'd admit her part in Mahikos's conspiracy against Pietas.

Better to face death from her son than his father.

Chapter Twenty-six

A sound to the left put Joss on alert. She hadn't hidden, but she hadn't been standing in the open either. She crept back along the canyon wall, waiting to see who might reveal himself. Had to be one of the men. All the women were in sight. She counted the male members of the Council.

All present. Then who...?

Beside a cluster of brush, Six eased onto the cliff edge. On one knee, he rested a fist against the ground and leaned out to take in the action below. A breeze tousled his dark hair. In profile, he had a strong chin and firm mouth. Lean, muscled body. The smile so quick to show around Pietas was missing up here. Six was all soldier. He might be a beta to Pietas, but on his own, he was alpha.

Interesting.

Then again, wherever and whenever Pietas showed up, he became the alpha almost by default. Everyone deferred to him. He didn't have to take control. People gave it to him.

Except Mahikos. Which always led to fireworks, and now--this.

Joss remained still, keeping Six in sight. Why was he here? Shouldn't he be with Pietas? What was this human up to? And why could she not read him?

Six pulled off his pack. After opening the flap, he reached inside and withdrew something. He'd turned enough for her not to be able to see. He shifted position and raised his hands, revealing a handmade weapon. Six nocked an arrow and drew back the small hunting bow. Excellent form. In a tournament, he'd win points. He might even be deadly against a human, but at this distance and with the size of the bow, he'd do nothing more than annoy an Ultra.

Although, if the point was distraction, that bow might be more than enough. It depended on how many arrows he was prepared to waste.

"Joss." Six didn't take his focus off Mahikos. "You can come out. I won't bite."

She showed herself. "Neither will I."

He never took his gaze off the target. "Good."

He said it as if the single word gave him great pleasure, the way Pietas always did, but she decided not to mention that. "Why are you up here?"

"Waiting for a signal. Pi sent me to cover him." He steadied his hand. "Although I suspect it was more to keep me out of harm's way and make me feel useful. No offense, but he doesn't trust Mahikos."

"No one with any intelligence trusts Mahikos."

"He was Chancellor. How did that happen?"

"Mahikos? Because people are afraid of him. There's an old saying, 'better the demon you know' and Mahikos is the people's favorite untrustworthy demon. Although Pietas is thousands of times better than his father, he's their second favorite. Father and son leapfrog the office. Now and then a token representative gets elected instead."

"Token?"

"Me. Half dozen others. Helia. Although when she's in office, it might as well be Mahikos because she does whatever he tells her to do."

Six gave a slow nod. "Gathered that."

"Did you?"

"Doesn't take eyes to see she and Pi adore each other. Walking across this world with him, I heard so many stories about her I thought I'd known her half my life." Six shifted position, tracking Mahikos. "It's just as obvious that Mahikos abuses her and she loathes him."

"That is not true! They've been married since-- You're wrong."

He snorted. "Some telepath you are."

"Excuse me, but being a telepath doesn't mean I know everyone's business. Helia and Mahikos both have strong shields. And," she added, "I have ethics."

Six lowered the bow and looked straight at her. "If you can't see how badly he treats her, you haven't been paying attention, telepath or not."

"You are dead wrong. Helia and I are best friends. I'd be the first to know if what you say were true." He couldn't be correct. Could he? Instead of firing off another retort, she turned her attention to the ongoing fracas.

Pietas remained implacable, standing in one spot, arms folded, watching. To his left, Dessy mimicked his stance. To his right stood Helia, stroking her cat. Members of the Council spread out and took up defensive positions behind them.

Mahikos screamed an obscenity and waved the torch.

Chapter Twenty-seven

Exhaustion was catching up to Helia. The temperature had climbed and the heat caused a wave of nausea to roll over her. When her knees wobbled, she lowered herself to the ground beside Pretosia. The cat rubbed its face along her chest and she hugged its thick neck. She would close her eyes long enough to stop their stinging. Block out the bright light.

How quiet it was. She could sleep here. She loosened her grip on the cat. So peaceful. When the darkness beckoned, she let herself drift toward it.

Chapter Twenty-eight

Joss shot to attention.

Helia had collapsed! Why? She'd seemed so alert.

Dessy rushed to her mother's side while Pietas spun around and raced toward them. He scooped up Helia and cradled her to his chest.

Swearing, Six pulled back his bow and tracked Mahikos as the man tried to join them.

Thankfully, the Council came between Mahikos and the family.

Six lowered his weapon.

Pietas conferred with Dessy and then with Erryq, who accompanied him.

Dessy eased through the line formed by the Council and spoke to her father. Mahikos responded at the top of his lungs but Dessy held her ground.

Armand and Philippe closed ranks behind her. The Councilmembers arrayed themselves behind them.

Just another day with the ap Lorectics.

Chapter Twenty-nine

"Mother?" The warmth of arms around her pulled Helia back to awareness. Pietas had picked her up and was walking. Concern marred his fine features.

"I'm okay." She touched his cheek. "Need a minute." Helia bit her tongue. How fast lies came to her lips. How did her son ever manage to tell the truth about everything? She wouldn't admit to being ill even when it had to be obvious to everyone.

"I'm sorry." Pietas drew her closer. "I shouldn't have brought you here. You're not well enough yet."

"Fine. Safe now."

"Yes, you're safe. I have you." He hugged her to himself.

"Down." She struggled against his hold. "Walk."

"Mother, you're in no condition to do anything."

"Fight. I fight."

"You always fight." He placed her in her pod and kissed her brow. The big cat settled along her side. "You're a valiant warrior full of honor."

"No." Tears scorched her cheeks. The concern in her son's face swam in a blur of tears. "No. No, I'm not."

Chapter Thirty

Joss stayed at Six's side as he tracked Mahikos.

The man swore with eloquent profanity. "Is it always like this?"

"No. They don't usually get along this well."

At that, Six swung his gaze toward her, his astonishment plain. After a moment, he blinked. "You're serious!" He recovered himself and returned to his quarry. "Wow, if this is the ap Lorectics *getting along,* I don't want to see them fighting."

"If you stick around, you'll have no choice. Before the peace talks, they'd avoided each other for almost a century, but a new Council got voted in and they elected Pietas as Chancellor. That made Mahikos Chancellor Emeritus. By common vote, Dessy had been runner up, so she was Second-in-Command. That meant they had to work together every day. There's non-stop arguing. Gets old, believe me."

"I do. Come from a feisty family myself. Someone's always on the outs." He gave a soft chuckle. "It's about to get even more interesting."

"How?"

"Above left. By the trees."

She shielded her eyes. "What are-- Oh, no!"

Against the bright dawn, a ridge of black revealed the silhouettes of over a dozen huge black cats.

Chapter Thirty-one

Sitting beside his mother's pod, holding her hand, Pietas sang once again.

Erryq kissed Helia on the cheek, patted Pietas on the arm and left the cave. Within minutes, Helia dropped into a deep, healing sleep.

As he sang, Pietas put away worries about his father and whatever mischief the man might instigate. The others could handle him. Pietas shifted position to better see his mother. With her so gravely ill, nothing mattered more than healing her.

After a time, Pretosia's ears flicked. The cat rose on its haunches, facing the cave entrance.

Turning to see why, Pietas found Tiklaus and two other cats approaching. He ended his song and stood to greet the cats. "Good morning."

The cats waited while Tiklaus continued alone, carrying something in its mouth. After reaching the end of the pod, the panther set down a dead rabbit.

Pretosia took a single leap and landed beside it, picked it up, and retreated deeper into the cave.

Tiklaus flicked its ears and another cat approached. After taking a rabbit from the cat's mouth, Tiklaus flicked its ears and the other cat backed away. Tiklaus set the rabbit at the feet of Pietas and nudged it toward him.

Pietas went down on one knee. "You hunted for me?"

The panther butted his chest, then looked back at the third cat. When it joined them, Tiklaus took the prey that cat carried and waited until it backed away. Once it had, Tiklaus swiped one massive paw at the pod and placed the second rabbit beside the first.

Gratitude swamped Pietas. It took a full minute before he trusted himself to speak. "And for my mother." He tapped a fist over his heart. "How you honor me! Thank you."

"Pietas!" Koliga called out. "Come see this!" He appeared at the cave's entrance, but then backpedaled, his brown-eyed gaze fixed on the three cats.

"Come in. What's going on? You sound happy."

"There's a whole troop of cats and they--" Koliga pointed to the rabbits. "I see you already got yours. They brought all of us rabbits. One apiece." He came inside. "Well, except Mahikos. When he tried to pick one up they snarled and lunged at him. He took off. Two more cats sit outside the camp. It looks like they're waiting for Joss and your human to come back. How did you get them to do that?"

"I didn't." Pietas motioned to the panther. "Tiklaus, you have no idea how much I appreciate what you've done."

Pretosia streaked past them and out of the cave.

Koliga peered toward the opening. "Where's it going?"

"Taking a well-deserved break, I imagine. That cat hasn't left Mother's side since it got here."

"Do they understand what we say?"

"I'm certain of it, but let's see. Tiklaus, as a favor to me, if I may pet you, nudge my right hand. If not, please nudge the left." He held them out.

"Oh, come on! That cat's not--"

Tiklaus chose the right side and Pietas petted it.

Koliga crossed his arms. "That was pure, dumb luck."

"Tiklaus, as a favor, will you please sit and then stand and turn around once?"

The cat took a lick of its chops, but then did as asked and eyed Koliga, its green gaze serene.

A soft swear word came from the other Ultra.

Pietas stroked the cat's sleek back.

Pretosia wandered inside and sat down. It licked one paw and started cleaning its face.

"How was breakfast?" Pietas started to offer his palm to the smaller cat, but checked himself. A soldier did not interfere with the troops of a different commander. "Tiklaus, may I pet Pretosia?"

The panther sneezed, which Pietas took for a yes. He held out his hand to the other cat and when it nudged him, he petted it and rubbed its ears. The animal flopped down on its back with no more dignity than a housecat. He rubbed its belly.

After a few moments of indulgence, Tiklaus stepped between them. While Pietas stroked the bigger cat's side, Pretosia stood and shook itself. With one leap, it landed beside his mother. Not a whisker went too close. The panther stretched out again and curled that long tail around Helia's head, then set one paw across her legs.

Tiklaus turned and the other cats backed away. Once they had, Tiklaus licked Pietas on the face and rubbed its nose under his chin, then turned and lumbered off, the others in tow.

Koliga stood aside and let them pass. "I can't believe how lucky we are to have them do this. If it's okay with you, I'll start skinning these rabbits and cooking them." He pointed to the ones near Pietas. "Is it okay if I come get those?"

Pretosia alerted, green eyes watchful, whiskers twitching.

"I'll bring them to you." He picked them up. "Here. Thanks, Lig."

The big cat closed its eyes.

"What's going on with my father?"

"Dessy worked her charm. You know how she is with him. He won't refuse her anything. She distracted him. While he wasn't looking, Armand and Philippe confiscated the bucket of pitch. Once he saw that, he gave up the torch. Said he was trying to make a point and wouldn't have done it."

"And your opinion?"

"Ever since we got here he's been..." Koliga made circling motions near his ear. "Not sure he'd have set the fire, but, Pietas..." He dropped his gaze and fidgeted with the rabbits.

Pietas gave him a minute before prompting him. "Go on, Lig."

"It's not my place."

"Councilmembers speak their mind. That won't stop because we have no formal chambers. Talk to me."

Koliga's face brightened but then he turned serious. "The penalty for attempted murder... I know he said he wouldn't have done it, but he could have. He didn't just attempt it out there by the pods. He had a knife at your human's throat. I know Ultras are at war with humans--or we *were*--but Six was a guest. Your friend. Mahikos had no right to attack him."

Pietas tapped a fist over his heart. "Lig, you honor me."

"I don't see any reason to fight this human. If he's your friend he can be mine."

"And in this, you honor yourself. Well said, my friend." He gave a quick tap over his heart. "Now, go on. What do the others say about the threat of murder?"

He grimaced. "Exile's harsh."

"I see." He suspected the man meant that telling the son his father should be exiled was harsh, but Pietas kept that to himself. "Is that what they say? That exile's harsh?"

"No, but... Exile's a full lifetime."

"True. Forty years. No more, no less. An Ultra lifetime."

"Too long, when we need every person we can get."

"No one is exiled without full Council approval, Lig. It must be unanimous."

"If a member is on trial, wouldn't he have to be voted out first?"

"Yes, he would. You're a fine councilmember. You know the law better than a lot of people."

Koliga stood straighter. "I pay attention, that's all. Okay, I'll go start on these. When are we doing the Mingle? I mean, I know Helia refused, but now that you're here and Mahikos is out..." He fidgeted. "We're doing it, aren't we?"

"Yes, we are. As soon as everyone's eaten. The Mingle will sap our strength."

Chapter Thirty-two

Pietas gnawed every morsel of meat off the bones and would have eaten those too, if he could. It had been a long time since he'd eaten. Erryq offered him part of hers. As tiny as she was, she ate little. He nibbled every bite. Each of them had left two bites for Helia. She would need food once she healed.

At Erryq's suggestion, all the bones went into a pot to be cooked for broth. Vaguely unsanitary, but Ultras were immune to disease. Besides, he chided himself, he was about to commit the most unsanitary act of all. Sharing blood.

Too weak to eat, Helia had taken a few sips of water.

Seeing her so listless drove Pietas to pace behind her pod while the others finished their meal. He'd been the one who insisted they finish eating. The Mingle took blood. He'd performed it on the battlefield under dire conditions and it had endangered everyone. Hunger made recovery longer, harder. But now he had to bite the inside of his cheeks to keep from shouting for them to hurry.

One by one, they gathered within the cave, except Marjo, standing watch. A good leader never pulled all his people in one place with no one to serve as lookout. Armand and Philippe had volunteered, but they functioned as a team and their strength could come in handy.

To help Pietas take part, Marjo had given him her blood kit, a pocket-sized tool that enabled battlefield transfusions. Every Ultra carried one, but his had been destroyed when he'd been imprisoned. All the others still had theirs.

Six had positioned himself where Pietas wanted him, near the mouth of the cave and away from others. Protected.

"Pretosia." Pietas stood back. "You're relieved. Thank you. Take a break."

Dessy chuckled. "Like it knows what you're saying."

The cat leaped down and sauntered over to her, took a sniff from boots to knees.

"Tas!" Hands up, Dessy took tiny steps back. "What's this thing doing?"

"Let's ask. Pretosia, did my sister insult you?"

The panther stared up at his sister, fangs bared.

Dessy backed away.

The cat continued to stare.

"Um, Tas, did it really know what I said?"

"Yes, and I'll prove it. Pretosia, please sit on my sister's right side and wrap your tail around her feet."

"No, that's okay!" Dessy went stiff as the cat carried out Pietas's command. "Um... Nice, kitty." She gave the cat a tentative pat.

Pretosia sneezed.

Dessy yanked back her hand, the look of fear on her face priceless.

The cat walked away, tail high, stopped and cast a glance back at Dessy. With a flick of its tail, the panther trotted from the cave.

His sister released a huge sigh.

Koliga whistled. "I wonder what other things they can do."

"I suspect we'll find out soon enough." Pietas motioned for quiet.

As one, the group of people faced him. Though he longed to snap out orders and put everyone to work, his focus had to be on his mother.

"Erryq, you represent Medical. Will you direct us, please?"

"Of course." She approached. "Is this the full ritual or a battlefield quickie?"

"Mother needs as much strength as she can get."

"Full it is. Let's put her pod on the ground and gather around her. We'll need to be sitting for this."

Armand and Philippe did the honors, placing the pod without rocking Helia. Everyone sat cross-legged on the floor in a circle. Pietas, Dessy, and Erryq sat closest to her.

Erryq faced the gathered Councilmembers. "There's a big bowl of water outside near the fire. When we've finished, place your blood kits in it and I'll make sure they're cleaned and returned to you." She placed her hands together. "Center and prepare."

Heads went down.

In silence, Pietas repeated his mantra and then closed his eyes and visualized himself on a storm-swept beach. He willed away anxiety, allowing it to recede on the tide. Gentle waves lapped at the shore, leaving calm in their wake. When he opened his eyes, his gaze collided with Six's.

Though at the exit of the cave, he was sitting opposite him. The ghost tapped a fist over his heart.

"Are we ready?" Erryq looked around the circle. "Good. Let us each share a word with our sister. I'll start." She took Joss's hand. "Hope."

"Serenity." Joss reached her other hand out to Koliga.

"Benevolence." He linked with Michel.

"Tranquility." He held out a hand to Armand.

Armand accepted. "Peace." He joined with his brother.

"Cherished." Philippe turned his hand palm up toward Dessy.

His sister accepted. "Comforted." In turn, she reached for Pietas.

He took her hand. "Healed." He took his mother's hand and then locked gazes with Six, willing him to see the bond.

Six mouthed one word in silence. "Loved."

Pietas released a breath. That one unspoken word did more to lift his heart than all the ones spoken before.

Erryq held hands with Helia. "The circle is complete. Let our blood mingle as freely as our hearts have mingled in love."

Each reached into a pocket and withdrew a blood kit.

Erryq went first. After inserting the syringe in her own arm and crimping the tube, she inserted the other end in Joss's arm. Joss then inserted hers in her opposite arm. Koliga helped her insert it in his and so on around the circle. Pietas accepted his sister's and then linked to his mother. He connected Helia to Erryq. Once all were linked, they took turns releasing the clamps between each person.

"So the Mingle begins." Erryq rested her hands on her thighs. "Rest. Soft talk. This will take some time. Our sister's need is great."

Pietas centered himself, eyes half-closed, silent. Aware of the others, aware of Six, hyper-aware of his mother, he settled into position to wait.

Time passed.

The sun crawled across the floor of the cave. No one moved. No one spoke.

How long had it been since he slept? Two days? Three? He'd not slept at all the night after his sister, Joss, and the twins had found him and Six. He'd been up most of the night before as well. Though an Ultra needed little sleep, they required some. He'd nap after the Mingle. After his mother was out of danger.

Erryq touched his arm. "It's time."

"Are you sure?"

"Look at her. She's reborn."

His mother's color was bright, the sallow tinge in her skin gone. The rebirth had left her vernal, vibrant, young.

Her eyes fluttered open and she gazed at him. "Thank you." She placed one hand on his arm and looked over at Erryq, closest to her. "And thank you. Where is my Dessy?"

"I'm here! Here, Mother." His sister yanked on the tubes connecting him to her.

"Slow down. Let me help you." Pietas assisted her with the blood link. "There. You're disconnected." He started removing the one from himself to his mother.

"Mother!" His sister crawled past him, paying no mind to the blood on both arms. She gripped the pod. "Mother! Are you okay?"

Helia cupped one hand around Dessy's cheek. "I am now."

"I was so worried!" When had he ever seen his sister shed real tears? She wiped her face, oblivious to those around her. "Don't try to do so much this time." She drew up the thin blanket and tucked it around her mother. "Just rest, okay?"

Helia gripped Dessy's arm. "You're bleeding."

"It's nothing." She extended her arms. "See? Already healed. We all ate well this morning. And we have food for you. Oh, Mother, there's so much to tell you."

Helia brushed back Dessy's dark hair. "I want to hear every word."

"After you've rested." She clasped her mother's hand in both of hers and leaned her cheek against it. "I'll tell you everything."

"We should go." Koliga started to rise, but Pietas motioned to him to wait. The others had all disconnected from one another.

Helia reached for Koliga. "I want to touch you. Thank you. Each of you."

One at a time, the other Councilmembers knelt beside her pod, hearing her thanks, assuring her of the honor of helping heal her.

When they had gone, Helia patted Pietas. "Now. How long are you going to keep me waiting? Don't you think it's time your human and I were introduced?"

A prickle of unease snaked down his spine. "Mother..."

"Go get him." Her eyes twinkled. "I promise not to do anything scandalous."

Chapter Thirty-three

So this was the person her son wouldn't admit he loved and was certain didn't love him back. That might be true, but she was going to find out for herself. How was her son ever to find a life partner if he wasn't looking for one? Six was mortal, so perhaps it wouldn't be him, but if a mortal could make her son happy for a while, where was the harm? She might not be able to nudge Pietas, but she might succeed in influencing Six.

It was what mothers did, wasn't it?

Helia had to admit, for a human, the man sitting beside her pod wasn't unattractive. Enviable smooth skin the color of caramel, almost-black hair, dark brown eyes. How she yearned to study his genetics in a proper laboratory. He was slender but strong. Had an easy smile.

She extended a hand and he took it. Gentle but firm grip. "My son tells me you saved his life."

"I take no credit for that." Six shot a glance at Pietas, who was sitting behind him, and then turned to her. "With his willpower? That man is impossible to kill."

"I'm sure he'd have everyone think so." She patted Six's hand. "Are you married?"

The fleeting look of panic in her son's eyes made her smile. He didn't trust her one bit.

"No, ma'am. Single," Six admitted. "I've been a soldier most of my life. Never had time to settle down."

"That's what Pietas always says. He's too busy."

Mouthing the word *mother*, her stubborn son shook his head.

"Six, family is vital. Do you agree?"

Dessy, who sat mending a uniform, looked around at everyone in the cave. She set down her work and paid more attention.

"Uh... I guess so, ma'am."

"Well, either you do or you don't." Helia stroked Six's hand. "How can you guess about something as important as family?"

"Yes. Family is everything. Do you mind me asking a question?"

"Go ahead."

"He says you're his mother." Six motioned over his shoulder toward Pietas. "You look more like a sister. To be honest, you both look like teenagers. I don't mean that as flattery. I'm being sincere."

"Thank you, Six. If my son would take better care of himself, he'd look even younger. He refuses to listen to his mother about caring for his skin or cutting his hair properly. 'I'm a soldier,' he says, as if that makes up for neglecting himself."

Her son sent a glance heavenward.

Helia patted Six's hand. "Our apparent youth is due to metabolism. When Ultras die, or come close to dying, we're reborn. We come back younger, stronger. It's one reason we're unbeatable in battle. We can be scary."

"I'll say. Pi bragged about how beautiful you are. That was the honest truth."

"Aren't you sweet?" She squeezed his hand. Six would have no idea that her physical touch charmed him. He'd like her whether he wanted to or not. It wore off quickly, but it was her most fearsome weapon in close quarters and other than her children, her favorite gift from Mahikos. Too bad her children had long since become immune. "Six, don't you agree a man should find time to settle down before he's too old for it to make any difference? Fall in love? Be happy?"

"Yes, ma'am. If he can."

Pietas motioned to Dessy, quite obviously asking her to intercede, but she made a slicing movement near her throat. *Not getting involved.*

Momentarily distracted, Six looked over at them and her children offered the "who, me?" smiles she'd seen so often during their childhood. With a puzzled look, he turned back to her, but glanced at them again.

"You were saying, Six?"

He focused on her. "Ma'am, no offense, but I don't see me finding anyone on Sempervia."

"And why is that?"

"Well... I'm human."

Helia squeezed his hand. "So you couldn't fall in love with one of my kind?"

"Oh, no, ma'am, that's not what I meant. I meant since I'm human, no one's going to want me. I'll die. Who'd want to fall in love, knowing that person would be gone and you'd miss them?"

"I see. You're worried one of us wouldn't be able to handle missing someone."

"Well, no, I didn't mean it that way." Six scratched his cheek. "I suspect an Ultra could pretty much survive anything, even heartache. But why risk that kind of pain for something that doesn't last?"

"That's considerate of you, Six. There's an old saying among our people. 'Immortals should never befriend mortals. Not because mortals aren't worthy, but because friendships last their lifetime. Missing a mortal friend lasts yours.' Over the last few centuries, our people have lost sight of that. No one befriends humans anymore, but we used to. Is that what you mean?"

"Exactly." He grinned at her.

"Perhaps it's not so much about an Ultra losing a mortal lover as it is about giving your heart to someone who'll leave you behind after you die."

"Maybe it is." His smile retreated behind a polite mask, but she'd poked a raw nerve and the backwash smacked her empathic senses like a rogue wave. His emotions churned like water under a paddling duck.

Centuries of experience kept her from reacting, but she took a moment to gather herself. "I wouldn't worry about it.

When you're ready, open your heart to the possibilities." She touched his arm. "Some of us believe love is the most important thing in the world, no matter who it's with. You might find your perfect mate in this camp."

Behind Six, Pietas rubbed his brow as if he had a headache.

"Six, doesn't love make the impossible possible?"

"Yes, ma'am. I'm sure it could."

"Good." She patted his arm. "My son thinks highly of you."

Shielding his face with one hand, Pietas glared a warning at her. My, my. He really *didn't* trust her.

"Pietas respects you and anyone who earns his respect has mine. I'm sure you can take care of yourself, but if anyone in this camp speaks unkindly to you, insults you, or hurts you in any way, after my son deals with them, they will face me. I'm sorry for the way you were treated when you arrived. Mahikos does not speak for me."

Her children looked at each other, eyebrows raised.

Six lifted her hand and kissed it. "Thank you, ma'am."

"I want to know everything about you. Do you know why?"

"No, ma'am."

"When you get to know someone, you fall in love with them. Not necessarily the kind that leads to marriage, but the kind between friends, companions, and co-workers. People you care about." She adjusted the covers over herself. "You understand?"

"Yes, ma'am."

Pietas was still studying her, but he seemed less distressed.

"My dear Six, as long as someone is loved, they're not forgotten. Someday, when you're 'gone,' as you put it, I want to remember you with love." She'd shocked this young man. His face showed it, although he was trying to hide it. She sensed his relief and a spark of joy. The compassion that was a part of his nature passed over her like a softly spoken word from a friend in a crowded room. Quiet, almost unheard, but reassuring.

No wonder Pietas loved him. How nice her son had made friends with such a man. She could sense nothing false within him.

"Don't you agree, Pietas? Love for Six will keep him alive in our hearts. I'm sure he'll live in yours." Surely, her noble son would not pick this moment to tell a lie. "Won't he?"

"Yes. He will."

There. She'd gotten her son to admit he loved the man. The rest would work out however it was supposed to. Lovers or friends, it was out of her hands, but she'd done her best to find her son someone he'd be happy with and she hadn't broken her word.

Her panther guardian trotted into the cave and halted. It seemed confused by her pod being on the ground instead of where it had been.

Helia held out a hand to the animal. "Pretosia, welcome back."

The huge cat came to her and rubbed its face on her hand. When she rubbed its ears, Pretosia bumped its nose against her cheek.

"I'm so glad you're back." She kissed the panther's nose. The impression of sunshine and clean air came to her. There was no smell of cat.

Pretosia took one tentative step into the pod, which rocked slightly. The cat lifted its paw.

Helia moved her arm to make room and the panther stepped in and stretched out beside her. She stroked the warm fur. "I'm tired, Six. I'm going to rest now, but we'll talk again. I have things to ask you."

"Yes, ma'am. I look forward to it."

"You're so polite. I admire that about you." Helia curled up along the panther's back and shut her eyes. "Let me sleep and then we'll go terrorize someone."

Six's laugh made her smile. "Pi, you were right." Though he spoke in soft tones, Helia could hear every word. "I am crazy about your mom. No wonder you missed her. Every guy wants a mom like that."

Chapter Thirty-four

Pietas stayed back, observing Joss from the shadows. In a different time and place, her white uniform and blond hair would have made her an easy target for snipers. With no one but themselves awake, she faced no danger. Still, his worry and the urge to shield her ran stronger than his knowledge that she could protect herself.

What was wrong with him? He ought to trust his people.

Still, he'd lost so much already. Losing someone close would hurt more than he could bear. Or perhaps it was losing *her*. Other than his mother and Dessy, there was no one else among his people he would miss the way he would Joss. Except Six.

Few women were as tall as he, but in some shoes, Joss was taller. Her warrior-level strength made them a good physical match. She'd taught him the tenderness most women wanted in bed and then taught him her own preferences. Thanks to her, he knew how to rein in his strength and be gentle when he made love. It was as close to lying as he ever got.

But with Joss, there was no pretense. How he'd missed that these long years.

When she was about to pass the area where he stood, he let himself be seen. "May I join you?"

"Of course." She glanced around. "Where's Six?"

He fell in step beside her. "Believe it or not, helping Dessy mend a uniform. The man can do anything. And who knew Dessy was domestic enough to sew?"

"We all know how to repair uniforms."

"I suppose so. I've never known her to go about it so... what is the word... industriously. Whose uniform is it? We all came here with just the clothing on our backs. I don't see anyone walking around without pants."

She chuckled. "Armand and Philippe had one extra uniform between them. You know how they are. Prepared for everything. They each had a sewing kit with extra needles and spools of thread."

"And Dessy is sewing for them?"

"She and the twins have been... Well, you know."

"*Ah*. Please! Tell me nothing more about that."

Joss unfastened her hair, let it fall around her shoulders and shook it loose. The blond waves caught the fading light and gave her the soft glow of a goddess, as feminine and powerful as if she radiated sunlight. She combed her fingers through it, giving him an odd look.

Pietas coughed. "Um... What's up?"

She gestured to herself. "You're asking me 'what's up'?"

What had he missed? "Yes. Why?"

"Because I asked you what was up, and you just stared at me."

"I did? Sorry. I was lost in thought."

"I see." Her coy smile said she did indeed. "So, Pietas, what's *up*?"

Now she was teasing him with double meanings and ambiguities. He'd love to join her in play, but until he'd learned what he needed, he ignored the temptation.

"Dessy says you're in charge of camp security."

"True."

"Has Mahikos returned, or attempted to?"

"No. I've kept a close watch. The twins reported no sightings. Your father's laying low." She pulled back her hair and fastened it again. "But we're not the sole source of security. I don't see him getting past them."

"Them? Who is 'them'?"

"I'll show you." She motioned for him to come with her. "Look over there."

On a promontory overlooking the pods, a panther sat beside a bare tree, scanning the area.

"You're referring to the cat?"

"Yes. Now look over there." She pointed in the other direction. On that side, another cat prowled beneath a tree on the trail leading to the pods. "They've been there all day. They switch every few hours. Every time they do, the big one that attacked Mahikos stands on the edge of the caldera where you first saw the pods. After the cats change places, it goes away. It's the changing of the guard. I can see what they're doing and I'm grateful for it, but they're so intelligent it scares me. They bump noses and then take up the position of the cat they're replacing. I think they might be telepathic, but with each other, not me. I don't pick up anything."

"They've done this all day?"

"Like clockwork. You know what this means, don't you?"

"Yes. I can get some sleep tonight." A yawn overtook him.

"I was going to say we should name them."

Pietas nudged his chin toward a cat. "We'll call that one Trouble."

Laughing, Joss poked him in the shoulder, but then kissed the spot. They stood eye-to-eye. "Pietas, I've missed you more than you'll ever know. We've been friends, lovers, partners, warriors. We've done everything together. When you weren't here..." Tears filled her eyes.

"*Shh.* I know. But I'm here now."

The shriek of a bird pierced the gathering dusk. They both turned, seeking the source. Above them on the caldera rim, the silhouette of a panther darkened the sky. The eyes reflected flashes of green fire. Beyond, a sprinkle of stars announced the oncoming night.

Pietas held Joss while darkness settled over the camp and the cry of night birds rose. Off through the grasses, a shapeless form moved. Green eyes glowed in the dim light and then vanished. Golden eyes took their place.

He toyed with one of her buttons. "When are you off duty?"

"I'm off now. I came out here to check on things once more before dark. Are you ready for a private lesson in how to shield?"

"I'm ready for a private lesson in anything you want to teach me."

"Oh, good." With a smile, Joss tangled her fingers in his hair. "Let's start with a memory test."

"A what?" He raised one eyebrow. "I remember everything. You know that."

"Yes, I do." She brushed hair back from his face and then touched his chin dimple. "But do you remember how I like being kissed?"

Chapter Thirty-five

Joss stopped by the camp to pick up a canteen of water and a bedroll, but had to wait while Pietas assigned Six guard duty and put him in charge of security for the night. He'd asked her for permission first. She ran security, but she was fine with it.

When he gave the order, every person in the camp had the same boggle-eyed *"he did what?"* expression. Ultras, protected by a human? Never happen, no matter how enhanced the human was. However, a Councilmember could not disobey a direct order from the Chancellor.

When ready to leave, Pietas tapped his heart in an Ultra salute. "Protect the people, Six."

The man tapped his heart the same way. "I serve."

Hearing him state the Ultra vow left a lump in her throat that the rest of the Council seemed to experience as well. Helia brushed at her eyes; even Dessy smiled.

Carrying her bedroll, Joss took Pietas by the hand and led him to the lookout point where she'd kept watch earlier that day. The small upper cavern wasn't visible from camp and had a recessed area big enough to sleep four. The spot had become a private getaway for amorous pairings. Dessy and the twins had claimed it before anyone else had a chance, fueling protests. When Joss attempted to solve the issue by drawing up a schedule, *that* fueled protests.

Earlier in the day, she'd let everyone know no matter what the schedule said, tonight it was hers. Like Pietas.

When they reached the cavern, she dropped the bedroll, pulled Pietas close. "Do you have any idea how much I love you?"

Pietas hugged her, smiling into her eyes. "I'm dying for you to show me."

Chapter Thirty-six

Sometime in the night, she woke to find Pietas still asleep. He hadn't slept in days, according to Helia and Dessy, and hadn't eaten since that morning. But, as in everything else he did, Pietas gave himself and held nothing in reserve. He made love the way he made war. He studied every weakness, pursued every advantage, and then conquered and commanded every inch of territory he claimed.

Her throat tightened and a flush of heat rose within her. The warrior she'd first taken to her bed as a beautiful youth had mellowed, strengthened, and settled, comfortable in his own skin in a way most men weren't. His utter confidence offered no resistance to anything. He pleasured her in any way she asked, as tender as she wanted or as rough as she needed.

He was, in a word, *amazing*. He'd always been her most unselfish lover and in the hundred-odd years since they'd last been together, that hadn't changed.

But afterward, she'd gone to cuddle with him and found him dead to the world. She let him sleep while she planned security for the camp and drew up a mental duty roster. Hours passed. She grabbed the usual two-hour nap an Ultra needed. When she woke, she lay there resting while the full moon crawled up into the sky and filled the small cavern with its silver light.

Pietas stirred and Joss stretched out and propped herself up on one elbow to better see him. In repose, he had the face of an angel. His cleft chin and strong jaw seemed at odds with his sweet face. None of the brutality he'd suffered-- throughout his entire immortal life--showed. He might have been an untried youth, sleeping in his parents' house, no knowledge of the world. The man she knew him to be on the battlefield, a warrior king capable of remorseless, barbaric savagery, remained hidden.

She admired both sides of his personality. Loved the man.

He turned and a shock-white hair fell over one eye. How could he have such white hair, yet have such dark lashes and eyebrows? Such a baby face. He looked so innocent. She brushed back his hair.

Without warning, Pietas gripped her arm. He flipped her over him, rolled on top of her and slammed her into the ground.

It knocked the wind out of her.

He wrapped his hands around her throat.

Centuries of training took over. In one fleeting move, she released a telepathic command to release her, hooked her hands over his wrists and pulled them apart, bucking her hips to throw him off balance. She then tucked her left leg outside his, pushed with her other foot, rolled him off her and scrambled to her feet. Gasping for air, she backed away.

He lunged toward her.

"*No!*" She threw out a mental push.

It shoved him back better than a side kick. Staggering, shaking his head, he crouched, ready to fight.

"*Pietas! Wake up!*" Though every instinct warned her away, she stepped into the moonlight and sent an image of herself into his mind, willing him to wake and see her. "*Look at me. Wake up! See me, Pietas. See me!*"

He blinked, shook himself like a dazed fighter. "Joss." He lowered his hands and straightened. "Jossie!" Regret twisted his face. "Are you hurt?"

Her air came back and she panted, nodding. "You--okay?"

He didn't answer her.

After she caught her breath, she went to him. "I shouldn't have touched you. You were asleep. I'm sorry. I knew better."

"No. I'm the one who's sorry." He drew away from her. "I hurt you." His teeth chattered.

"Are you cold? I can hold you." She reached for him.

"No! No," he repeated, calmer this time. His distress hung between them thicker than rancid smoke, soiling everything it touched. He trembled, but backed away from her. "I could have killed you. I'm not safe, Joss. I should go."

"No, Pietas, stay. Please." She did not get between him and the way out. *I love you. I want you to stay. I'm safe with you. I'm not afraid.*

He looked up at her. "You should be. I hurt you." He touched his own throat and motioned toward hers. "I put marks on you." Through their mental bond, his disgust with himself stung her as much as it must have stung him.

She did not shield. "I'm a warrior. I've had worse in practice." The adrenaline of battle had kept her focused, but now it occurred to her they wore nothing but Sempervian moonlight. Taking her time, Joss lifted her arms and unfastened her hair. She shook it out and let the soft curls fall over her shoulders. "I'm fine, Pietas. Stay. Please."

The war she'd sensed within him raged, but at last desire nudged aside self-anger.

He stood up straighter. "I hurt you."

"Don't blame yourself. I can take anything you do to me. I can defend myself. I knew what I was getting into with you. I know you. I got careless." She stood before him. "May I touch you? Please, Pietas. Look at me."

Sorrow filled his eyes. Remorse eddied to her, dirty water clouding a fresh stream. "Joss, the last thing I wanted was hurt you."

"I know that. You didn't do it on purpose. I forgot myself. You weren't abusive. It wasn't your fault." She held out her hands. "Let me hold you."

His ragged breathing calmed. He gave a single nod.

She flattened her hands on his back and drew him up against her.

Slowly, he wrapped his arms around her and tightened them.

Joss leaned into him. "I'm sorry I put you through that."

"I shouldn't have tried to sleep."

"*Shh!*" She set one finger on his lips and held his gaze. The moonlight silvered his hair and turned his turquoise eyes as gray as his sister's. "You're not invincible. You have to eat, sleep, laugh and make love. You can't be all war. I want you to be free to do those things. I stepped outside the bounds you were ready to handle. It's my fault and it won't happen again." She leaned up and kissed him.

He slid one hand through her hair, wrapped it in his fist. "I love touching you. Making love to you. I know we're rough during play but this... This wasn't right."

She rested her head on his shoulder. "I have no regrets except that I didn't stop and think. I knew better." She squeezed him. "Forgive me?"

He slid his hands down her back. "If you forgive me."

She moved so he could see her smile. "Done."

Pietas studied her, his intense gaze searching, judging. As if he'd found what he sought, he let out a sighing breath. "Thank you."

"Thank *you*."

"Joss." He drew her back into his arms. "For the record, I know how you like to be kissed and I am *never* going to forget." He crushed his mouth against hers.

Chapter Thirty-seven

Once the camp slept, Helia slipped out of her pod.

Her panther guardian rose as if to follow.

"Pretosia," she whispered, holding a hand before its nose. "Stay. Guard Dessy."

The cat peered toward Dessy's pod, then lay down and set chin on paws.

After petting the panther, she kissed its nose. At the cave's opening, she paused to make sure the cat hadn't followed.

Pretosia picked up its head and stared at her, but lay down again.

Heart in her throat, Helia tiptoed over to the upright pods and listened. Nothing but the crackling of a fire broke the stillness. The night air chilled like a lover's contempt, slipping beneath all her defenses. She rubbed her arms to warm herself.

On the other side of the pods, Marjo stood watch. When they'd first arrived, the woman had refused to walk a beat during her watch. She'd complained since they were alone on this world and anyone who needed protecting slept in a cave behind her, it wasn't needed. Since Pietas had arrived, she'd walked every shift.

Dangerous to shirk duty around Pietas. Even more so to complain. As much as Helia admired her son's attention to detail and obedience to command, she recognized it as the influence of Mahikos. He had instilled in their children by force what he'd created within her genetically.

They obeyed on instinct. She obeyed an inner compulsion. In both cases, weak as he was, Mahikos ruled them.

Until the children were thrust out, like Pietas, or escaped, like Dessy.

Marjo got up from the campfire and walked toward the pods, which gave Helia an opportunity.

She paused to ensure the cat had not followed, double-checked Marjo was out of sight, and then raced toward the lower waterfall and past it.

After months of illness, unable to do little for herself, the Mingle's restoration left her eager for freedom. How good it felt to have her speed and strength. Her energy. Her drive.

She reached the brackish part of the caldera, near the marsh. No one in camp went there. In sunshine, the soggy ground stank of rotted vegetation. At night, a thick cloud hovered.

Around the bend, however, hid a sheltered spot with trees, grass, and pockets of fresh air. A fetid getaway but once there, no one intruded. She'd never visited on her own. Mahikos had carried her, but she knew how to find it.

Tonight, she'd reach it on her own. She needed no one's help. Would not be carried like a child or an item to be placed where someone else thought it fit.

Mahikos's voice came to her before he walked out into the light.

Loathing for this man rose within her. He had always controlled her. Forced her to do his bidding. He'd kept her captive, chained to himself and his desires.

When he beckoned, her body responded. When he commanded her, she could fight him, resist him, hate him, but in the end, her inner compulsion left her unable to refuse. When he promised her a thing, she believed him, knowing he lied. Knowing he'd use her. Knowing he'd take and never give.

But she believed him anyway.

While he partook of pleasure wherever he fancied, she was bound to him. She could never be with another. When he beat her, she could no more run from him than the sun could go dark at noon.

He'd promised he'd stop hurting her if she gave him complete control over their children. She must allow him to rear them as he wished, without interference. Said it was for their own good to rear them as soldiers.

He'd created them. They were his experiment, not hers.

She resisted. She was a mother. A mother protected her children. That was why she wanted them, to give protection as she had never been protected.

Mahikos hit her harder, more often. Bruised her. Cut her. Starved her. Hurt her in so many ways she lost count.

Then, he threatened to destroy the children. Painfully. Permanently.

She capitulated.

Better they live with a tyrant than not at all. It broke her heart, but once she hardened herself to their misery, her own lessened.

Now, he swore to her, once he became king on Sempervia, he'd give her what she wanted most. He'd finally set her free.

If she helped him get what he wanted. Once he possessed the power he sought, Mahikos would remove her shackles. The technology existed on this world, hidden, part of the bargain he'd made to come here. He'd drawn maps, shown her.

Gaining her freedom now depended on helping him gain the power *he* wanted. To do that, she must help him destroy the one thing standing in his way.

This, she could control. It was her decision. Her choice. One promised her freedom. The other promised suffering.

She could side with Mahikos. Gain her freedom.

Or suffer by siding against him with their son.

With a smile, Mahikos held out his arms.

Helia ran to him.

Chapter Thirty-eight

On his side, Pietas opened his eyes to sunlight streaming into the cavern. The bedroll was empty. No scent of Joss remained and her side held no warmth. Cold stone lay behind him. He remained still, taking stock. His empathic senses found no one near. Physically, he hadn't felt this rested in years, even in a comfortable bed. Ultras didn't need long periods of sleep. He napped in some out-of-the way spot and he'd taught himself to sleep standing up. When had he last slept this late?

He turned onto his back and crooked one arm over his eyes. The usual pain in his shoulders didn't happen. He reached up, reached to the side, turned his head in both directions. He took stock of every part of himself; feet, legs, hips, back, shoulders, head. No pain. Anywhere. After well over a year of constant pain, relief made him feel younger.

What had happened? On his fingers, he ticked off recent changes. He'd found his people. His mother was safe. He'd made peace with his sister. His father would be dealt with. He'd discovered a tribe of panther allies. He'd eaten. Slept, apparently, for *hours*. He'd had raw, unbridled sex with a woman he'd adored since forever.

He cracked a smile. "Had to be the sex."

When he tried to tuck both hands behind his head, the motion sent twin daggers into his shoulders. He caught his breath, lowered his hands and took slow, deep breaths. The pain eased, but knowledge of its reason remained.

Freed after fifteen months of captivity with his arms bound behind him, he hadn't recognized the two blackened sticks as his own arms. His loathing of humans had never been so deep or so all-encompassing as at that moment. They had destroyed his body.

With Six's help, he'd regained most of what he'd lost. Pain still owned his body, but waking this morning pain-free showed him that one day, the cruel master could be banished. Once more, he would be free.

He crooked first one arm, then the other over his eyes. He could make that motion without difficulty, but couldn't reach behind him.

Pietas lifted his arms, pushed his palms toward the roof of the cavern, and stretched. Taking it slow, he reached back. Pain robbed him of breath. He panted until he gained control, and then tried again. And again. After ten times, he lowered his arms to his sides. Instead of lingering, the pain subsided. Good. *Good.*

As he sat up, a black bird with an orange beak hopped into view, pecking the dirt. Another landed, its flaring wings sending up a pinch of dust. As a child, Pietas had once sent a tendril of chaos toward a bird and it died. He'd practiced with Dessy until he could send so small a trickle, it was less than a whisper along the skin.

Curious, he tested his ability on the two birds hopping about.

Squawking and flapping, both streaked toward the sky.

Once on his feet, he found a metal canteen. He sniffed, tasted, and drank it. He attached the canteen's carabiner to a belt loop and prepared to set out. Joss had created a bower for them in this place and removing the bedroll would wipe away proof they'd spent time together. He hesitated, but left everything as it was, intending to return in the evening. He started back to camp.

He hadn't gone a hundred steps before his inner soldier nagged him about leaving signs an enemy could follow. *Stop being paranoid. There's no one out there.* Fifty steps later, he spun around and returned.

After shaking out the bedroll, he folded it and tucked it under his arm. He checked one more time for any items they might have left behind. Satisfied that he'd secured the area and their presence had been erased, he set out.

Too much time had passed without drawing the Council together. He needed to discover what they had accomplished so far. The cryopods could not be left as they were. He needed to know how much time they had before they all opened and what steps had already been taken. Other than a camp for themselves and a half-hearted attempt to clear out thorny weeds--which appeared to be a failure--he could see nothing of value.

That would end today. They needed a decisive, straightforward plan of action. If they couldn't come up with one, he would give one to them.

Upon his return to camp, sly looks darted his way from the Ultras gathered around the fire. As little as he indulged in pleasure for pleasure's sake, he refused to feel guilty for it now. But knowing everyone knew what he and Joss had been up to brought heat to his face anyway.

Had they been overheard? Once they were alone he'd given no thought to such things. This was not some random soldier assigned a task.

This was Joss. She would have shielded them.

When he entered the cave where his mother slept, he came up short. All the pods were empty. He stowed the bedroll and strode back out, seeking her.

"Morning." Koliga glanced up as Pietas approached, but then returned to sanding what appeared to be part of a pod. "You sleep well?"

"I did, thanks. Do we have--"

"Any food? Yes." He pointed toward the central campfire. "They saved you some rabbit. The panthers delivered again today."

Pietas acknowledged a beckoning wave from Michel, who stood near the fire. "Did they?"

"We'll get spoiled, if they keep that up."

"Have you--"

"Seen the human? He's with Joss." Koliga pointed. "Over by the pods."

"And--"

"Your mother's with them."

"Lig."

"Hmm?" He kept grinding with the stone.

"I wasn't aware you were--"

"A telepath. Me either." He looked up. "But I've been picking up thoughts ever since you got here." Koliga set down the flat stone he'd been rubbing over a raw metal edge and picked up a rag. "Weird, huh?"

"I imagine so. Although most telepaths don't--"

"Finish sentences for pe-- Oh." His cheeks darkened. "Sorry."

"No problem. Ask Joss. Some sort of code."

"Code, huh?" He rubbed one edge and peered at the metal. "Okay. I'll ask her."

"What are you making, Lig?"

"What do you say it is?"

"A bathtub."

Wiping his hands, the man chuckled. "I'm sure everyone will want to try it out as such, but it's a boat."

"To use where?"

"There's a huge lake in the caldera and it's full of fish. A river too. If we can transport it, maybe we can get a few boats out of here and take them overland to bigger rivers. Once all the pods are open, we need to find a use for them."

"They connect when standing up to make shelter, don't they?"

"Yeah, but we don't need half a million of them."

"Good point. Oars?"

"We have a few tools, so I was able to cut down a small tree. I can get two oars out of it. This thing is big enough for two rowers."

"What do you know about the pod situation?"

"I've been in and out of all the delivery units. Even the upended ones. Wanted to see if I could open one at a time. Not possible, by the way. But I did figure out how to use one of the built-in functions. There's a narrow, flat area on the top and bottom of each pod. Made that way so they won't roll when stacked on pallets. Set one atop the other and trigger this mechanism and it releases surface hydrocarbons. Those ignite methane nanobubbles, allowing the stacked pod to bond with the ones above and below it. It's permanent."

"Perm--" His voice cracked. Pietas coughed, chest tight. "Permanent?" Darkness bundled itself around him. The ground tilted.

"Pietas!" Koliga jumped up and steadied him. "What happened?"

He regained his balance. "Don't worry over me." He withdrew from Koliga's touch. "We need to be sure that doesn't get triggered. We don't want any--" His voice cracked again. "We don't want anyone...trapped."

"Oh, that won't be a problem. There's a failsafe. It won't work if there's a living occupant inside." Koliga sat down and picked up the stone again.

"Is that useful?"

"Very." He hefted the stone. "I can grind and polish with it. It's quite hard. Wish I could find a use for that stupid thorny plant growing everywhere." His dark skin showed no blush, but the warmth of embarrassment emanated from him. "Oh, you meant-- Sorry. Bonding means if we stack the pods of the dead and seal them, we can make a wall for protection from the elements and create a memorial at the same time."

"A memorial. How fitting!" Pietas tapped a fist over his heart. "You're a genius."

"No, I'm an engineer." Koliga eyed the metal edge.

"Then you're a genius engineer."

"Thanks, but I didn't invent this process." He looked up at Pietas. "I refuse to quit and I keep going over a problem until I figure out how to go around it or I make it work. Which is why the Toil class elected me to the Council. Not because I'm a genius." He went back to polishing and sanding as if Pietas were not there.

At the campfire, Pietas greeted Armand and Philippe, Michel, Erryq and Marjo. Michel handed him a small metal bowl full of roasted rabbit pieces and Erryq filled his canteen.

He tore into the meat. The juicy flesh quieted his hunger.

"Wish we had coffee." Marjo sipped from her own container.

He swallowed before speaking. "We will before long."

"You have coffee?" Marjo set down the canteen and came to her feet. "Where?"

The other Ultras perked up, dogs hearing their master's step.

Pietas wiped his mouth. "Six found it."

"What?" Marjo glanced around. "That human has coffee? Where? Is it here?"

He lifted one brow, took his time choosing a piece of meat. "*That human* has a name."

Tucking dark hair behind her ear, Marjo clenched her teeth. "*Six* has coffee?"

He took the last bite, chewed thoughtfully.

"Pietas, come on! Does he have it or not?"

"Not on him."

Her shoulders sagged. Around the campfire, the other Ultras slumped back into morose disinterest.

"But," he continued, "he discovered coffee trees about a day's walk over the summit." He motioned toward that direction. "He knows how to harvest and prep it. His family worked on a coffee plantation when he was a boy."

"That's some serious skill." Marjo rubbed her hands together. "Might be worth letting him live."

"I'll pretend you didn't say that." Pietas downed the water.

"Didn't say what? Here." Marjo handed him a cloth. "It's damp."

"Thanks." While he wiped his face and hands, she refilled his water from a larger container. He hooked it to his belt. "Appreciate it. Okay, I'm off to find Six." He cast a wave. He hadn't taken ten steps when Marjo called his name. He turned back. "Yes?"

"You know..." Marjo smirked. "He's with Joss." She folded her hands before her, looking pleased with herself.

How little she knew about Joss's honor, or his friend. "I heard."

Chapter Thirty-nine

Halfway down the twisting trail to the pods, Pietas came upon a stubby, leafless tree. As he got closer, the thickest lower branch revealed itself to be a branch with a panther stretched out atop it, chin on paws. The majestic animal regarded him with supreme indifference, yet a clear challenge.

He halted, recognizing Tiklaus. As he would with any sentry, he maintained military protocol and kept his distance. The panther tribe deserved no less honor than any of his troops.

"Pietas, requesting permission to pass."

The cat gave him a serene blink and sniffed in his direction. The telepathic link they'd shared before re-engaged without effort. This time, a barrage of impressions flooded his mind.

Fight. Pain. Cage. Pain. Fight. Hunger. Thirst. Pain. Fight. Pain.

Pietas reeled under the psychic impact. He stumbled back and bent at the waist, sickened. These animals had endured cruelty beyond measure even before they'd been caged and shipped away as unwanted cargo. Their captors hadn't put them in stasis during transit. They'd been caged. Tormented. Ignored. Starved.

"Keep them hungry," echoed through his mind. One human had fed and watered them too little, too late. When he ventured too close to the cages, they took him down together, tore out the man's throat to silence him, ripped him apart, then dragged chunks of him through the bars of their cages and feasted. The connection was so strong between himself and the cat, Pietas smelled the blood, tasted the flesh.

He choked back bile. He, who had once bitten chunks off a hated, vile enemy.

For killing the human, the tribe had been punished the rest of the trip.

Pietas could count the means of death he feared on one hand. Being eaten by panthers went straight to the top. Not even an Ultra could come back from that. Perhaps consuming Ultras was what the tribe had been created to do.

Once on Sempervia, the panthers had been scattered, abandoned, each dropped in a different location and left to fend for itself. Tiklaus had been released in a forest near Pietas and Six.

The panther had watched him. Waited. The entire tribe had made its way here, to this place.

No. Not just *here*.

To *him*.

Why? How? He hadn't known he'd be here himself.

Through their connection, Tiklaus revealed an image of Pietas in a clearing, head back, arms outstretched, mouth open in a silent scream.

It had happened the night he'd learned the truth of how Ghost Corps made ghosts. Needing time alone, he'd stormed off into the trees and released a howl of empathic rage.

Unintentionally, he'd alerted his people he was near. Alive. Joss confessed later, *"It woke us all up. Even across a mountain range. I think the whole world felt that."*

The morning after, he'd encountered Tiklaus and they'd touched each other's minds for the first time. Panther and Ultra bonded.

That howl had alerted the other panthers as well.

Tiklaus, was the tribe sent here to eat Ultras? Or...me?

The connection shut. The panther rested one front paw over the other, somber and silent. It half-closed its green eyes.

Though his mind churned with possibilities and questions, Pietas accepted the decision not to answer. If there was one thing he understood, it was the importance of giving honor where it was due. Tiklaus had revealed much. This was not the time.

"Tiklaus, thank you for the service you and your kind have provided for my kind. I'm grateful. I do not take it for granted. Thank you for breakfast as well. That's two rabbits I owe you so far."

In one swift move, the panther rose and leaped down, landed on front feet and pushed off with the back ones. It loped toward him.

His heart hammered. As he did in battle, Pietas braced himself, stood his ground and refused to flinch. In an intuitive act of trust, he relaxed his warrior's stance, opened himself and dropped his hands at his sides.

Tiklaus halted before him, rose on hind legs and set both paws on his shoulders. It rubbed its nose along the side of his face, a pet happy to see him.

Pietas rubbed the cat's head and round ears. "You're huge at a distance. Up close you're monstrous. Scary monstrous." He gripped the animal's ruff. "But in a good way. I'm glad you're my friend."

The panther licked his face, dropped down to all fours and bumped into his legs. It hooked one paw around a knee and pulled.

Pietas tucked and rolled, ending on his back with the panther atop him.

Play. Chase. Tickle.

Pietas laughed. "You want to play!" He set his hands on either side of the panther's snout, leaned up and kissed the cat on the nose. "Biting is okay, but, mind you, no drawing blood." He rocked the animal's head back and forth.

Tiklaus rammed its nose up under Pietas's chin. The scratchy warmth of a wet tongue dragged along his jaw. The panther gave him two more licks and then pounced, nothing more than a kitten with a favorite toy.

It almost knocked the wind out of Pietas. He rolled in the dirt with Tiklaus, rubbing and tickling, hugging when he could manage to sneak an arm around the beast. The panther rolled onto him, which pulled one arm farther than he could move without pain. Pietas made no sound and did not pull back.

Tiklaus ceased all movement and sniffed his pained shoulder. The green-eyed gaze came to his.

"It's okay, my friend." He petted the panther. "I'm good."

Tiklaus went back to their rough play. More than once, the beast fixed its mighty jaws around his arm without pressure. It licked his hand and drew his thumb into its mouth, eyes closed like a suckling kitten. The intimacy triggered a connection.

Images, impressions, memories merged. In captivity, before the ship, a worker came every day with food. The man played. Scratched ears. Tickled. Pet. Chased. Aboard ship, isolated and in pain, Tiklaus longed for him. An image of the man's face hung before him, so clear, if they ever met, Pietas would recognize him. At the shared memory, tears filled his eyes.

Tiklaus released his hand.

He stroked the panther's face. "I will play with you every day. I promise."

Flipping onto its back, belly exposed, Tiklaus huffed twice.

"You want a belly rub." Laughing, he rubbed with one hand and stroked with the other.

Tiklaus lolled on its back, legs spread wide, the position trusting and submissive. The big cat sneezed and then rocked to its feet, shaking its head. Claws retracted, the panther batted at him, knocked Pietas onto his back and then flipped itself down beside him. Tiklaus wrapped its front legs around his arm and gnawed at it in gentle play while the hind feet kicked him without injury. Claws flashed, but did no harm.

Now I know how a chew toy feels. He blew out a breath.

When the panther draped itself over his chest, Pietas struggled to slide out from under but could not get up. The animal weighed less than he did, but with no visible effort, it kept Pietas from rising.

"I concede, my friend. You win."

The panther ignored him.

"Tiklaus, off."

Nothing.

"Off, *please*."

The panther yawned, opening a huge maw. Fangs flashed.

Pietas tried a signal that worked with sparring partners and asked for release by double-tapping the panther's side.

The cat stood at once and stepped over him. It shook from nose to tail, then sat and groomed itself.

He stood and brushed himself off. Standing beside Tiklaus, who reached him mid-thigh, Pietas took pride in knowing this sweet, playful cat was also the snarling ball of animal rage that had nailed Mahikos to the ground.

Pietas ensured no one was on the path in either direction before he knelt and scratched the cat's ears. "Who's a good kitty?"

The animal sneaked in a lick of his hand and face and flopped down on its back.

"My Tiklaus, that's who. Tiklaus is a good kitty." He rubbed the smooth belly. "Yes, you are! Such a good, big kitty. You're my kitty, aren't you? Good, good kitty."

The panther accepted the attention, one paw twitching. After a moment, it stood and shook itself. A purring sound rumbled from its chest. It sat, licked one paw and added a lick of Pietas's face as well.

He chuckled. "Thank you for the bath." He hugged the panther's neck. "You have as soft a heart as I do but you don't show it either. Pact, my friend. I won't tell if you won't." He kissed Tiklaus on the nose.

The panther bumped its head against Pietas, then bounded to the tree and up it. It resumed a nonchalant pose, as if none of their boisterous play had happened.

After standing, Pietas brushed off dirt and shook it out of his hair. "*Ugh*. I need a shower. How I miss soap and towels."

The panther yawned, crossed one paw over the other and set its chin atop them. The serene gaze flicked over him, then away.

"Don't look so smug. A few licks and you're clean. I need a bit more."

Tiklaus emitted a low rumble. The animal came up on all fours again and leaped from the tree. The ruff around its neck bristled. This time, it jerked its head toward Pietas and took off in the direction of the pods.

He followed.

Two minutes down the trail, Tiklaus crouched, tail lashing.

Squatting beside the cat, Pietas studied the area ahead. "What is it?"

The panther took one slow, creeping step, then another.

Keeping low, Pietas followed. As they reached the curve where the trail led down to the pods, he and the panther both stopped.

A grating growl rumbled from Tiklaus. The sound ended in a threatening hiss.

At the bottom stood Helia, Dessy, Joss, and Six, engaged in conversation.

Sneaking around the pods behind them was Mahikos.

Chapter Forty

"You! Stop!"

Pietas? Helia whirled around, but as close to the pods as she was, the sound of his voice seemed to come from everywhere at once.

"If you move"-- he bellowed --"I will let the panthers eat you!"

He knew! Robbed of breath, she clutched her chest. Pietas knew she'd betrayed him. She'd bathed and scrubbed in the icy falls to remove Mahikos's scent, but Pretosia had smelled him on her and told the other panthers. How else could Pietas have known?

Pretosia crouched low, looking up, past her.

Helia shielded her eyes. Above, halfway up the cliff, standing with arms folded, stood her son. In the direct morning light, Pietas was a blazing tower. A flaming sword. A god of retribution.

"Hey! You!" Six yanked out a knife.

Helia stumbled in her haste to obey. Her daughter caught her.

Brandishing the knife, Six passed her. "Back off!"

"Who do you think you're talking to, human?" Mahikos beckoned to Six. "Let's finish what we started."

The presence of Mahikos meant her son had been speaking to his father, not her. Unbidden, tears coursed down Helia's cheeks. Pietas didn't know. If he knew, he'd stop her. She'd never be free.

Six squared off with Mahikos.

"Six, no!" He was no match for Mahikos. If her spouse slaughtered him, Pietas would never forgive her. He wouldn't keep her close. "Pretosia, help him! Protect!"

Her guardian let out a yowl and two panthers raced past them and flanked Six. Once ahead of him, they crept toward Mahikos, snapping and growling while he backed away, hands outward.

He yelled at her to call them off.

She clamped both hands over her ears.

Pietas shouted as he descended the steep trail.

Mahikos screamed back.

The panthers snarled and growled.

She jammed her hands harder over her ears. The heat beat down on her, sapping her strength. The world existed half a step away. Sound echoed. Bright spots blinded her. Helia closed her eyes, willing herself into the dark sanctuary of sleep. Hiding where no one could find her. A world where no terror dogged her days and no regrets haunted her dreams. A world where she lived free.

Dessy's alarm washed over Helia, but it was Six who caught her and guided her as she crumpled.

"Here. Sit down." Once Six seated her, he stayed close. "I won't touch you."

Pretosia sent up a howl that ended in short huffing barks. It sounded so alien Helia opened her eyes. The panther licked her face, then howled again.

Pietas and Mahikos shouted.

"Mother!" Dessy knelt beside her. "Are you sick?"

Joss joined them. "Helia, you're pasty white. Dessy, I can't read her at all."

The shouting match between Pietas and his father continued unabated.

Pretosia bumped its head under Helia's chin, whimpering and licking.

"Move, Pretosia!" Dessy shoved the panther aside.

The great cat snapped its jaws and snarled.

"All right!" Dessy scrambled back. "Don't bite me!"

Pretosia took up a position between Helia and Dessy. The cat's neck thickened and its fur stood on end.

Unable to speak, Helia clung to the animal's neck.

Making little whimpers, it licked her face.

Joss moved up behind Helia. "Take my hands, Dessy. Pretosia won't bite us. We're here to protect your mother." The two women wedged Helia and the cat between them.

Helia broke into tears as the warmth and quiet of Joss's shields rose around them. It locked out the torrent of hatred and contempt spiking between Pietas and his father.

While the fight raged above her, Helia slumped against her panther.

Pretosia gave two sharp huffs, more bark than growl. Helia felt the sound rather than heard it.

Within moments, another panther sat beside Helia. A third braced her other side. Pretosia leaned on her chest.

How unworthy she was of their devotion! She'd betrayed her son and he would soon know it. Pietas would sense it. He would know. He'd hate her.

"I'm as useless as a mortal!"

A look of insulted disbelief flickered in Six's eyes.

Helia covered her mouth. She hadn't meant to say those words aloud. Six had protected her and she'd insulted him.

He didn't speak, but the small shake of his head said everything.

"Mother." Pietas stooped beside her and placed one hand on her shoulder. "We need to talk."

Helia hid her face.

Chapter Forty-one

Pietas stood back and allowed Joss and Dessy to assist his mother to her feet. They dusted off her uniform and stood with her between them, arms around her.

Mahikos paced while two panthers eyed his every move. Tiklaus prowled back and forth near Pietas, chest rumbling, ears flat. Another panther touched noses with Tiklaus and then took up a place between the other two. Pretosia and two more panthers remained at Helia's side.

"Tiklaus."

Licking its chops, the panther turned and looked at him. A message came through their bond, not in words, but Pietas understood. *Feast!*

Oh, how he'd like to grant the panther a meal. But he must obey Ultra law.

Pietas squatted and the panther trotted to him. "He will be punished. Our kind must do other things first." He made sure Mahikos was watching before he continued. "If the sentence is death by panther, I promise, you get first bite."

Tiklaus sneezed and leveled a glare at Mahikos.

His father broadcast no emotion, but a twitch in the jaw revealed his fear.

Pietas rose and paced before his father. The man had returned--so he claimed--to offer a solution to the problem of releasing Ultras from the pods. Though Pietas had no faith that was true, he owed it to his people to listen.

"For now, Father, stay out of camp and away from the pods. I'll consider your offer but if you come back before I give you permission, I'll let these panthers eat you."

Mahikos puffed out his chest. "How dare you threaten me?"

"Not a threat. Promise." He touched the panther. "Tiklaus. Please tell your tribe to escort him away and keep him away."

The panther gave a low-pitched yip and the three panthers facing Mahikos advanced.

His father retreated.

"They won't eat you, Father, unless you refuse to leave."

Mahikos backed away, never taking his gaze off the panthers. When they didn't come closer, he turned and ran.

Pietas folded his arms and stayed until the man was out of sight.

Tiklaus slapped its tail back and forth on Pietas's legs. Their bond made the meaning clear.

"I know, my friend." He dropped down to one knee and stroked the panther's neck. "I'm sorry. I wish you could eat him too."

When Pietas returned to his mother's side, mixed emotions stuttered from her, reflecting confusion and exhaustion. She still wouldn't look at him. How like her to take on too much. The walk down here followed by the argument she'd witnessed had weakened her.

"I'm going to carry you." Pietas lifted her.

"No, put me down." She pushed against his chest. "I'm too heavy. I can walk."

"Mother, any lighter and you'd blow away in the wind." He carried her toward the steep incline. "Stop fussing. You overdid it, as usual. You're not walking up that hill."

"But--"

"Mother, I am *not* putting you down."

"I'm sorry. I'm so sorry!"

"*Shh.* It's not your fault. It's Father's."

Despite his assurances, his mother wept. When he'd been a child, he'd seen her cry many times. Then, he'd been powerless to comfort her, having no ability to intercede or protect. Now, at least he could wrap her in his arms.

Though she wasn't heavy, carrying her up the incline put pressure on his shoulders. His hands numbed and his arms screamed in agony.

He broadcast an illusion of himself as a healthy, vital man in his prime. Not the damaged shell he'd become.

Who would follow a king plagued by weakness?

Before his imprisonment, the task would have been trifling. Now, sweat trickled down his face.

"Pietas." His mother tapped his chest. "'We're at the top. Put me down. I can walk."

He let her slide down but had too much pain to open his arms. "Hold on to me, Mother." He rested his face against her fair hair.

Tiklaus and Pretosia had shadowed them along the trail. The cats sat and cleaned their paws. Pretosia gave Tiklaus a lick on the cheek and the bigger panther gave one back.

Pietas fought the tremble of exhaustion, forcing it back with pure will. *No pain defeats me. I am unstoppable.* His shields wavered, tall grass in a storm. Any minute, they would fall and everyone would see how weak he'd become. How damaged. *I am unstoppable. I am unstoppable. I am--*

Joss hugged them both. The momentary interruption threatened to topple his illusion, but then Joss slid her shields over his and strengthened the image he broadcast. Her intimate touch shored up his ability, adding a level of protection higher than anything he'd experienced alone.

"I'm with you," she sent. *"They don't need to know how much it hurts."*

He willed her to feel his gratitude. His pain eased and he took a deeper breath. His sister joined their group hug and her touch lessened his pain even more. He reached out and gathered her close.

Dessy squeezed him. "Did we ever do a group hug before today? Ever?"

"Yes. You were young." With one hand, his mother caressed first his face, then Dessy's. "When you were babies. Toddlers. When I held you both." She didn't say it, but Pietas knew the rest.

When your father didn't know. When your father wasn't around. When your father wasn't looking.

When he wasn't there to tyrannize them.

Pietas would expel the man from the Council and oversee a fair trial. He'd hear what the man had to say. He'd listen to the proposed solution. He'd make sure to comprehend every detail.

Once he did, he'd employ the most valuable lesson his father ever taught him, used in every battle. He'd extinguish weakness, tenderness, love, or mercy. He'd send in his troops and savor their victory.

He'd bond with the panther tribe as they hunted Mahikos down, ripped him apart, masticated every chunk of raw flesh, and slaked their seething lust for his blood.

Chapter Forty-two

This lowly cave was a far cry from the luxury of the Council's flagship, the *Uurahkal*. Though Pietas could not yet prove his father's collusion with the humans and their treachery, it was a fact that humans had destroyed the magnificent ship and slaughtered its entire crew.

They were gone. Every single person. All gone.

He'd hoped his own ship would take vengeance and his troops would release him. When time passed and no one freed him, he feared for the fate of *Soomus Bellum*. We Are War: the finest contingent of soldiers in all of the galaxy. Never in its hundreds of years had it faced so vile a threat.

And he had been helpless to assist them.

The gritty scrape of sand underfoot careened him back to the present, with its barren rock walls and dirt floor. For the trial, they'd removed everything from the cave.

Armand and Philippe entered with Mahikos between them and the three proceeded to the deepest end. The cavern ceiling rose no more than a handspan above the twins' heads.

His father remained calm and confident, as if he were the one who'd called the Council meeting. He was fit, in his prime after a rebirth less than three years before. As was his custom, he'd shielded himself. No emotion leaked, but he held himself as he always had, cocky, smug, above it all, bored by whatever happened around him.

The other Councilmembers entered and stood side-by-side, facing the man. Six remained at the exit. Last to join them, Helia walked in with Dessy, took a spot between her and Pietas. Though she revealed no emotion, he sensed a fine tremor of fear running through her.

He squeezed her hand, shielding his murderous thoughts and savage hatred. If she saw the violence he planned for his father, she'd try to stop him. Not out of love for Mahikos, but because it was his mother's nature to soothe and mend, not destroy.

His father would not leave here unpunished. The knife Pietas had in his pocket made that promise a solid guarantee.

As War Leader, he made life and death decisions over the enemy every day. For him, passing judgment on this man would be closer to joy than hate.

In the pod aboard the transport ship, Pietas had borne over a year of unrelenting pain, hunger, thirst and confinement without asking for so much as one drop of water. It was not time in that pod that had taught him to suffer in silence.

That had been drilled into him as a child. If Pietas could credit his father with one thing, it was the knowledge that begging meant he'd suffer worse.

Oh, yes. His father taught that lesson well.

Now that everyone had arrived, Pietas stepped forward. "I am Pietas. I serve."

One by one, each councilmember voiced their name and the Ultra vow.

Mahikos said nothing.

Dessy came up next to Pietas and set one hand on his arm. "Father insisted since you were missing, he was in command as Chancellor Emeritus." She addressed the Council. "As Lieutenant Chancellor of the High Council, it's my duty to request reinstatement of Pietas ap Lorectic as Chancellor. All in favor?"

A unanimous "aye" sounded.

"Thank you, Dessy." He bowed to her. Pietas took time to meet the gaze of each person in the room, including Six. "I accept command."

Koliga raised his hand. "I vote Mahikos ap Lorectic be removed from the Council."

"Is there any discussion?" When no one spoke, Pietas nodded. "All in favor?"

The instant and unanimous response accompanied a pulse of emotion. Had it been directed at him, Pietas would have cringed. Mahikos drew himself up with such pride, you'd think he'd been elected instead of disgraced.

"The vote carries. Mahikos ap Lorectic is hereby removed from the Council and stripped of all rights and privileges. We are gathered to bear witness against Mahikos for one count of assault, seven thousand counts of attempted homicide, and one count of homicide."

His father's aplomb faltered. "Seven thousand?"

"That is how many Ultras would have perished had you set that unit on fire. Assuming it had not spread to the others."

The man rubbed his brow. "I had no idea there were so many in those things."

"You are not on trial for being uninformed. Not even immortals have enough time to recount your failings in that regard."

A snicker sounded from the back of the room. When Pietas turned in that direction, Six gave a shame-faced smile and mimed zipping his lips.

Mahikos dusted off a sleeve. "I murdered no one."

"Did you not? I call a witness." He turned and motioned to Six.

"Point of order," Mahikos interjected. "A human cannot testify! Mortals have no voice on the High Council."

Pietas tapped one finger against his lips. "You challenge the testimony of a human?"

"I do." Sneering, Mahikos lifted his chin.

"Are you suggesting a mortal has no right to justice? You? After all the work you did to bring the Ultras into peace talks with humans? Now you claim humans have no place?"

"I do. No human has the right to judge me. Only an immortal."

Oh, how satisfying to hear that claim. Once more, he nodded to Six, who stepped outside the cave.

The ghost returned seconds later and ushered in Tiklaus and the fourteen other members of the panther tribe.

Mahikos almost fell over himself backing away, but Armand and Philippe prevented him from leaving.

Tiklaus padded over to Pietas and sat. Pretosia rubbed Helia's hand, then joined the others as they spread out. All the cats watched Mahikos.

"You can't bring those animals in here!"

"According to you," Pietas indicated the tribe, "they have every right. These are immortal beings."

"Im--" Mahikos sputtered a laugh. "Don't be ludicrous! They're animals!"

"Even humans protect their animals from unlawful killing." Pietas stooped beside Tiklaus and laid one hand on its back. "Tiklaus is immortal, intelligent and sentient. Like the other members of the tribe."

His father cast a wary eye on the panthers.

"I'll demonstrate their cognitive abilities. Tiklaus, this is the proof I told you about. Are you and the tribe ready?"

The panther made a low huffing sound. The tribe encircled Pietas.

"Tiklaus, you are number one. Please demonstrate you understand our language and also numbers by asking every other member of the tribe to sit after you do."

If the panther communicated, it was out of hearing range for Ultras. Once Tiklaus sat, every other panther took a seat.

"So they know a trick." Mahikos jutted his chin at them. "That proves nothing."

"Tiklaus, please ask those standing to circle the panther sitting on their left and then sit facing the opposite direction."

As the panthers carried out the command, the pleasure of the other Ultras fed through to Pietas. Erryq clapped her hands in delight.

Mahikos, who had always been fair, paled. He swallowed. "It's still a trick."

"Is it?" Pietas clasped his hands before him. "Tiklaus, this is a difficult request, and I hope you will forgive me for asking. If you see the man who stabbed you, will you stand before him, please? I promise he will not hurt you while I am here."

The great cat flicked its tail and then trotted straight to Mahikos, sat, and angled its head upward. The man jerked back.

"Does the accused request a *trick* of this panther?"

"No." Mahikos made shooing motions. "Take him away now."

"Tiklaus, you may stand down."

After a few tail flicks and a growl, the panther returned to Pietas and paced, head turned toward Mahikos. The tribe's growing bloodlust coursed through Pietas, a river of retaliation piling high behind a dam already bulging with hunger for retribution.

Three of the panthers crept closer to Mahikos.

His father backed away.

Tiklaus, Pietas sent. *They must wait. Soon. I promise.*

With tail straight out, the alpha cat hissed a warning. The three panthers halted, but laid back their ears and hissed in return. Tiklaus launched full force into the trio, snarling and snapping.

Councilmembers scurried to safety.

Yelping, the panthers rolled onto their backs and remained there while Tiklaus sniffed each in turn. Upon reaching the last one, Tiklaus bared fangs and growled. The cat remained on its back, tail flicking, but turned its head. Tiklaus nipped its ear, causing it to yip in pain. The alpha sniffed the wounded ear, licked it, and nose-bumped the other cat.

Tail between its legs, it submitted.

With a swagger, Tiklaus returned to Pietas.

The trio slunk back to the pack, snarling at each other like brothers fighting over who was to blame for their whipping.

In silence, the Council resumed its former position.

Tiklaus sat and wrapped its tail around Pietas's closest leg.

He placed his hand near the cat.

Tiklaus nudged it. *Promise.*

Thank you. Pietas folded his arms. "Does the accused deny killing this immortal opponent?"

"It was self-defense! That animal had his jaws on my neck."

"Self-defense?" Pietas indicated Tiklaus. "If you recall, the panther was protecting me because you tried to stab me in the back. Had we deputized the tribe before that moment, it would have been murder while on duty. Count yourself lucky. The penalty for murder is death in like fashion. Committing murder while the victim is on duty requires the punishment twice. One of our most honored decrees is 'The front must not fall. A death on duty weakens us all.'" Pietas turned to his sister. "What lawgiver am I quoting, Dessy?"

She folded her arms and faced Mahikos. "Our father."

The man put his head down.

"The victim identified the attacker. The attacker has himself admitted to stabbing the victim."

"I killed an animal!" Mahikos threw out his arms. "An animal has no rights in this court and you know it!"

With a rumbling snarl, Tiklaus stood.

Mahikos stumbled backward.

While the twins subdued the prisoner, Pietas stroked Tiklaus. "We will now proceed to the verdict. Does the Council require privacy for discussion?"

No one spoke.

"No privacy, then. What say you on the charge of murdering another immortal?"

Around the cavern, all beheld Mahikos with resolution on their faces as they spoke in turn. His mother looked down, then lifted her gaze once more and cast the last vote, making it unanimous. "Guilty."

Though his father remained silent, the look he gave Helia promised recompense. She stared back with the fearless pride of a queen.

How Pietas wished she had found that resolve before now, but he closed his thoughts to the past.

"Mahikos ap Lorectic has been found guilty of murdering another immortal. What sentence does the Council require?"

Koliga stepped forward. "Death in like manner." One at a time, they all agreed.

"Thank you." Pietas motioned to them. "The sentence shall be carried out immediately." He stooped beside Tiklaus.

"No!" Terror erupted from Mahikos. He backed away. "You can't allow that animal to attack me!"

Armand and Philippe gripped Mahikos by the arms and brought him under control.

"You can't do this!" Mahikos jerked and fought, but the twins held him fast. "This is barbaric! Pietas, stop! You have far too much honor."

"Honor?" Pietas stilled himself. "What do you know of honor? You, who sold our people's freedom for the price of power?"

Brief recognition flared, then hid behind ill-disguised fear.

Pietas allowed himself a smile of satisfaction. The father worried over what the son knew. Good. "Do not depend on the honor of others when you possess none."

"Pietas, be reasonable!"

"Reasonable? As you were with my sister and me when we were children? Forcing us to stay at lessons until we slept at our desks? Marching us in the cold without shoes so we'd be tough? Locking us out in the snow with nothing but a worn blanket?" The combined pity of the Councilmembers swept over Pietas but he blocked their concern.

"And because of it, you two are the finest soldiers in the galaxy."

Pietas took a step toward him. "One evening, you kept us up learning tactics and then sent us to bed less than a minute before the day started. You made us get up again. You forced us through hours of work the entire day. That night, you set us on watch and made sure we stayed awake. The next day, you drove us through more grueling work. Tell the Council why you did that, *Father*."

"It was for your own good, you ingrate!" Mahikos let out a theatrical sigh. "You never appreciated anything I did for you!"

"Did I not? Was I not required to thank you for every single thing? I had to thank you when you sent me to bed hungry after every thrashing you said I deserved."

"I beat you because you disobeyed. Be a man and own up to it."

The man's scorn lashed over Pietas, sharp as the sting of a whip. Accustomed to the pain, he bore up under the empathic attack without a twitch. The anger that rose within himself at the man's arrogance, though, tightened a noose around his chest.

Five short steps to reach that vile tormenter. Tear out his throat.

"Pietas." Joss's mindvoice touched his, her strength an armored glove over his own iron fist. *"I promise. I'll help you kill him."*

Pietas flexed his hands.

"No, my love. After the trial."

He ground his teeth. *"Now!"*

"No, Pietas. Bring him to justice. Make him pay. Make him confess to the entire Council."

Pietas sheathed his anger like the blade it was. He spun around and went back the place where he'd been standing.

Tiklaus stood and nudged his hand.

He stroked the cat. "As usual, Father, you bait me into an argument to avoid discussing the truth. You put Dessy and me through two days of misery, working us harder than soldiers as a gift for our birthday. To show us what good soldiers should expect."

"And look at him!" Mahikos faced the Council. "Look at him! Have you ever known a more magnificent soldier? *I* made him what he is. *I* trained him. *I* created him."

"Liar!" Pietas smacked a fist against his chest.

The entire tribe scrambled to its feet, fangs bared.

As one, the Council stepped back.

A furnace of rage erupted within Pietas. "You get credit for nothing I did! Nothing!"

Tiklaus crept up beside Pietas, chest down, hindquarters raised, poised to pounce.

The acrid smell of urine--not the cats'--permeated the air.

Pietas flung out an arm, pointing at Dessy. "My sister and I give you no credit for what we are." He smacked his chest again. "We are everything you are not!"

Tiklaus hissed.

"We are soldiers by our will, not yours! Our skills. Not yours! Our reputation as stone-cold killers?" Pietas straightened, chin lifted. "Yes. That I will lay at your feet. Every time I kill a human, instead of his face, I see *yours*."

Helia gasped.

Mahikos did not look up.

Pietas faced the Council. "It was Dessy's and my sixth birthday. He locked Mother away for two days so she couldn't interfere with our *gift*. She clawed the door so hard, trying to get out and protect us, she left bloody grooves in the wood. My father forced her to fill them with putty and paint over them."

His mother hid her face against Dessy's shoulder.

With a sharp intake of breath, the Council turned toward Mahikos. The fury ebbing from Joss toward his father was gratifying.

"Yes, expect me to be reasonable." Pietas stabbed his forefinger into the palm of his other hand. "Like father, like son."

Taking his time, Pietas strolled across the cave floor. His regret was that Mahikos would come back from death. At least...this time.

"Son!" Sweat soiled the man's already dirty uniform. A dark streak ran down one leg where he'd wet himself. His wild-eyed gaze pleaded with the others. "Think this through. You don't want to do this."

Oh, but he did. He'd dreamed of the day he'd humble this man, lived for it for centuries. He'd be denied no longer. "You have been sentenced to death."

The man panted faster than a cornered animal. "Pietas, don't do this! Don't let those animals loose on me!" He jerked and bucked, but the twins gripped his arms, preventing him from breaking free. He trembled in their grasp. "Son, please! This is barbaric! They'll rip me to pieces!"

Pietas got in his face, holding the terrified gaze. "The verdict is murder of another immortal. The sentence is death in like fashion." He withdrew the knife from his pocket.

Relief spiked, but faded with a whimper.

Pietas knew a thousand ways to kill with a knife. None pleasant.

"No! Don't do this! I'm your father!"

Had Mahikos savored his children's impotence, his children's begging the way Pietas now savored his? Dark, haunting, brimming with terror. Delicious. "Though I've trotted out your sins as a father for everyone to hear, you are judged today for the murder of Tiklaus. I do not stand before you as your son. I am your executioner." He pressed himself against the accused and angled the knife before his face. "Take a good look. See the rust? The dull edge?"

Mahikos shut his eyes.

"Look at it!"

Face screwed up in fear, the man squinted.

"When you cut my friend, *Father*, you used this weapon." In one swift move, he flipped the blade, caught it in his fist, and rammed it straight into the remorseless pit of his father's heart.

As the light faded from the man's eyes, Pietas gave the knife one savage twist.

Chapter Forty-three

Pietas wiped blood from his face. He relished his victory even as the stench of death rose in his nostrils. Wrapping his arms around the inert body, he lowered it to the floor.

As one, the panthers surged closer. Their riptide of bloodlust dragged Pietas from the shore of sanity into the churning hatred of berserker rage.

Pain. Chains. Cages.

Horrified screams rent the air.

Blood!

Pietas grabbed the corpse by one arm and dragged it toward himself and the tribe. They surrounded the body, each member snapping and snarling.

People shouted. Voices rose. Words mutated into noise.

A call arose. A plea. A need.

Blood. Justice. Vengeance.

He tore open the man's shirt.

The tribe cried out all at once.

Jagged pain ripped through his left leg. He clutched it. He'd taken no wound yet he recognized the pain--a vicious kick. An Ultra had kicked one of the tribe.

Someone gripped Pietas by the arms, dragged him up, away.

No! Bad! Bad!

The tribe converged on whoever held him. They dropped him again, screaming.

The moment Pietas was released, Tiklaus and the tribe surrounded him, licking his face and hands, nudging him toward the body.

Duty! Blood!

He crawled back but Koliga had crouched over the corpse, risking bites from hungry jaws. Pietas shoved him but Koliga grabbed onto the body and refused to release it. The man spoke, but the sounds held no meaning.

Pietas fought to speak, but the tribe's feral mind-link held him captive. He had tribe-words. *Blood. Duty. Promise.*

Tiklaus wedged itself beneath his arm. *Blood! Duty!*

Pietas gripped the animal's ruff and set his face against its snout. Neither had words: emotion, need, hunger--those ruled.

Vengeance bound them. Duty to their own kind separated them.

If he refused the blood-ritual, he lacked tribal honor.

If he fulfilled the blood-ritual, he lacked Ultra honor.

Pietas. Joss's thoughts intruded into his. She went down on one knee beside them. *Help me understand. What do you need?*

His joining with her weakened his bond with the tribe, yet their clamor for vengeance still inundated. Surely, she saw it. *Ritual. Help.*

Her calm became his. Her strength girded his. Her resolve underscored his. *You must do this. Right now, their honor is more important than ours.* Joss touched his cheek, brushed aside his hair. "Everyone, get back!" She stood, began moving people away. "They won't eat him. It's blood-justice."

Pietas opened himself to Tiklaus, presented a heart-vow to honor his promise. The link eased, loosened, freed him. Words returned. He motioned to Koliga.

"Move."

With a look toward Joss, Koliga climbed off the body and scuttled aside on hands and knees.

Pietas pressed one hand into the gore on his father's chest, then held out the dripping hand to Tiklaus.

The panther crept forward, casting glances at the Ultras.

"They won't stop you. I give you my word."

The cat came to him.

"Taste your vengeance." He remained motionless while the big cat licked away the blood.

The animal ended with a lick on Pietas's wrist and then sat. Blood debt paid, the rancor and ire faded.

Tiklaus immediately shifted attention to a cat that lay on its side licking a wounded flank. After touching noses, Tiklaus licked its face and glared at Michel.

The tribe beheld the man as well, ears up, tails out.

Pietas pushed himself to his feet. "I guess we know who kicked the panther."

Gaze downcast, Michel remained where he was.

Pietas approached him. "Why?"

"I thought they were going to eat him." He still did not look up.

"You damaged the bond I had with them. It sent them into a frenzy. I nearly lost control."

Michel peeked up. Eyes the color of dark honey beheld him without fear, but full of shame. The gaze lowered again. "I'm sorry, Pietas."

"Injuries in the tribe are paid with blood. That panther has the right to draw yours."

Michel's head popped up, mouth open. "I just wanted them to stop."

"I didn't understand the need for blood until Mahikos died. They are one. Hurt one, you make enemies of them all. You must appease them."

Michel lifted one shaking hand and rubbed his face. "If-- If I let him bite me, will that work?"

"Try."

"Should I-- Do I have to do anything? Say anything?"

Pietas took in the tribe, but sensed nothing from them beyond resolution. "Try an apology. They understand."

Michel dropped to his knees beside the injured panther.

The cat blinked at him. A sense of forgiveness, of comradeship permeated the air as sweet perfume. The tribe settled, watching. Tiklaus came to Pietas, sat beside him and butted his hand.

He rubbed the cat's ears.

"I'm sorry," Michel told the other cat. "I acted without understanding what you needed. I was wrong. You can bite me." Squeezing his eyes shut, he offered his hand.

The cat leaned closer to Michel, sniffed his palm, then rested its chin in his hand.

Michel lifted one eyelid, then the other. A smile crossed his face. "He forgave me! Look!" The animal nudged his hand. "I promise." He stroked the cat. "I will never hurt you again."

The tribe dismissed its agitation all at once. Calm skimmed the room in a wave.

Tiklaus stretched out, chin on its front paws.

Held in Dessy's arms, Helia wept while Joss stood beside them.

Pietas crossed to the women. "Mother."

His sister motioned for him to wait. "Not now, Pietas."

His mother hid her face and cried with renewed vigor.

"Mother--"

"Not now!" Dessy rocked their mother, sheltering her close. "This is not the time. Let her grieve."

How could anyone grieve over Mahikos?

Joss came around from behind the women and took his arm. She led him away a short distance. "She isn't grieving over him."

Did she hear his every unspoken word? Between her and the ghost, he could have no private thoughts whatsoever.

"You'll just have to get used to that. Try not to look at her."

"Used to-- Never mind. Why not?"

"It's not your father she's grieving over."

"Then who?"

"You."

How was it this woman could speak in riddles and expect him to understand? "What are you talking about? I'm quite alive."

"Not as she's perceived you. Today, she saw what your father made you."

"Are you telling me she didn't know I was a killer? Half the galaxy knows that."

Arms around their mother, Dessy led her from the area.

"Pietas." Joss linked one arm through his. "She'd never had a personal view before. I was connected to her when you killed him. Your anger--" She squeezed his arm. "It overwhelmed her. I'm sorry, Pietas, but she was terrified."

"Of me?" He slapped his chest. "Joss! I would never hurt her!"

"I know." She released him. "But for that instant, she didn't."

"I need to go to her. Explain."

She squeezed his arm. "No. You need to let her deal with her emotions. Dessy will be there. You finish what you have to do here." Joss sent him a mental caress. *"Perform your duty to Six."* She crossed the cavern.

Pietas took a moment to calm his mind and gather his thoughts.

When he had, he returned to the body. Lifeless, Mahikos looked small, weak. Not the tyrant who'd towered over him as a child. For one instant, he longed to kick the man as his father had kicked him as a young man. Instead, he bent and yanked out the knife. It dripped with blood.

"Six, will you come here, please?"

His friend picked his way around the others. When the ghost reached Pietas, Tiklaus walked around the human, sniffing his legs. Though Six kept an eye on the animal, he showed less fear than he had before. The cat sat at Six's feet and wrapped a tail around his legs. It gave Pietas a serene blink.

Six lifted one hand, hesitated, and then gave Tiklaus a single pat. The panther arched beneath the ghost's hand.

"Well, well. Looks like you're the pet now."

"Very funny." Six patted the cat again. "Nice kitty."

Tiklaus sneezed.

Six yanked back his hand. Keeping an eye on the cat, he sidestepped. "Look, Pi, I'm sorry you had to do that to your dad. I know he deserved it and you had to, but--" Wincing, he looked up. "I'm just...sorry."

"Thank you, my friend, but that man was never my *dad*, merely a sadistic drill instructor. How like you to have pity on a man who would have killed you without a second thought." As he, himself, would have done at one time. He took no pride in the realization. When everyone looked their way, Pietas placed the bloody knife across his palms and offered it. "By our law, you have no right to address Mahikos in trial, but as a warrior, you have the right to wear your enemy's blood."

His back rigid, Six looked from the knife to Pietas.

"*Mira*, Six. Watch." Holding the weapon in one hand, he motioned bringing the blade across his own chest like a sash. "It's not required. The point is to remind your enemy you bested him. You won. It'll dry as black as the mask I wear. Whether you wear his blood or not, this is yours to keep. But I'd sharpen it first." He offered the weapon again.

"Bested, huh?" Six accepted the knife and dragged it from his own left shoulder toward his right hip, once for each side of the blade. Scarlet smeared his chest. He stuck the knife in his belt and then crossed his arms, head held high.

Pietas gave a nod.

Armand and Philippe were on their knees petting a panther.

He crossed to them. "You two pulled me away, didn't you? It was you they attacked."

The twins looked up. Armand nodded. "This one--"

"--attacked," Philipped concluded.

"Were you hurt?"

"Fine." Armand responded. "The cat--"

"--is our friend," Philippe finished. They both continued petting the panther, which licked each of their faces in turn.

Even at a distance, the bond forming among the three had a tangible presence. How appropriate that one panther chose to bond with them both.

A guttural cry meant his father had entered the burning agony of rebirth. "Good. He's reviving."

The man writhed, grimacing. Mahikos never made an attempt to shield others from his suffering. How weak. He displayed pain as if it were a badge of honor, instead of shame.

Six sucked air over his teeth. "Geez, that must hurt."

"Rebirth is worse than electrocution. Humans think because we come back from death, dying doesn't matter. They have no idea."

Mahikos cried out. He never had been good at bearing pain, only dishing it out.

"How long does this go on?"

"Rebirth?" Pietas wiped his hands on his shirt, but it was bloody as well. "Until after midnight."

"Really? Geez! It didn't take you that long. In the pod or after you came out of it."

"Pardon?" He drew back.

"You died so many times during the voyage. I lost count, but you never thrashed around."

"Six." He leaned in closer, lowering his voice. "Did I cry out?"

"You?" Six swore. "Never! But I felt it every time you died. At first, I thought the ship was haunted."

"Haunted?"

"My skin crawled worse than passing a graveyard in the dark at midnight." He shuddered. "Wasn't till I realized you were awake in that pod that I put two and two together and realized I was feeling you die."

"I had no idea you could feel that. I'm sorry."

"What could you do about it? Worst thing I ever experienced. Knowing you went through that, over and over because I was 'doing my job' as a ghost."

"Six!" Pietas clutched a fist over his heart. "You mustn't blame yourself. The traitors who locked you in with me-- they're responsible for what we both suffered. I'm glad it was you I ended up with, but I'm sorry they betrayed you in order to betray me."

"No way, Pi." The man held up his smallest finger, measuring the tip of its dirty nail with the other hand. "That much. That's how much honor they have compared to you. You owe me no kind of apology. No kind whatsoever."

How he treasured this man. He would never get over the luck of gaining such a beloved friend from the ranks of such a hated enemy.

Six adjusted the hang of the knife in his belt. "Do I ever want to go through that again? No. A hundred times no. Him, though?" He jerked his head toward the body on the floor. "Whole other story."

"So you don't have the same feeling now? You're not experiencing his death?"

"No. Maybe I ought to feel sorry for him, but I'm having trouble doing that."

He tapped Six's chest. "Don't lose sleep over any pain he suffers. He deserves worse."

"Go clean up, Ultra." He made a face. "You're covered in his blood. Got to stink."

Pietas chuckled despite the situation. "Yes, it does." He held up filthy hands, pulled out his shirt and examined it. "I need a shower. Like to burn these clothes."

Six patted a pocket. "Firestarter's handy. I'll help." He popped over to his backpack, which rested near the cave wall, and returned with the metal box holding their last sliver of soap. "Gonna take scrubbing to get that off your skin."

In truth, his skin would slough off any foreign matter but he didn't have the heart to spoil his friend's generous gift. He accepted the box and gave Six a quick bow.

"Finished?" Joss took his hand. "We can visit that waterfall and bathe."

Six lifted one eyebrow. "We?"

Joss gestured between herself and Pietas. "This we."

The man's mouth twisted. "Spoilsport."

She shot Six a bemused look. "Ready, Pietas?"

He accompanied her to the exit.

"Pi!"

He paused and turned back to Six.

The ghost turned toward Mahikos. "You're just gonna leave him there?"

He puzzled over the question. "He's being punished."

"Punished. So that's justice to Ultras? You kill him and then let him flop around and suffer?"

"Told you." Pietas grinned at Joss. "He's a softie."

Six motioned to himself. "Standing right here. I can hear you."

Joss tapped Pietas on the chin. "I think he's sweet."

He snorted. "You would."

"You two *can* see me, right? I'm not an *actual* ghost."

"Tiklaus." Pietas stooped. When the cat came to him, Pietas went down on one knee. "My friend, will you keep watch over Six while I'm away?"

The panther nose-bumped his chin.

"Thank you." He stroked the panther, meeting Six's gaze. "He needs protecting."

His friend made a comical face. "Whatever."

"We won't be back tonight." Pietas stood and took Joss's hand. "Get some rest. In the morning, Father stands another trial."

"Another one?" Six swore under his breath. "Wasn't that enough payback?"

Pietas scoffed. "Certainly not. I owe him far more vengeance than I can unload in one killing. But tomorrow, he'll account for a worse crime."

"What's worse than murder?"

"We have no hope of leaving this world for many lifetimes. *Centuries.* He knew it would happen. He planned it. He marooned us here so he could be king."

Mahikos twitched and drooled. One by one, the Councilmembers looked down at the man with disgust.

Pietas made a dismissive gesture toward his father. "At his next trial, it won't be me he has to face."

Chapter Forty-four

Pietas stripped and carried his bloodied clothing into the cold pond. Once he was knee deep, he stopped and drew a deep, calming breath, letting the peace of the moment sink into him.

Like a thousand quiet children whispering, the fall of water softened the chirp of crickets. Above, the glimmering stars shone down on a world made gray by the rising moon. Its light cast lengthening shadows, turning the waterfall into a slice of silver on inky velvet.

He held the bloodstained shirt and pants--long since borrowed from Six--beneath the numbing water. The falls beat the soil and blood from his skin. He angled the shirt this way and that, but the bloodstain's outline remained. Soap might help, but why waste it on himself? The small metal box sat untouched on a boulder back on the pond's edge.

Joss, who had stopped by the camp to pick up strips of cloth to use as towels, arrived and waved to him. She set down her bundle, stripped off her uniform and draped it over a big round boulder. Nude, she waded toward him.

If she hadn't been a warrior, she'd have been a brilliant dancer. Full of grace, lithe, supple, smooth, she possessed generous curves in all the right places. The dimming light deepened her body's shadows.

Halfway to him, she hesitated, turned around and went back. Pulling at a fastener in her hair, she worked it through tangled golden curls and tucked it into a pocket on her uniform.

Water splashed around her calves as she waded toward him, running fingers through her hair. Her pale curls released in a cascade of silver, catching the moonlight.

He tossed his soiled shirt and pants over a boulder, freeing his hands. Had there ever been a more beautiful woman on any planet in the galaxy?

Joss looked straight at him, her pleasure at his thoughts washing over him.

He opened himself to her rising desire and sent a *sidere*, the most intimate telepathic caress. Among all the lessons in pleasure she'd taught him, this delighted him the most. Sending her an unexpected *sidere* across a room always sent a flush of color to her cheeks. He loved the game of sitting in a meeting while some speaker droned on about *whatever* while he and Joss secretly engaged in loveplay.

More than once, they'd left a room and met in some hidden, out-of-the-way location for a silent, lusty tryst. He grinned at the memories that evoked.

Joss joined him in the icy deluge and pressed her body against his. Her warmth next to his cold skin sent a blast of heat through him. She lifted her mouth to his in a leisurely kiss.

When they broke apart, she touched his chin. "Thank you."

"For?"

"The *sidere*. And for thinking I'm beautiful."

"The *sidere* is pure pleasure. You can't thank a man for knowing the truth."

She beamed up at him. "I *adore* you." Taking his hand, she drew him deeper into the falls--and behind it, into the dark.

Pietas jerked from her touch and burst back into the air, gasping as if he'd held his breath too long underwater. Heat flooded his face. Why could he not face one moment of darkness? Was he a useless chi--

No.

He put the epithet far from him. A man must take credit--or blame--for his own actions. He was damaged. He'd turned into a craven, horror-stricken, useless coward fearing monsters under the bed. What a--

Stop it, Pietas. You are no coward.

He flinched at the presence of Joss in his thoughts. If only he could spare her from his cowardice.

Joss stood before him. *You have never been a coward. You will never be a coward. Ever. Look at me.*

He turned away. "Don't pretend I'm not damaged."

"Of course you're damaged!" She put herself in his line of sight. "Look at me."

"Joss, don't." He turned away.

"Pietas, you spent over a year imprisoned in Stygian darkness. Of course it damaged you. That doesn't make you useless, a child, or a coward. It makes you vulnerable."

"I can't be vulnerable!" The cold air bit his skin. "I'm a king."

Anger sparked from her, not at him but at those who'd betrayed him. "I know you think so, but a king with no heart and no fear is no king."

He hesitated.

Pietas, please. Joss touched his arm. *Let me hold you.*

Not worthy of you, Joss. You should go.

I am never going to leave you! You are more than worthy! Tears spilled onto her cheeks. *Ultras don't suffer the loss of limbs. They grow back. But your sense of self, of who you are, even what you are-- They stole that from you. Please don't let them get away with it.* She brushed away tears. "Fight back! Let me help you. You *are* worthy! Please don't let them win!"

"*Shh.*" He cupped his hands around her face. "Don't cry. I'm not worth crying over."

"No!" Joss threw herself into his arms. "That's not true, Pietas."

Her anger on his behalf shamed him. How could he let her down?

"You're not letting me down. You're facing what humans face when they're injured. Sometimes they can't come back from it. They fade away. Humans kill themselves because the pain never stops. *You* are a fighter." Joss gripped his arms. "Nothing defeats you. Nothing. You will beat this. Don't ever say it's cowardice. It's self-protection, and that's all it is. Your mind refuses to allow you to put yourself in any situation where you might be trapped. You can overcome your own mind."

"Joss... How can I lead our people when I'm afraid to take one step into the dark? I'm not fit to be king. I'm not the man I was."

"Of course you're not the same!" She brushed back his hair. "You're better than you were. Look how you restored your relationship with your sister. The old Pietas would have never done that."

That part might be improved, but look at him. He was a mess.

"You are not, but you could learn some new skills."

"Skills?" He frowned.

She took his hand. "Let's start by showing you how to escape if you're ever trapped again."

That he could use. "What do I do?"

"Begin by taking stock of your surroundings. It's safe where you are. You can breathe. You can take a shallow breath, can't you?"

"Yes."

Take one with me. She breathed in and out and he copied her. *Now another.*

He took it.

Look into my eyes. You are safe here, Pietas. This is a safe place. No one will hurt you here. You can breathe as deep as you want. Take a deep breath now and let it all out.

He did as she asked.

Good. Take another. Let it all out. You can go anywhere you want to go. You're not confined here. She merged her thoughts with his. He was not-her, not-him, but them.

At her thought-suggestion, he sucked in another big breath, closed his eyes, and released it.

Let's go for a walk.

Alongside Joss, he followed the falling water. It cascaded over rocks and gathered at the fall's base, then splashed over one edge to flow down the caldera's sides. It trickled alongside the trail partway down to the pods, ran off to one side and fell not far from the towering units. On the lowest level, it skirted around them and out into the crater basin.

They strolled along a narrow path, following smooth stones. The water had carved a wider track in other seasons and they ambled along its dry banks. Tall grasses rose on one side and he dragged one hand across their tops as he walked. They tickled his palm. The quiet of the caldera at night released calm. The scent of grasses came to him on a gentle night wind. Far up on the caldera's rim, two panthers sat side by side, their silhouettes stark against the moon's light. From down here, they seemed unreachable.

As they did on every world, nightbirds swooped overhead, scooping insects from the sky. Orange and lavender slashed the western horizon, fading into rich, royal purple and up into darkest black, a backdrop for the diamond-white scatter of unrecognizable, alien stars.

Pietas opened his eyes--and flinched. He'd been standing on the floor of the caldera and now he was halfway up it, back at the waterfall's base in ankle-deep water. He blinked a few times.

"What was that?" He turned to Joss. "How did you do that?"

"That, my love, is how a master telepath does a *kueshda*."

The telepathic quest he'd attempted earlier bore little resemblance. He shook himself. "You took me out of my own skin. I've never experienced that before."

Joss extended both hands and he accepted them. "I didn't keep anything back. You needed to escape."

"Can you teach me to do that?"

"I couldn't have before, but I can now. You're ready."

"Six is always saying, 'Wow.' It's all that fits."

"I'll teach you how to do a deep *kueshda* on your own. In case you're trapped."

"Thank you."

"Knowing you can get out, even if only in your mind, helps you bear it when you're confined. Pietas, no one can take your mind from you--unless you let them."

"I'm sorry."

"Don't ever apologize for being hurt." She squeezed his hands. "You were injured, physically, emotionally and morally."

"Morally?"

"You knew our people would surrender if you did but you had no other choice. You blame yourself for us being here." She touched his chin. "Am I right?"

He clutched a fist to his chest. A hard knot formed in his stomach. "That memory invades me. It's a cancer. Can't force it away but can't stop looking at it. Plays in my mind over and over. How could I have won? What else should I have done? How did I fail? Why couldn't I see the truth? Why couldn't I make anyone believe me?"

She moved aside a lock of his hair. "If one of your soldiers had been in the same situation, would you have punished him?"

He wanted to say "yes" but could not. "It's not the same thing."

"What's different?"

"I don't expect as much from others as I do myself. I should have been better. Stronger. Faster. Wiser."

"You aren't at a point yet where you can forgive yourself, but one day you will."

"Never. I destroyed our people. I deserve no forgiveness."

Joss moved into his arms, soothing him with her warmth. "You believe that now but one day you'll understand. It might take time, but you have plenty of that. You need to let yourself face the memory and accept that it was out of your hands. You are *not* a god." She met his gaze. "You're immortal, not infallible. You're worthy and you can heal. You will heal."

He stood there in the moonlight, holding her, naked, freezing in ice water, marooned on an alien planet with insurmountable odds to face. Yet with Joss at his side, he counted himself the luckiest man in the universe.

"How I love you. Thank you for those honest thoughts."

He kissed her. *I love you.* He slid his fingers through her wet hair. "Joss, when we first connected, I caught a glimpse of what's behind the waterfall."

"It's a great spot."

"So I saw." Pietas swallowed. He wanted this. Wanted freedom from fear of any *thing*, any *place.* "Take me there."

She hesitated, but didn't question. Joss released one hand and led him back toward the falling water, then behind it, into a pocket with walls carved smooth by the falls. The rush of water quieted. Through reflection and refraction, the chamber held light yet was cut off from the outside. Like looking out through frosted, moving glass.

Not confining at all.

"Joss!" His voice echoed. He could breathe. The chamber held plenty of air. The top soared far overhead. "This is huge. Impressive. How did you find it?"

"Luck, pure and simple."

"You have a knack for finding private places."

"Telepath. I'm happy being alone. Plus, no wind." She held one hand beneath the falling water. "It's quiet here and the water is less cold."

"Cold?" He grinned. "Who's cold? Seeing you, definitely not me."

She broke into a huge smile. After twisting her wet hair into a tail, she tossed it behind her. Water droplets glistened on her skin and sat like jewels on her lashes. She brushed them away. Flattened, darkened by water and swept back from her face, her gorgeous hair took second place to her huge blue eyes and generous mouth. The cold water had darkened her lips, left them wet and inviting.

"The way you're looking at me..." Joss trailed fingertips up his arms, "I don't need telepathy."

"No?" He cupped her chin, leaned in, and dropped a kiss on one side of her mouth. *Maybe so, but feel free to tell me--* he kissed his way across to the other side *--if I miss a spot.*

Chapter Forty-five

The moon was setting when Pietas and Joss emerged from the hidden cave. Holding her hand, he lifted it to his mouth and kissed it. Once they reached the water's edge, Joss unfolded a cloth and handed it to him. They toweled each other dry.

He helped her towel her hair and gather it. Once she'd pinned it up, he drew her to him.

She turned and kissed him. "I have a surprise for you." She tapped him on the chin. "And no, not *that* kind of surprise. Here." She picked up a bundle of khaki-colored clothing and held it out to him. "Put this on."

"What is this?"

"A Councilmember field uniform. Dessy and Six have been working on it for a couple of days."

"They did this for me?" He handed her the pants and slipped on the shirt. Longer than his usual, but otherwise, it fit well. After getting out of the water, he dried his feet and then took back the pants. The waist had room to spare but the pant legs hung to the tops of his feet. "I'm in my own uniform. This is wonderful! I look like an Ultra again."

"Turn around. Let's see you."

He turned in a slow circle.

Joss clapped. "You look gorgeous."

"You're the one who's gorgeous." He pulled her naked body into his arms and kissed her. "Thank you for this."

"I'm the delivery person. You should thank your sister and Six."

"I will." He released her. "I can't believe Dessy did this for me. Six, I could see. He has a servant's heart." He slid his hands along his uniform. "Which I love about him. But Dessy? I'm stuck saying 'wow' again."

"Your sister loves you, Pietas. You should never forget that." She pulled on pants and drew on her tight-fitting undershirt.

He held her outer uniform shirt for her. When she turned to face him, he slid the backs of his fingers along her skin. "Need help with those buttons?"

"Thank you." She pushed his hand away. "I can handle this part."

He smirked. "So could I."

Laughing, she shook her head at him. "Shall we rescue your other clothes or leave them for the water to beat into pieces?"

They still hung over a rock beneath the falls. "They're rags. Six won't want them back. Not now." Pietas ran his hands down the smooth cloth. "So these belonged to Armand and Philippe?"

"Philippe donated the pants. Armand gave the shirt. Or was it the other way around?" She paused. "Anyway, we looked but no one in camp has shoes your size. You could use the twins' shoes for a catamaran on the lake."

He chuckled. "I don't mind going barefoot. Although Six pointed out if someone mentions Father, I step on something or twist a foot."

"Really?"

"Happened several times while Six and I were hiking. One day as a test, he randomly slipped in the word 'father' and I tripped both times. Unsettling that he has so much influence."

"Yes, it is." She took his hand. "You want to try sleeping for a while? We'd have to go back to camp. The upper cavern is taken. The twins wanted to go up there with--"

"Stop. I do *not* want that picture in my head."

They arrived in camp a short while later to find Michel on duty by the fire. The pods had been moved back inside the cave. Koliga slept in the one Mahikos had used. Pretosia perked up and regarded Pietas from his sleeping mother's pod. Off to one side, Tiklaus lay beside Six, who slept on the ground, his backpack serving as a pillow. The cat looked at Pietas, then went back to sleep.

"Joss," he whispered. "I thought you said Dessy was with the twins." He pointed. "She's in her pod."

Joss glanced around. "I guess they went alone. That's odd."

Michel waved to them from the side and they joined him. "They're not alone. They took your father up to the other cave."

The back of his neck tingled. "Did they say why?"

"To take care of him. Thing is, he had recovered, but they insisted he needed personal attention." Michel shrugged. "I wasn't telling them no."

"I see." Pietas headed for the moonlit the trail leading to the cavern.

Joss slipped her hand into his. "I'll go with you."

"Thank you, but I'll handle it." He stopped, kissed her, and drew her hand to his lips. "It's my responsibility. Stay here. Get some time alone. I know you need it." He touched her cheek. "I'll be back."

He waited until she walked away before resuming his pace. If the twins were doing what he thought, could he stop them?

He'd prefer to watch. Or help.

Chapter Forty-six

Constant shielding kept voices out of Joss's head. For the most part. Since the trial, that had dwindled to never. Shielding required energy, gained through sleep and food. The best rejuvenator, time alone, had disappeared since Pietas arrived. Also, largely thanks to her desire for him, sleep.

Tonight, with the camp resting and Pietas checking on his father and the twins, she had a rare moment to herself.

After the trial, the frayed emotional state of the Council had blasted through every vestige of her protection. She'd isolated Pietas to calm him not merely for his own good, but also hers.

In the past few days, he'd gone from a fledgling telepath to a powerful one. She could no longer shield against his thoughts.

How had he gained the ability so fast?

She'd learned the rudiments of shielding within days after her creation. Joss had studied, practiced and honed her telepathic skills for centuries. She'd mastered her craft, but Pietas had reached an astonishing level within days. Nothing in her experience explained the rapidity of his change.

Some outside force was at work. But what?

Across the camp from her, the darkness itself moved.

She caught her breath.

With a flash of green, a panther padded past.

She released the breath and rubbed her eyes. Were the panthers strengthening his telepathy? Perhaps the bond he'd developed with Tiklaus had altered him.

She poked the campfire's embers with a stick. Sparks rose, bright in the cool night air.

A scuffling noise preceded Six's human scent. Moments later, he ambled into view, bow in hand. Scratching himself, he yawned. Upon seeing her, he halted. "Oh, sorry. Thought I was the first one up."

Joss motioned to the ring of flat-topped stones circling the fire. "There's plenty of room. I don't mind."

Tiklaus peeked around the upright pods, then disappeared behind them.

With another yawn, Six plopped down near her. He set down his bow and held out his hands to the flames. "Cold in the cave."

"I bet. You know, Six, you're the single person whose thoughts I can't hear. It's refreshing."

"You hear everybody?"

"Unfortunately."

"Must suck to be a telepath. I'm not even close to being one and I get tired of it."

"Tired of...?"

He tapped one finger to a temple. "Overhearing Pi."

She tossed the stick into the embers. "Overhearing. You mean his thoughts?"

"Yeah." Six rubbed his hands together. In the firelight, his dark eyes looked black. "But just Pi."

"Just..." Like a lock with the right key, the mystery of Pietas and his enhanced ability tumbled into place. "You can hear Pietas but you can't hear anyone else."

"Yeah."

"But he can't hear you."

"Weird, huh?" He yawned again, stretching both arms over his head.

"Not at all. No one can hear a *plenos*."

He froze, arms up. He lowered them in slow motion and wrapped them around himself. "A what now?"

"A *plenos*. In ancient proto-languages, it meant ample or full. It became amplify. In Naro, the Ultra language, it means to amplify or enhance psy-powers. Or, in this case, a person who can do that."

Six cast a look behind him, back at her. He pointed to himself. "Me? I amplify telepathy?"

"Yes. A *plenos* amplifies abilities in one person--his *lemma*--to a great degree, and to a lesser degree, the abilities of others."

"Some kind of telepathy booster."

"I suppose that's one way of seeing it, but you boost other psy-powers too. Clairvoyance, apparitions, extra sensory perception."

"I don't have ESP."

"True, but you enhance it in others."

"Don't say that. That's not true."

"I'm afraid it is."

"No, it isn't!" He leaped to his feet and headed away from her.

"Who was it, Six?"

The ghost stopped, and without turning back, swore in Spanish.

"Six." Joss leaned one hand on the stone beside her. "Whom did you frighten? Was it when you were a child?"

"No one. I didn't scare anybody. Don't know what you're talking about." He stood there, silent. After a moment, he turned toward her. "Look, it wasn't my fault! I was a baby. How was I supposed to control anything?"

She motioned to the place where he'd been sitting. "Why don't you sit down and tell me about it."

Six stared at her but then perched on a rock, feet tucked up close, arms around his knees, face hidden.

How frustrating not to know what bothered him. Was this what human counselors faced? How could they help someone without knowing the problem? She called on all her patience and waited for him to say the first word.

"I've never told anybody about this. I don't want it broadcast."

"I'm good with secrets."

Though he didn't speak, she felt him take her measure. "My birth mother."

"You frightened her?"

"Yeah."

"What happened?"

"I didn't know until shortly before I became a ghost. I'd gone home for good-byes. I knew if I died they'd tell my family I was missing in action. I'd never see them again, so I went. My birth mother was there."

"I see."

"She told me why she'd abandoned me as a baby. The real reason." In the firelight, his eyes blazed with pain.

"Go on. What did she say?"

"After I was born, every time she held me, she could see ghosts."

"Spirits?"

He bit his lip, nodding.

"And that frightened her."

"Wouldn't it scare you?"

"I imagine it would. She said that's why she didn't stay?"

Six swallowed. "She called my *abuela* to come get me. Left. Never came back."

"Oh, Six!" Hands pressed together, Joss brought them to her lips. "I'm sorry."

He kept his head down, not looking at her. "Said she came to see me because she wanted to know if I was still cursed."

The ignorance of humans! "What did you say?"

"Told her what she could do to herself." He cracked a smile. "She jerked back and went all who-do-you-think-you-are righteous on me. I told her she gave up the right to judge me the day she put her newborn baby down on the floor and walked out on him." He cracked his knuckles. "Felt kinda good, saying that."

"I bet."

"I thought she was full of it when she told me that ghost bit. But since I'd already signed up to be Ghost Corps..." He shrugged. "Thought she'd had an omen, maybe. But that didn't give her call to leave me on the floor like trash."

"You must have been furious when she said that."

"You think?" He braced his elbows. "I never met a telepath until Pi. Since we got here, where you guys are, his thoughts have gotten stronger. I can't *not* hear him."

"That's because of me."

He looked up.

"Plus you and me in combination, Six. Either one of us has abilities on our own, but when you combine a master telepath and a *plenos*, it's putting fuel on a fire. Anyone in the vicinity with even a smidgen of psy-talent will develop it."

"So the others? Are they getting...?"

"Koliga is. He asked me about it this morning. Said Pietas told him not to finish people's sentences."

"What happens to his ability when I die?"

She'd grown accustomed to Six being there. He'd become one of them. Yet he wasn't. Enhanced, but not immortal. A deep yearning swept over her. One of the worst things about human friends was missing them before they were even gone.

"His ability will fade. Over time, he'll return to the way he was."

"Oh." Six rubbed his eyes. "Guess he'll have to find another... Sorry. What am I?"

"*Plenos.* We might not find another for hundreds of thousands of years."

His face screwed up in confusion. "Why?"

"You're as likely as ice on the sun." Joss picked up a stick and poked the fire. "Less than one in tens of billions. In my lifetime, I've read about two. Never thought I'd meet one." The fire blazed up and she added a bigger stick. "Ironic, isn't it? I'm the master telepath and you're the *plenos*, but we can't hear each other. Or can you hear me?"

"Nope." Six shook his head. "Quiet."

The flames danced, bright orange in the darkness. "Did you get any sleep?"

"Thought I wouldn't, but the minute everyone else slept, I was gone."

Neither of them spoke for a time.

Six gathered a few pieces of wood, brought them back and began stacking them in the fire. When he finished, he dusted off his hands. "I have a coffeepot in my survival kit but I ran out of coffee three days after we landed. Been using it to boil water. Sure could use a cup right now."

"I try not to dwell on the things I'll never have again." She rested her elbows on her knees. "Too depressing."

"Oh, you can have coffee. I spotted a grove of trees a day or so before we connected with you guys. Just needs harvesting and prep work."

She sat up straight. "Are you serious?"

"Yeah."

"How wonderful! How long does it take?"

"Once the beans are ripe, you have to pick them, sort them, spread them out in the sun and let them dry. That takes a few weeks. Then there's hulling and cleaning. Some more sorting. After that, you roast them and they're ready for grinding."

"Roasting? Like in an oven?"

"We can make stone ovens. They're easy. The grinding will take equipment, but Lig says he can build a grinder from things we have in camp."

Joss put away her knife. "That's something good to look forward to. But we can't start until we make headway on the cryopods. Those are a priority."

"I work better with coffee."

"Me too."

Six rubbed his chin. "Does Pi drink it?"

"He pretends to when everyone else is having some, but he pours a splash into his cup, stirs in half a dozen sugar cubes and licks the spoon."

"So no priority for him."

"Sadly, no. He'll put it low on the list of must-haves. Although... He might if he knew it would make me happy."

"What makes you happy?" Pietas strolled into view, Tiklaus beside him.

"Coffee," they said in unison and smiled at one another.

"I see." He reached down and scratched the cat's ears. The huge animal leaned into the caress. "Once we free everyone, have food laid in and shelter built, sure."

"Told you." Six shot Joss a look.

Pietas dropped down beside her, leaned closer and gave her a kiss. The cat stretched out at his feet, chin on paws.

"Hey." Six gave a thumbs-up. "Uniform is lookin' good."

"Thank you." He ran his hands down the front. "I hear you helped with this."

"Glad to. Tell me you trashed what you had on before."

"I left them by the waterfall. Didn't think you'd want them back with *his* blood on them."

"You're right about that, but you're wrong about the coffee. It's low priority for you, but it's high for us."

He frowned into the fire, looked at Joss, back at Six, his handsome face puzzled. "Why?"

"Armies run on coffee. It's how you start the day. You work with it in your hand."

"I've observed that. I assumed it was habit."

"It's more than that," Joss added. "It's camaraderie. Soldiers reminisce over coffee. Even Ultras use it to wake up. The caffeine doesn't affect us, but it's part of the ritual."

"So you don't need it for nutrition. It's for relaxation and morale."

Six mimed drinking a cup. "It's a thing."

"How many beans would we need per pot?"

Six rubbed his chin. "If we all drank it, and rationed it to a pot a day, we'd need at least two small bags per week."

"How would we bring back enough beans to make it?"

"Best bet, you'd pick them there, lay them out to dry, hull them, and then bring back what's left. Less weight to carry. By volume, half the weight of coffee is hull. More efficient use of resources. We could transport it easier. You said you left the shirt and pants by the waterfall. We could sew up all the openings except the tops and use them as bags. Lig and I were talking about sewing some of the material from the pods to transport crops. He knows how to build looms, but we'll need lumber and other tools. We'd have to make looms anyway. Our clothes won't last." Six stood and stretched. "You two hungry?"

"Famished."

"Breakfast, coming up." Six picked up his bow. "I'm going hunting." He patted his thigh. "You coming, Tik?"

Tiklaus nudged Pietas's hand, bounded over to Six and trotted alongside him.

"Tik? Tik?" Pietas threw up his hands. "That man nicknames everything."

"Yes, he does. He's in love with you."

He hugged her. "It, not he."

"Your friend is hardly an it."

Pietas stiffened. "I thought you meant Tiklaus."

"How odd you didn't know I meant Six."

He studied her in silence.

She hadn't heard his mindvoice since he'd arrived but until this moment, hadn't noticed. "Impressive shielding, Pietas." She released his arm. "What are you hiding?"

"Mother said he loved me as well." He slid his hand into hers, entwining their fingers. "I assured her she was wrong. I know him. It's respect. Honor between men. I've lived so long, gender distinctions have far less importance, but I can respect them in others."

He was a master at not answering direct questions. "Everyone in camp has fallen in love with you at one point or another."

What an endearing blush he had. "Flattering, but untrue." He drew up their hands and kissed hers. "My parents and sister are here."

"Other than your family, then. Although your sister might be an exception."

His startled gaze flew to hers. He narrowed his eyes.

"Pietas, you haven't kept up with her over the years. I have. Did you know she's never taken a lover who isn't tall and has blond hair and blue eyes? The twins are a prime example."

He withdrew his hand, cheeks darkening. "What are you suggesting?"

"I'm suggesting her girlhood crush on her big brother never faded. She's unconsciously chosen lovers who at least superficially resemble you. Or her father."

"Don't be insulting." He stood and held out his hands toward the fire.

"You should ask her about--"

"I have no intention of asking my sister any such thing."

"Pietas, hear me out. I'm trying to--"

"Forget it, Joss! I'm not asking that."

"Pietas?" Dessy approached them from the left. "Not asking what?" When he didn't respond, a mix of panic and mistrust rolled off her. "Joss? What's going on?"

Michel and Koliga walked into the clearing, speaking to one another. They halted and cast curious looks from Pietas to Dessy and then Joss. An awkward silence fell over the gathering.

His sister frowned. "Pietas? Is something wrong?"

"It's the trial." He turned his back on the fire. "It's postponed a week."

"Why? Is Father all right?"

"He's dead, Dess. He can't get much worse than that."

"I should check on him."

"Don't worry over it."

"Where is he?"

"I said, don't worry about him!"

The young woman flinched.

Pietas cast Joss a withering you-caused-this glance. "I shouldn't have shouted at you, Dess. Don't worry about

Father. Believe me, the twins are taking good care of him. Stay away and let them handle it."

The hint of satisfaction in the way he spoke told Joss his words had double meaning. She bit her lip to remain quiet.

When Pietas walked away, Dessy went after him. "Wait! Tas, where are you going?"

He checked his speed but did not stop. "Hunting with Six."

Chapter Forty-seven

Pietas spent a fruitless hour searching for Six before he thought of trying a *kueshda*. Having a skill didn't mean its use came naturally.

Crossing his arms, he stood under a tree and calmed his mind. He drew on what Joss had taught him about conducting a psychic search. He had viewed the general area from above, so picturing the canopy of trees took no skill, merely memory. As he had the night he'd made such vivid contact with Tiklaus, he searched for movement instead of detail. A disturbance to the east caught his attention.

He eased through dense scrub and entered the deeper forest. Scuffling sounds drew him. In a small clearing, he found Six, a rabbit dangling from his fist.

The man lifted the dead hare. "Gutted and ready. Breakfast for one."

Tiklaus pranced into view with two rabbits in its mouth and dropped them onto a pile of other prey.

"Show off." Six set his rabbit atop the pile.

The panther sat and groomed itself.

"Impressive, Six. There must be a dozen here. How many are yours?"

"Shut up."

Pietas chuckled. "That many?"

Six set about gutting one the rabbits Tiklaus had brought.

The cat took a sniff, sneezed.

"Okay, Pi. Why are you here? Thought you'd be with your girlfriend."

Tiklaus trotted over to Pietas and nudged him on the leg.

He stooped to pet the cat. "At least someone's glad to see me."

"Had a fight, did you?"

"No. I thought you could use some help."

With a scoff, Six stuck an arrow back into the quiver behind his shoulder.

"What does that mean?" Pietas stood.

"What does what mean?"

He imitated the scoffing sound.

"Oh, that? That's me saying you're full of--"

"Six! Why are you giving me grief when I came out here to help you?"

"Giving you--" The man lifted his hands, palms outward as if shoving him back. "Okay, fine. *Whatever.* You came to help me hunt rabbits." He prodded the pile at his feet. "There they are."

"What's wrong, Six?"

"Wrong? Nothing. Everything's perfect." He swept back his hair and began rearranging the dozen carcasses side by side. "Tik, I promised you first choice. Take your pick. Seeing as how you caught all but one."

The cat sniffed the long row, chose the one Six had caught and tossed it up in the air. It came down into the panther's jaws. Tiklaus carried it over to one side, stretched out on its haunches and began gnawing off the head.

Pietas was hardly squeamish about death, but seeing those fangs and knowing the purpose for which the cat had been designed left him queasy.

Holding the rabbit in its mouth and between front paws, Tiklaus gazed at Pietas. He could swear the cat dipped its head in acknowledgment.

Six tied the legs of the first rabbit together. "What did she say?"

"Who?"

"Your girl."

"My-- You mean Joss?"

"Unless you've picked up one of the other women since I left."

Stifling the urge to snap a retort, Pietas made a fist. "What did she say about what?"

"It's obvious you had a fight."

"We did not."

Six fixed him with a stare. "I thought you didn't lie."

"I do not. I did not argue with Joss."

The man studied him. "Define argue."

Why had he spent an hour looking for this man? Pietas refused to clench his teeth. "What makes you so sure I argued with anyone?"

"You're kidding me." He indicated Pietas's body from top to toe. "You're vibrating like high-powered machinery."

"Six!" He tightened his hands into fists but then flattened them atop his thighs. "I did not have a fight back at camp, but I am about to have one here."

"If not a fight, then what happened?"

Sputtering incoherent words, Pietas stomped across the clearing. Near the edge, he stubbed a toe on a bare tree root and hissed at the pain. Bracing one hand on the tree, he examined his skinned toe.

"*Ah*, I see. It was your father." Six wiped one hand on his jeans. "Should have guessed. Okay, give. What happened with Daddy?"

"He is *not* my daddy! I did not argue with him."

"Oh, really?" Six raised one eyebrow and looked pointedly at Pietas's feet.

The realization he had once again hurt a foot while talking about his father brought Pietas up short. Why did he *do* that? He straightened and then dusted off his hands.

The ghost went back to tying rabbits. "It's obvious something went down. You came all this way to find me, but now you're gonna pretend nothing's wrong? Come sit by Uncle Six and tell him what happened."

"Uncle Six?"

The man gave him a droll look.

"Fine!" He dragged himself over to Six and dropped down beside him. "They killed him."

Six continued looping cord around rabbit legs. "Who killed who?"

"Whom. Who killed whom."

"Seriously?" Six braced himself and looked over at him. "Grammar? Now?"

Pietas raised both hands in apology. "The twins. Until the trial, they didn't know Father was abusing us. They spent sixteen years making sure we were safe, only to find they'd been protecting a monster from prosecution while he abused two innocent children and hurt their mother."

His friend swore under his breath. "Are you saying they *kill*-killed him? Was it perma-death?"

"Six!" He drew back. "How can you say that?"

"Pardon me if I don't sympathize with that cutthroat. Literally." He drew a finger across his own throat.

"I'm not saying he doesn't deserve it." Pietas rubbed the tight spot between his eyes. "But I let them do it. I even encouraged it."

Tiklaus roused itself and padded over to him. The cat butted beneath his chin.

He scratched its ears. "I'm Chancellor. Lawgiver. Judge. If I dishonor the law, what does that say about my honor? I let them murder without repercussion. I put a stamp of approval on the same thing for which I tried Mahikos."

"I get it, Pi. You think you're condoning murder."

"Yes." He stroked the cat, but then halted. "What do you mean I 'think' I am? Don't you think I am?"

"Did you know it was happening but you decided not to stop it?"

"They'd already killed him." When Tiklaus nudged his hand, Pietas resumed stroking the silky fur. "When I got there, he was recovering."

"Well, then you didn't have anything to do with condoning it."

"No, I didn't. At least, not that death."

"Um, Pi? Explain 'that' death."

"They'd killed him on Armand's behalf. Once he heals they're going to kill him again--for Philippe."

Six clapped a hand to his forehead.

"I know." Pietas stroked Tiklaus under the chin. "I shouldn't let it happen."

"No, I suppose not." Six swore again. "Too bad. If anyone deserves it..." He broke off, folded his hands and leaned elbows on his knees. "Maybe you misheard. The way those two share words, you could've made a mistake."

"I wish I could agree. Unfortunately, I obtained clarification. I even told them about a case where someone did that and made sure the person was fully healed before they started on him again. I told them it was blood-justice."

"I could see you saying that. Seems to me it is."

"You do?"

"He used them to hide what he was doing. I've heard a fraction of the abuse he put you through, and in my opinion, he deserves death."

How gratifying to hear his friend defend him. "Thank you. But does he deserve to die twice?"

"If he's done what you believe he's done and betrayed your people, he deserves to die and never come back. In my opinion, you shouldn't stop them. You made sure the panthers got blood-justice. Why not the twins?"

Pietas contemplated the situation. He'd left the man to the twins' mercies. Mahikos lay in a broken heap, twitching, drooling bloody spittle, crying out as his bones snapped and popped, knit themselves together and reformed. Painful to hear. Agony to suffer.

Pietas had been through it, dropped from the air chained inside his pod. He'd slammed into the ground, bounced and rolled down a hill; all while being smashed side to side like a pebble in a can.

If immortality was a blessing, the torment of rebirth was its curse.

Could he wish that pain on his father -- again?

For hundreds of reasons, he told himself. Through a haze of remembered beatings, starvations, forced marches, and confinements, a voice broke through. Pietas sat up straight. "What?"

"I said, how did they kill him?"

"They pummeled him until they broke almost every bone in his body."

A string of Spanish swear words mixed with a few choice ones from other languages. Six tied up the last rabbits. "I wouldn't want those two mad at me."

"Nor would I." His father had been beaten to death by two men he trusted. Two men he had used as pawns as he had used his own family. Used his son. "So why do I feel guilty?"

"Because it's not your father you're worried about."

"Then who am I worried about?"

"Don't you mean 'about whom am I worried?'"

So, his friend did know proper grammar. Good. Despite the situation, he smiled. "Seriously?" he echoed.

With a wry grin, Six stood and picked up the string of rabbits. He worked at fastening the rope to a stout pole.

Pietas rose and brushed off his new pants. "So what is it, Six? Why am I feeling guilty?"

"First, you're worried about what'll happen if the others find out you knew but you didn't do anything to stop it."

"You're saying I should tell them."

"I wasn't finished."

Pietas reached for the rabbits but Six pushed his hand away. "Let me. You'll get blood all over your new clothes. I'll carry them."

"I can--"

"Just say 'thanks, Six' and let it go." He set the pole on his shoulder, allowing the line of rabbits to hang behind him.

Pietas clenched and unclenched his hands. "Thank you, Six."

"There, don't you feel better?"

"No."

"Didn't expect you would."

Tiklaus raced ahead and disappeared into the brush.

"You figure it out yet, Pi?"

"What?"

"The second reason you feel guilty."

"Because I didn't stop them from killing my father."

"Pretty dense, Ultra." Six elbowed him. "Do I have to spell it out for you?"

He rubbed his temples, fighting a headache. "Apparently."

"You can't accept feeling angry, so you label it guilt. You've felt it so long you can't tell the difference anymore."

Pietas halted in his tracks. "That's preposterous. Of course I'm angry. Who wouldn't be? My father used me. He used my sister. My mother. Every single one of us. He's selfish, hateful, egotistical, maniacal, and he'll stop at nothing to get his way."

"You and I both know your father deserves every lick he gets. You're mistaking guilt for anger because you're angry with your mother."

Pietas threw up his hands. "My mother? How could you say that! What are you, some kind of psychiatrist? 'Your problem's with your mother, Pietas.' Ludicrous. For your information, I love my mother. She's the most gentle person I've ever known. No one could blame her for what happened. She's as much a victim as my sister."

Six squinted at him. "Interesting. You see your mother and sister as victims, but not yourself."

"I failed them. I should have been stronger. I shouldn't have let him hurt them."

"You were a kid. It wasn't your job to protect them. It was your mother who should have done the protecting."

The world went white. Sound hollowed. "Six, that is not true. He hurt her."

"Okay, so maybe your mom was afraid. Maybe she was threatened. But beyond being a trained scientist and a warrior, she was a mother. I know you love her. I love her and she's not even my mom, but she stood by and let you and your sister suffer."

"No." Fury coiled its twin tails of ferocity and rage around his heart. Pietas forced himself to breathe at a normal pace, refusing to submit to base emotions. "You heard how she tried to get out. Her fingers bled, Six! She suffered as much as we did."

"Oh, I don't doubt that. At least that *one time*. Somehow, someway, she should have stopped him. Killed him. Gotten you and your sister out. How? No idea, but my *abuela* would have found a way and she was an old woman. In your heart--" Six paused. "Pi, I'm sorry. I know you don't want to hear this and you don't want to believe it. In your heart, your anger isn't with your father. Your anger's with *her*."

Where heat had unfurled, the chill of winter's ice now resided. He drew himself up, chin lifted. "You dare say that to me?"

"It's true. You know it."

He could not pull in enough air to breathe. "What I know"-- he forced out --"is if I'm angry with anyone, it's an idiot who'd blame my mother."

The man had the gall to look at him as Pietas were a disappointment. "Look, Pi--"

"My anger is with you."

"I'm sorry, but--"

"Save it! I should never have come out here. Why I wasted time looking for you is beyond me."

Six reached for him but Pietas knocked his hand away.

"Do not touch me, human."

"Pi, don't do this."

"My name is Pietas. *Pee-ah-toss*. Get it right!"

"You need to listen."

"No." He drew himself up. "I need to protect my family."

"Will you listen?"

"No!" He backed away. "Do not come near me. Ever. Do you hear me?" He turned and walked away. Near the forest's edge, he paused, but did not look back. "I should never have let you live."

Chapter Forty-eight

Putting Six's lies far from him, Pietas walked, paying no heed to direction. He refused to consider the man's hateful, twisted words. How could an Ultra be so blind to human failings? There was no room for liars or humans in his life, and that ghost was both.

Pietas had been desperate. It was that simple. The ghost had taken advantage of the situation. The man had made a pretense of friendship.

In a moment of physical deprivation, Pietas had mistaken the ghost's so-called kindness for friendship. He'd let his guard down.

How could a human be anything but duplicitous?

Out in the forest, Tiklaus kept pace with him, but did not come close. The cat appeared on first one side, then the other. It sat in the path ahead of him and when Pietas reached the spot, stood and put itself beneath his hand for petting.

Promise.

He stooped to scratch the panther's ears. "I'm sorry, Tiklaus. I know I promised to play, but I'm not in the mood right now." He kissed its nose and continued walking.

Promise.

"Yes, I know, I promised."

The cat bumped the back of his knee, knocking Pietas off balance. He kept himself from falling, but once he faced the cat, it sneezed and pawed the ground.

"What is wrong with you?"

Promise. Play. Chase. Tickle.

"Fine. I can see you won't be put off. We'll play." He took off his new shirt and tossed it over a low bush, then got down on his knees.

The cat came to him, rubbed up under his jaw. He rough-housed with the cat, wrestling, pulling its ears and rubbing its whiskers. By the time he'd worn out the cat, Pietas had worn out himself. He remained on his back, chest heaving.

"Best exercise partner ever." He rested on the sweet grass beside the panting animal, petting and stroking. Pietas leaned on one elbow. "You need a name for me the way I have for you. If you call me by name, I'll stop and play." He stroked the cat. "Do you understand?"

Tiklaus stared straight into his eyes and blinked. *Do.*

A command understood and carried out. A type of, *"Yes, sir."*

"You understand. Thank you, Tiklaus."

The green eyes blinked lazily, watching him. *Promise.*

"I'd like to know the name now, please. Name me."

The cat put out one huge paw and set it on his hand. *Promise.*

"Thank you. I'll wait. But don't bump me from behind anymore."

Tiklaus lifted its paw and set it back. *Promise.*

"You want me to promise you something?"

Do. Promise.

All at once, the meaning struck him. His throat tightened so hard he couldn't breathe. He sat up. "You mean you already have a name for me. I am Promise."

Do. The cat sat opposite him. *Keep. Promise.* It put out a paw and Pietas took it. *Keep. Care. Protect. Promise.*

"How you honor me!" The cat's paw held in one hand, Pietas tapped his other over his heart. He tried to speak, got choked up and had to start again. "May I never fail to live up to my name in your eyes."

Chapter Forty-nine

Joss stopped sharpening her knife and listened, sure she'd heard whistling. Though she searched the aether, she found no trace of Pietas. He wouldn't be whistling anyway; Six would. The *plenos* displaced no psychic space, making him untraceable to telepaths, but his human scent, faint as it was, preceded him. With it came a hint of animal blood.

The ghost's head appeared first as he came up the incline. He whistled some merry tune, sauntering with that easy stride of his. When he caught sight of her, he slowed, the whistling stopped and his usually cheerful face rearranged itself into one of somber concern. In silence, he continued toward her.

No sense of Pietas behind him, though surely he would be. She stood and stretched up on tiptoes. No sign of him on the slope near the falls.

"Hi, Joss." Six had a pole over one shoulder and a dozen rabbits hung from it. He manuevered it around and stuck the end on the ground. "Still hungry?"

"Famished. Although I sincerely miss food I don't have to skin first, these look delicious. Nice and plump."

"Thanks. Tik caught them."

"All of them?"

"I helped. I stomp around and when the rabbits run away, he catches them. I mean, it catches them. Pi insists Tik's not a he."

"Where is Pi?" She gasped. "Oh, I meant-- Where is Pietas?" She sidled closer to him. "I can't believe he lets you call him that."

"Yeah, well..." Six scratched his neck. "He and--"

"Six!" Koliga called to him. "You brought breakfast!" He came over and examined the long string of rabbits. "What a great catch!" He gave a loud whistle, summoning the others. "Food!" he bellowed. "Need some help over here!"

Marjo popped around the upright pods, took a quick look, and waved to the others. She jogged over. "About time. We were starving."

"Hey, Six!" Michel came running. "Wow! Look at this catch!" He slapped him on the back. "Thanks, buddy." He took the pole. "Lig, let's get started on these. Marjo, get the fire going."

"I'll help."

"No, no." Michel squeezed Six's shoulder. "You did the hunting. We'll prep." The three shot big grins toward Six and headed for the campfire.

Erryq waved at Six as she joined the others.

Six had perked up when greeted, but now his shoulders slumped.

Joss indicated the slope on the opposite side, leading down to the pods. "Want to walk with me?"

"Yeah. Why not?" He fell in step beside her.

They walked without speaking for several minutes. Six stumbled but quickly caught his balance.

"What happened?"

"Big rock there." Six pointed. "Didn't see it."

"You know that's not what I meant."

He stared straight ahead and kept walking.

Joss kept pace beside him. "I might not be able to read you like I can the others, but you're broadcasting signals anyone can see." She clasped her hands behind her.

"Such as?"

"Head down, no smile. Not your usual loquacious self."

He lifted his hands. "You're worse than Pi. I don't understand half the words you people use."

"Talkative."

"Oh." He shrugged. "Me and Pi had a fight."

As if she hadn't guessed. "I see. Want to talk about it?"

"Not really."

"Is that why he's not with you?"

"Yeah."

They walked a bit further. "So where is he?"

He shrugged, glancing up at her. "Took off. Told me to stay away from him."

"So a serious fight."

"You could say that." Six stuck his hands in his pockets.

Without speaking, they walked halfway down the incline. Joss tucked an errant curl behind one ear. "Tiklaus with him?"

Six nodded.

She slowed and stopped, and he faced her "You know, Pietas has been mad at all of us at one time or another. All of us have been mad at him. It doesn't mean the end of your friendship."

The ghost looked away from her, his mouth tight. He swallowed, twice. "He called me--human."

Joss waited for him to say more.

He didn't face her. "I've tried to be better than that."

"Better than human, you mean?"

He glanced at her, the hurt in his eyes affirmation enough.

"Six, our people have been at war for centuries, but I happen to believe humans are noble creatures."

He gave her studious attention. "You do?"

"Given the opportunity and education to make good choices, they usually do. Much of the hatred between my kind and yours is borne of ignorance."

"Yeah." He rubbed his neck. "Seen that. They taught us lies about you." He added, "I mean you, collectively."

"I got that."

"Sorry."

"Don't be." She touched his arm, indicated the way back to camp, and they started back up the long slope. "It's been good, having you here. Before getting to know you, I think the Council thought humans all had tails."

Six glanced behind him. "I try to keep mine hidden."

Joss laughed aloud. Taking his arm, she leaned into him as they walked. "Pietas will come around. Give him time."

"I hope so."

At his wistful expression, she squeezed his arm. "Wait and see."

"I made him plenty mad."

"Did you?"

"Told him something he didn't want to hear."

Which could be almost anything. Pietas was as hard-headed as they came. If she asked what they'd fought about, he might evade or stop talking, so she waited for him to begin.

"About his mother."

"I imagine that set off a spark."

"More like a bonfire."

Oh, how Pietas needed this man's lightness in his dark life. "Tell me what you worry will happen."

His face screwed up. He scratched his neck. "I 'as kinda hopin' you'd tell me."

"Give you my opinion, you mean?"

"Yeah."

She stopped again and he took up a space before her. "Pietas is quick with praise and slow with anger. Once his temper flares it burns hot. Generally, though, after he's thought through a situation, he comes around. I'd never heard him apologize until he did to you. In private, yes, to me. Always. He's big enough to admit when he's wrong. In your case, I think he was trying to show us how much you meant to him."

"Oh, he's not gonna apologize. Not for this. I'd be surprised if he didn't kick me out of camp."

Worse than she'd thought. "Do you owe him an apology?"

The ghost remained silent for a time. "Don't see how. I told him the truth. Can't apologize for that, but I'm sorry it hurt him."

Before she could speak, a tide of emotional uproar cascaded over her. While with Six, she'd dropped her shields.

A jab of reflected outrage and fear tightened her chest to the point of pain.

She gripped Six's arm.

"Joss!" He steadied her. "What's wrong?"

She clutched her chest, rebuilding her shields as she gathered her breath.

Dessy hurried into view, shielding her eyes. "Joss!" The young woman waved both hands. "Joss! It's Father!"

Chapter Fifty

At the sound of falling water, Pietas sought its source, wending in and around trees and fallen logs. Bird calls increased as the sound heightened. A cool mist enveloped him long before he found the source. A forest pond and waterfall burst into view all at once.

"Look, Six, a--" Pietas silenced himself. He'd spoken out of habit, accustomed to having the human at his side, sharing every detail of every day. He'd soon break himself of *that*.

Tiklaus slunk into view and approached the pool's edge. It drank, waded into the liquid and watched a moment. With a snap, it pulled out a fish and carried the wiggling creature up onto the bank. The cat chewed off the head and finished the rest in three bites.

Shorter than the falls in which he bathed, this one cascaded over rocks the size of a small shuttlecraft and plunged into a clear pool so blue it rivaled the sky. A riot of plants grew around it; huge purple flowers with yellow centers that stuck out at crazy angles, a bird-of-paradise-type plant in electric blue, and a tumble of bright pink blossoms shaped like bells. Clustered in such a small area, the surfeit of floral scent glutted his senses.

Turquoise-backed hummingbirds skittered in and out. In the trees, birds chirped and called. One made a plaintive *weet-weet-weet* that resembled a fire drill aboard ship. Another answered with the *whoo-oop-whoo-oop* of a collision alert. Were they mimicking sounds heard aboard a ship? Had they been transported as part of terraforming?

He'd have to ask his mother about protocols.

Thinking of her brought Six's words back to mind. He shoved the loathsome memory back out again.

Tiklaus padded up to him and dropped a fish at his feet. The shiny bluish-green creature flopped around on matted grass. Two jagged tears opened its middle, thanks to the cat's fangs. It would die whether Pietas ate it or not.

He withdrew his knife, picked up the fish, and sliced off its head. He tossed that to the panther, who caught and downed it in one snap. Pietas removed the tail and dropped it.

Tiklaus gave it a sniff and gulped it down. After a healthy sneeze, the panther sat and groomed itself.

The rest Pietas cleaned and ate raw. He'd grown used to uncooked fish while hiking with--

No. He banished the name.

Staying outside the falls' splash zone, he washed his hands, cupped them and took a drink. Making a face at the fishy taste, he stripped. After hanging his clothes on a bush, he stepped into the frigid water and ducked under the short falls.

He climbed out, thoroughly chilled but clean. After sluicing off water, he squeezed as much out of his hair as he could reach. The dry pants stuck to his wet body but once he'd pulled them on, he set his feet apart, and took a deep breath.

Tiklaus sat nearby, alert, watching.

Pietas counted to twenty, breathing in and out, slowly, evenly. Relaxed, he brought fist to palm in a warrior's salute. The flat, mossy ground around him afforded plenty of room. The heavy shade and twining plants imparted calm, quiet.

Shifting his weight, he centered himself. He dropped his hands, turned them palms down and drew them up slowly before him, leading with his wrists. At shoulder height, he opened his hands palm outward and drew them back. He visualized a large ball of blue energy before him, cupped his hands around it, and pushed it, taking his time, thinking of form during the move.

With no more speed or force than falling snow, he eased through the meditative routine, each step as familiar as his own heartbeat. Like snowflakes, each layer built on the last, adding weight and power. A relentless fall of snow would cover mountains.

When he finished, his mind was at rest and his thoughts at ease. It had been too long since he'd practiced. The energy now residing within him had balance, harmony. He should teach it to Six.

He groaned. That intolerable human invaded every aspect of his life!

Calm ended, Pietas snatched up his shirt and donned it. The canteen Joss had given him was empty, so he filled it from the falls. The liquid had no taste, simply a clean feel on the tongue. He drank the entire contents, refilled it and clipped it to a belt loop. If he'd had this canteen while crossing--

"Stop it!"

He would not think about the long trip with-- He clenched his hands.

He needed control. Pietas braced himself against the driest side of a moss-covered boulder and focused on the clamor of birds and water. Though not tall, the falls sent sheets of water in strong rivulets, beating itself upon rocks below as if determined to shatter them. Where it frothed at the edges, the bubbles popped with the faraway tinkle of children's laughter.

An alien sound.

He'd never laughed as a child. His father had forbidden such nonsense and even his mother warned him and his sister not to laugh. *"Don't get into the habit. You might slip up when your father can hear you."* They'd both taken pains to avoid laughing. He might be amused now and then, but laugh?

Not until he'd met---

He groaned in frustration. Why must *every* recollection bring up that name?

Laughter was overrated anyway. A human weakness. He needed none of it. Pietas tore himself away and trudged back the way he'd come.

By the time he approached camp, the afternoon sun sent prickles of heat over his back and shoulders. He stopped at the lower waterfall to refill his now-empty canteen and take a drink. Once he'd filled it again, he washed his face.

Tiklaus, who'd remained at his side, lapped water. The tribe sent up a howl, and the cat streaked off, racing up the hill.

Pietas climbed the slope.

Everyone had gathered around the campfire. As one, they looked at him.

Six stood to the left of Joss. Beside her sat Armand and Philippe. Arrayed in the center, Erryq, with her flaming red hair contrasted with Marjo's and Koliga's dark skin. Dessy and his mother took up the far right.

Bloated and swollen from the beating, his father sat at Helia's feet and leaned against her. Bruises the color of old eggplant splotched his battered face.

"Pietas!" His mother braced both hands on her hips. "How could you let them do this to your father?"

Half turned away, Six refused to meet his gaze.

Joss covered her mouth with both hands.

Heads bowed, the twins did not so much as glance at him.

Dessy folded her arms.

"Well?" his mother demanded. "What do you have to say for yourself?"

Mahikos tipped back his head, looked down his nose at Pietas, and eased into a leisurely smile rampant with smug contempt.

Chapter Fifty-one

While his mother continued to berate him, Pietas remained calm, focused on the enemy at her feet, the serpent who'd whispered temptations in her ear. Mahikos had sullied her. Pushed her back to his own side and into bondage to his lies.

No matter.

Pietas was here now. He would save her.

He might be damaged but he'd survived. Nothing could destroy him. Nothing could stop him from saving his mother from this tyrant.

Again, his mother demanded he answer her.

He endured her rebuke and continued to observe his father. *Look away from the cold eyes of that snake? Never.*

"Pietas!" Helia screamed his name like a curse word. "Answer me!"

He would give no reason for allowing that fiend to suffer. The man deserved worse. Far worse.

That demon she called lover had deceived her. Used her. Twisted her heart. Set her against her own son.

For that, Mahikos would pay with his immortal life.

I will end him.

"I said answer me!"

He remained silent.

Helia stepped out from behind Mahikos. "Don't you dare ignore me, Pietas ap Lorectic! Look at me! Don't you dare disrespect me. You answer your mother!"

He changed his focus, then. If she knew him, she'd know silence marked his nimble mind at work, seeking the best angle, the best offense, the best chance for his lightning-fast reflexes to home in on the prey.

Patience rewards the hunter.

Low rumbling behind him meant the panther tribe had arrived. Seconds later, Tiklaus brushed up against his hand, then sauntered closer to the other Ultras and gave one short, barking *huff*.

Pretosia rose from its place and nudged Helia's hand. Without a backward glance, it followed Tiklaus.

"No..." Lifting a shaking hand, Helia took a faltering step after the small panther. "No one is loyal anymore."

Shaking her head, Dessy turned away.

Helia dragged a scathing look down Pietas's frame, whirled around and took a place beside Mahikos.

The man held up an unhealed, twisted hand.

Helia accepted it and stood behind him.

"Forget him." Mahikos's voice grated like metal scraping across rock. The twins had crushed his esophagus and it hadn't healed yet. "That boy's always been a failure." A retching cough tore from his throat. "And a coward."

His mother looked straight at Pietas. Her silence said more than words.

Mahikos turned Helia's palm toward him and kissed the center. "I should destroy him and breed you with another. This time, you might give me a child worth rearing. I'll just have to keep you pregnant until you do."

Like a panther's claws, a storm of black fury shredded every scrap of control. No sound, no taste, no smell.

One duty.

One focus.

One target.

Pietas wrapped his hands around Mahikos's throat and slammed him into the ground, bashed the man's head into the rock.

The hated snake eyes bulged, staring up in stark terror. Unhealed broken hands slapped uselessly. The twisted mouth contorted, gasping. Veins popped up on the red face.

Pietas accepted the pain tearing through his shoulders, down into his arms. Welcomed it as an old friend. Let it drive him.

He drew back one hand, stiffened his fingers and jammed them like a spear into the throat beneath him.

Again. Again. And again.

Hot blood spewed into his face.

He punctured skin. Jabbed flesh. Tore muscle. Ripped sinew. Gripped bone.

The world went black.

Chapter Fifty-two

The sound of a waterfall soothed Pietas in sleep. The warm softness beneath him offered rest. He relaxed on his mother's lap. She stroked his hair. He breathed easier, knowing she held him.

As children, he and Dessy sometimes lay on either side of her, their heads on her lap. When they weren't allowed to go outside, they'd take turns using the gift of illusion to create images for one another. His sister would conjure the likenesses of birds, while he favored dragons.

The image of a bloody throat and screaming face jolted him awake. He opened his eyes under a clear sky.

"*Shh.*" His mother pressed a cool cloth to his face.

He gripped her hand. When he levered himself into a sitting position, darkness closed in like a nightmarish tunnel. He held still for some time, aware she spoke but unaware what she was saying. When the blackness receded a bit, the world swam into focus.

It had not been his mother at all, but the petite Erryq. Her fiery tumble of red hair shone in the sunlight. None of her cute sassiness showed. She sat with hands folded, placid, demure, better behaved than he had ever seen her.

His head ached as if he'd slept on solid stone instead of a pleasant lap. "I dreamed-- There was-- Was any of that real?"

"You mean killing Mahikos?"

He nodded and an instant stab of pain made him regret it. "Feels like someone clobbered me."

"Sorry."

Intending to massage his neck, he reached up but pain in his shoulders stopped him. Bracing his back on a boulder, Pietas struggled to his feet. Splinters of hot pain shot through his head. Darkness blanketed his vision. Nauseated, he bent at the waist.

"Pietas, here!" Erryq, who barely reached his chest, wrapped an arm around him. "Lean on me. You shouldn't be up. Joss says you have a skull fracture. She's hoping it's just a concussion but it looks bad. She said it would've killed a human. You're supposed to rest."

"I can manage." His knees buckled. Bracing himself between the boulder and Erryq, he sat. Taking shallow breaths eased the nausea. Nothing assuaged the headache. He leaned back against the stone, wincing when his wound touched it. "Who cracked my skull?"

"Sorry."

"Stop apologizing."

"Sor-- I mean, yes, sir."

"Who hit me?"

"Me. I'm sorry, Pietas. I didn't mean to hit you so hard."

"You?" Concentrating made the pain worse. He rubbed the space between his eyes. "I had no idea you possessed that kind of strength. Was it a sledgehammer?"

"Rock." The tiny woman looked everywhere but at him. "Sorry."

"*Stop* apologizing."

"Sor-- Yes, sir. I'm sorry. I'm trying. I just-- I'm sorry." She covered her mouth.

He closed his eyes. "Where's my father?"

"Um... He's-- He's um..."

He forced his eyelids up. "Erryq, I'm not going to kill him again. At least, not today. Where is he?"

"With Dessy and your mother in the cavern."

He leaned forward, head in hands. "Is he perma-dead?" He held his breath, hoping. When she didn't answer, he met her gaze.

She gave one negative shake.

Six's favorite swear word came to mind, but Pietas refused to voice it. "How big was it?"

She squinted at him. "How big was-- Oh! You mean...the rock? That big." She indicated a size wider than her two hands. "I'm sor-- I mean... I didn't-- I wasn't trying to hit you that hard. I just-- I panicked. I'm sorry."

What irony. The unstoppable Bringer of Chaos laid low by a petite woman with a big rock.

"Pietas? How do you feel?"

"Don't worry about me."

"Joss told me if you said that, it meant I should."

How well the woman knew him. "No need. Although it doesn't feel like it this minute, I assure you, I'll live." He took care leaning back against the boulder.

"Pietas, lie down. Put your head on my lap. I'm softer."

He hesitated, but pain drove him to accept. "Thank you." He stretched out again and turned so he faced away from her. "Much softer."

She stroked his hair without going near the injury. "Everyone was trying to pull you off him but no one could get a good grip. Armand and Philippe tried to keep them from stopping you. They wanted him dead. Your shoulders and arms must be killing you."

His shoulders ached all the time. Nothing new. He pushed up his sleeves. Bruises ran the entire length of both arms. "I wish you hadn't stopped me. I meant to perma-kill him."

"Your mother was hysterical. She kept begging us to stop you." Erryq drew back the hair on his forehead and placed a cool compress there. "I'm sorry, Pietas. I panicked and grabbed the rock. I didn't mean to hit you so hard."

"Stop apologizing, Erryq. You were doing your duty. I don't hold it against you."

"You don't? Really?"

"You carried out duty with honor. I respect that. You need fear nothing from me."

She squeezed his shoulder.

It hurt, but if he said so, she'd apologize again. He closed his eyes against the brilliant spots filling his vision, but it did nothing to block the spectacle of light.

"You shouldn't sleep. That's what Joss said but maybe it would help you."

"No, it wouldn't." He asked the question nagging him. "Did the ghost try to stop me?"

"No. He kept clear of everyone. But he looked--" She didn't continue.

"He looked what?"

"Scared. Like he'd never seen you kill before."

"Oh, he'd seen me kill. I took out seven of his comrades before I came for him."

"Not like that. Not in frenzy. I'd never seen you lose it like that and I've been with you in a fight. All of us together couldn't stop you." She stroked his hair. "You were magnificent."

Magnificent. Not the word he'd have used. "*You* stopped me."

"The rock stopped you. I just held it. I hated having to hit you."

He patted her hand. "I'll live. Where's the ghost now?"

"Helping the others move two pods up to the upper chamber."

His eyes sprang open. "Why? Whose?"

"Armand and Philippe. After what they did, your mother said she didn't trust them."

"That's ridiculous!" He pushed himself up, but nausea swamped him. Bright sparkles appeared. Gingerly, he put his head back down. "They did nothing wrong."

"Where is he?" His mother's voice, distant, carried urgency. "Where have you put my son?"

He forced himself to a seated position.

"Pietas, don't." Erryq tugged at his arm. "You need to rest. You're in pain."

"Stop it." He pushed her hand away. "Pain is my ally."

"But, Pietas--"

"I can't let Mother see me like this. I have to be strong. She needs me." He pushed himself against the boulder, and clinging to it, got to his feet. His stomach lurched but he ignored it.

Joss's voice carried to him, too low for him to understand the words. His mother answered, her tone strident, angry.

Had pain altered his perception? He could understand none of what they said.

Erryq pleaded with him but he blocked out her words. If his mother needed him, he must go to her.

"Helia, please, don't!" Joss's voice came through clearly, from close by. "He's grievously wounded."

How could Joss say such a thing? He was an Ultra. A warrior! An Ultra did not need protecting. One did not coddle a warrior. Tend to wounds, yes. But fuss over him?

Never.

"Joss, move. I want to see my son for myself."

"Listen to me. This isn't the time. Let him rest."

Pietas braced himself against rock, forcing open his eyes. Light filled his vision. Sparkles danced into view. He wiped involuntary tears.

Weak. Weak!

"Joss, get out of my way!"

If his mother was taking time to see him, he must not let her see him falter. He must eradicate every vestige of weakness. He stood straight. He must not look weak. Not before her.

Where were his things? This room held no tables. No chairs. Nowhere to sit. "Erryq, where are the chairs?"

"The what?" She squeezed his arm. "Pietas, your eyes look odd. The pupils aren't the same size. You need to sit down."

"There's nowhere to sit. Bring in the chairs." He could not welcome his mother in a place like this. "She'll be angry. I can't make her angry."

"Who, Pietas?"

He tried to answer, but pain seesawed through his head.

"There's my little soldier," His mother's voice whispered in his memories. *"Soldiers don't cry, do they, Pietas? You're my brave boy, aren't you? Mother is so proud of you."*

He forced himself upright. He couldn't let her see him in this condition.

When he brushed off his shirt, he found it stiff. Blood had drenched him. He brought up one hand, then the other. Drying brown flakes had caked his hands and under his nails, between his fingers. His father's blood must be all over his face.

"You're unkempt, Pietas. Don't be such a disappointment."

He scrubbed at his hands but could not get them clean.

"Do not come to this table with dirty hands. Dirty children get no supper. Get out of my sight."

Helia came into view around a boulder, her bright hair like a white flame in the light. How beautiful she was. She wore intelligence like a crown.

Pietas came to attention. Out of habit, he tried to clasp his hands behind him, but his wounded shoulders allowed no such movement.

"Mother, I--"

Her slap almost knocked him to his knees. Pain lanced through his head, stabbing down into his neck and shoulders. Staggering, he fumbled for support against the boulders. He used them to right himself while she railed at him.

He'd let her see him soiled. Dirty. How angry she must be! He must clean himself up. "Mother, I'm sorry. I hadn't had time to bathe, but I will."

"You did this! You caused this! You fix it!"

In his pain-addled state, he struggled to follow her reasoning. The waterfall made its soft roar nearby. He could bathe there. The pounding water wouldn't hurt that bad. He'd suffered far worse.

"I'll go clean up and--"

She slapped him again.

He fell backward. When he cracked his head against the stone, darkness drew him into its embrace. He slid to the ground.

On hands and knees, he listened, silent, aware she spoke but unable to understand her words. Sticky, interlaced cobwebs of memory dried and cracked, falling away.

She'd struck his face, but his chest ached as if she'd taken a fist to his heart. His vision swam, blurred, faded. A cold knot tightened in his throat. Light bloomed around the edges of his vision.

Holding on to the boulder, he climbed to his feet, dimly aware that Joss and Erryq were staring at him.

"Pietas!" His mother stamped her foot. "You ungrateful brute! You did this to your father! You fix it!" She lifted her hand.

Heat rose in his face as he brought forth Zip. To him, time stopped. Up to now, he'd used the pseudo speed only against his enemies. Before she could strike, he gripped her wrist.

She flinched. To her, the grasp would seem abrupt.

"Mother, you will not hit me again."

"You fix this!" Helia tugged at his hold on her. "This is all your fault!"

He drew her against him, restraining her the way one would a petulant child. "Stop it! Explain yourself."

"Let go of me!"

He gripped her shoulder with his other hand and kept her immobile. Despite blinding pain, he still possessed Compulsion. As upset as his mother was, she lacked personal control. That weakened her immunity. The moment he sent the first tendril, Helia ceased resisting.

"What is my fault?"

"No one will help your father. He needs the Mingle but no one will take part. They're all too afraid of *you*."

"The Council? Afraid of me?" How he wished. "They acted wisely. No one should help him. He deserves to die."

Her mouth formed a silent O. She struggled to free herself. "How can you say that?"

"I killed him for a reason."

"Because you hate him! You've always hated him!"

When he released her, she stumbled. He made no attempt to help her.

"No one on the Council will help that snake because he deserves nothing."

Helia gasped. She tried to strike him but Pietas intercepted the blow.

"Enough of this!" He gripped both her wrists. "Woman, you become tedious. Don't you see what he's doing? He's using you. You've stopped hating him and gone back to defending him. Where is your backbone? Where is your strength?"

"How dare you say that to me? Yes, I went back to him. He needed me!"

Like getting ice water in the face, hearing those words. He released her as if burnt. "*He* needed you? Where were you when *I* needed you?"

Rubbing her wrist, she turned. "He was right. *You* are a cold, heartless monster! You appreciate nothing. You're a disgrace."

He had never been her good little soldier.

He had always disappointed her.

He had not lost her love.

He'd never had it.

The unwanted memory of Six telling Pietas his mother never protected him crept into his thoughts.

Pain seeped down into his chest. The air grew thin. He could draw in only enough for shallow breaths.

He stood on some fathomless precipice, his life hanging in the balance, and he had no choice but to go over the edge.

All that remained was whether he'd jump or be pushed.

The response he wanted formed in his thoughts. He'd prefer to keep the words inside, but he set them free.

"Mother, you are a fool."

"You have the insolence to stand there, covered in your father's blood, and say that to me? What kind of son have I raised?"

The brightness that had plagued his vision eased, but behind it crept the blackest ink. How could she not see the truth? The world constricted.

"If you had ever had the courage to stand up to Father, you'd have raised a different son."

She gasped. "How dare you! You have no idea what I went through, protecting you."

Those words pierced to the heart.

"Protecting." With a scoff, he patted his chest. "When did you ever protect me?"

"Your father was right. You're nothing but a merciless killing machine!"

"I'm sure Father would recognize such a creature, since he is one." He pressed the fingers of one hand against his brow, fighting the pain threatening to burst his skull. "He's poisoned you against me."

"It's not poison. It's truth. I watched you try to tear off his head. You tried to rip out your father's spine through his throat! I'm so ashamed of what you've become!"

Pietas dropped his hand and lifted his throbbing head. Darkness closed in around the edges of his vision.

Ashamed of *him?*

His entire life he had bent to her will. He had done every single thing his mother had told him. Learned every lesson. Borne every punishment. Suffered untold agony to save her.

And now, after she'd honed him into a warrior half the galaxy feared, she viewed him with shame?

"You should be proud, Mother. I *am* a merciless killing machine. Exactly what you and Father made me. But I should be ashamed of myself. I made a grave error. All my life, I thought you brought me strength. You brought me nothing but weakness."

"Do not speak to me like that!" Helia lifted her chin. "Don't come near me! Not until you've come to your senses and shown proper respect for your father."

Darkness gathered. Strength ebbing, Pietas pressed his back against the cold, impervious boulder. Fighting to remain on his feet, he clawed the heatless stone. Enveloped in darkness, he slid to the ground.

He reached out to his mother but then tightened his hand into a fist and tapped the middle of his chest--not his heart-- in grief.

Helia disappeared into the encroaching night.

All the light in his world faded.

Chapter Fifty-three

Rubbing her bleary eyes, Joss leaned against the opening of the upper cavern.

For two days, Pietas had slept, face down, arms tucked beneath his chest. The blanket roll where he rested was as smooth as when she'd left him that morning. He hadn't moved all day except to turn his head. The erratic flicker of his eyes behind closed eyelids indicated life. The vibrant leader who'd survived over a year of the most brutal confinement imaginable now lay still as death.

Dessy visited after breakfast every morning and sat beside her brother, stroking his hair. If he was aware of her presence he gave no indication. He didn't respond to Six's twice-daily visits either. With two exceptions, all the others came to see him, ask about him, touch him. Each one sat beside him and stroked his shining hair, as if that physical connection reassured them he was still with them.

Helia stayed with Mahikos.

Joss had loved her like a sister. She'd thought they were close. How had she not seen that Mahikos had twisted and manipulated her? Helia was not the woman Joss had cherished. This woman was alien to her.

Yet she could not get past the image of Helia attacking Pietas. Who in their right mind did such a thing? The woman had either tremendous courage, or incredible stupidity. Maybe both.

Each night, Dessy returned and looked in on her brother. She'd hug Joss and smile, but wouldn't speak. When pressed to tell Pietas the truth, she'd shake her head and find a reason to escape.

Armand and Philippe, who slept nearby, took turns guarding Pietas and following Dessy. Separated by duty, the twins couldn't speak.

After another two days, the fist-sized knot on Pietas's head went down. That night, he opened his eyes.

Giddy with relief, Joss supported him and gave him water. As Pietas drank, he looked up into her face as if trying to place her. Already slender, he'd become gaunt. The moment she let him lie down, he shut his eyes and slept.

For two more days, he awakened long enough to eat or drink, unless Tiklaus visited. Unlike Dessy and Six, the cat refused to be ignored. It butted Pietas with its head and patted him with an insistent paw until he woke.

At first, Pietas did little more than pet the cat. Once he'd healed, physically at least, he wrestled with the animal and put up with being mauled as if it were an everyday occurrence. Perhaps it was. The cat's fangs and claws ceased being a concern after the first visit. At the end of their "play" he had nothing worse than a few minor scratches that soon healed.

He talked to the cat like they spoke the same language. Tiklaus never made an outward response, but the keen eyes watched every move Pietas made.

Each time she observed them, a lump formed in her throat and she had to cover her mouth to keep from crying. What broke her heart were the glimpses of Pietas as he had been. Broken, yes. Damaged and alone, but alive, full of hope and striving for the future.

He'd become a shell of his former self. Once the cat left, the new, silent Pietas returned, shutting out every person and every thing.

While the world turned and time moved on, he slept.

Though he spooned her when she slept beside him, he did nothing more than hold her. Passion had never driven Pietas. Honor had. It had been like that since she'd known him. Even when he was younger he'd given more than he'd accepted, as if being loved was as foreign to his nature as breathing water.

Seeing him like this, it was she who breathed water. At night, after everyone was asleep, she climbed the cliff so the wind would carry away the sound of her crying.

In the cavern below, Mahikos fought for every breath, his ragged, torn throat healing layer by layer. Though Helia begged the others to share blood, no one complied.

There was a time Joss would have opened every vein to help her. Given her own life to save him simply because Helia asked. Not now. Not after hearing what he'd done to Pietas and Dessy. Not after knowing Helia allowed it. Not after seeing her attack Pietas.

Not after overhearing his fearful thoughts of being less than perfect. Of being a young child forced to drill like a soldier for long hours without rest, then sent to supper without having time to wash, and being forbidden to eat.

Her beloved king had lain crumpled, covered in dried blood, forsaken by the person he loved most in all the worlds. Tears rose unbidden and she dashed them away, furious with herself. Tears would not help Pietas.

She had to fight for him. Stay at his side. Support him. Bring him out of this lethargy and despair. Heal his broken spirit and mend his broken heart.

Pietas had lost his mother.

Joss had lost her dearest friend.

Helia was a scientist and a warrior. One of the most educated women in history. How had she let herself be swayed by that madman? How could she not have protected her children? How could she have been so cold and cruel to her son?

Since Mahikos had sworn he knew how to save those still encased in cryopods, the Council allowed him to remain in camp until he healed. After that, he'd be allowed to prove he knew what to do. If he failed, they'd hold him accountable.

But no one--no one--would help him heal faster.

While Six didn't offer to donate blood, he did take Helia water. She pulled back from him at first, but no one else had offered her anything. She took it. Pretosia brought her one rabbit each morning, but went away again right after. Six skinned and cooked the hare each day.

"Six?" Joss took his arm. "Tell me you don't feel sorry for her."

"Pi wouldn't want her to go hungry."

"He wouldn't want you to side with her, either."

"I'm not." Six picked over the meat. "She might have been a victim once, but she accepted the enemy's lies. I'm sorry if it's harsh, but from where I sit, she deserves Mahikos. After seeing how she abandoned Pi... She turned on him, Joss. She treated him like he was the enemy. I can't feel sorry for her. Even so--I won't let her go hungry. Not if I can help it. Pi wouldn't. She hurt him, but he'd see to it she was fed. I'm not doing this for her. I'm doing it for him."

When she didn't speak, he looked up at her.

"You're liked by everyone in this camp, Six." She squeezed his arm. "And you're a good friend to Pietas."

He pulled away. "I wish he believed that." He went back to what he'd been doing.

Joss approached the pod where the comatose Mahikos fought for every breath.

Helia, seated beside the man's inert form, did not look at her. "Either have pity and help him or go away, Joss."

"Pity? For him? He deserves nothing of the kind. You, however..." When she didn't continue, Helia looked up. "I worry about you, my friend."

With a scoff, Helia turned her head. "You were never my friend."

The placid indifference Joss picked up belied the anger on Helia's face. Joss had always assumed Helia's attitude of indifference was her true emotion. For the first time, she recognized it for what it truly was: an impregnable shield.

"How long have you hidden who you really are?"

Helia stood and after tilting back her head, met Joss's gaze. "How long have you known me?" With that, she walked away.

* * * *

Each day, Mahikos's body knitted itself back together.

Each night, a little more of Pietas unraveled.

Joss sat on the blanket roll and leaned on the cavern wall. While she watched, Pietas rolled onto his back and opened his eyes. One tear slid down over his temple. She had the impression he hadn't realized she was there. He scrubbed both hands over his face and sat up, drew up his knees and hung his arms across them.

A perfect picture of melancholy and depression, he sat in silent isolation, his thoughts shielded as if encased in iron. Not one emotion leaked.

The lie that had sustained him his entire life had shattered at his feet. His brilliant turquoise eyes had lost their sparkle. She'd welcome even a smidgen of their former joy.

The first time she'd seen him, he'd been sitting just that way. Abandoned, cold, wet, grimy, his shock white hair unkempt, frizzed and curling in the wet weather, pants torn, shirt so thin it looked more like a layer of dirt than cloth. When she'd spoken to him, he'd come to his feet with as much pride as a decorated war veteran.

He'd been all of sixteen, yet those beautiful turquoise eyes looked back at her from an ancient soul filled with pain. Her heart had gone out to him. Bruised and beaten he might be, but his ego was still intact. Since she'd known him, he'd never lost faith in himself.

Seeing him now, listless, mute, focused within... She wanted to scream for him to wake up. He had to come back from whatever pit held him prisoner. He was their hope!

No one else could pull them out of this state. No one else would have the will. If Pietas did not rally, their people would perish. They'd suffocate in those cryopods and waste away to nothing. Trapped within the very units that kept them alive throughout their treacherous journey to exile.

Without Pietas, the Ultras would vanish from the universe.

Permanently. Eternally. Forever.

He had never once lost faith in others. He'd always believed others wanted the best, as he did. His loyal troops would follow him over a wall into hell. If Pietas was going, they were going. If they fell short of his level of perfection, it puzzled him, but it didn't stop him.

That day so long ago when she'd first taken his hands in hers, her gift had revealed his path. Greatness. Might. Towering strength, in body and mind. Willpower beyond anything in all her centuries of experience.

With that single touch, she'd known legends would be written about this boy, once he became a man.

He must not lose faith in himself now. Not because of his mother's infidelity to her children. There had to be some way Joss could reach him. Some word she could speak that would restore his shattered faith.

All her life she'd searched for ways to quiet the mindvoices of others. A means of blocking the ocean of noise that filled her every waking moment. Yet here she sat, not an arm's length from her lover and king and he was silent as stone.

Joss stuffed a knuckle in her mouth and bit down, shielding as hard as she could, forcing back tears.

Pietas stood in one fluid movement and strode out of the cavern.

Heart pounding, she leaped up and went after him. At the opening, she ducked back inside and stayed in the dark, out of sight.

The legendary Bringer of Chaos and the ghost called Six faced one another across a gulf of mere handspans--and half a galaxy of hurtful words.

Six slid his canteen off over his head. As if approaching a feral beast, the man lifted it toward Pietas, easy, by small degrees, unhurried.

For long moments Pietas stood there, unmoving, unspeaking.

The image blurred. Joss wiped away tears.

At last, he reached out, accepted, and took a deep drink. Without a word, he walked to the edge of the cliff and sat, legs over the side.

Six settled in beside him.

When Pietas offered the canteen back, Six smiled.

Epilogue
An afterword from Pietas

Our master engineer, Lig, and his three-person crew have set sail in two small pods-turned-boats lashed together.

The day before, Tiklaus and Pretosia came before me. With great patience and many false starts and stops, they conveyed the message that Pretosia wanted to go with them. Koliga, Dessy, Mahikos, and Helia would need protecting. Tiklaus made it clear this was not for Helia's sake, but for Dessy's. Though my parents were kin, the panthers only considered my sister such.

Dessy was my blood, therefore part of the tribe.

Tribe protected tribe.

Pretosia would not go without my permission. Tiklaus had not assigned the duty, but approved. Who was I to argue?

My father had no patience with children. No reason to assume he'd tolerate a cat. Claws and fangs are no guarantee of protection against treachery and deceit. The fact that Pretosia is immortal does not make me rest any easier. The party will cross an enormous inland ocean. It is a long swim to shore.

Michel, Marjo, Six and I helped carry the boats down the outer side of the caldera and through the forest to the river. There, we stood on the shore until the party was out of sight.

They're heading for a vast, inland sea my father swears harbors a hidden city on its farthest banks. Left by the planet's terraformers, it holds tech and machinery which he promises will provide release for our people.

If anyone will know how to make use of tech or repair it, it's Lig.

When terraformers leave a world, they take everything, erase every vestige of their presence. Except on Sempervia? Why, unless it was planned?

Which proves what my sister and I believed. Our father conspired to come here. How else would he know about such a treasure?

I don't trust the man when he's in full sight, let alone out of it, but once again, the Council has overruled my wishes.

His complicity will be brought up at his trial, after he returns. If his promise is true and he can save our people, it might win him lenience from the Council.

Not me.

If he doesn't return as promised, I will hunt him down like the dog he is and kill him.

Every day.

Until his suffering bores me.

How I wish I could imprison him in a pod and seal him up in the middle of the stack. I'd let him rot there. A fitting end.

My mother would never forgive me.

I long for the bliss of ignorance, of being special to her, of holding esteem as her son, but thinking you are loved when you are not is embracing a lie. I must be as honest with myself as I am with others.

I must accept the truth: Trust is a lie when the person you trust is faithless.

For days before he left, I'd seen my father sneaking looks at me, one hand at his neck. Realization that I'd noticed him watching would show on his face and he'd drop his hand and look away. Right before he left, I happened to catch his eye and mimicked a bobblehead. His immediate fury was a delight to behold.

My wish for him is to never forget the sight of me hovering above him, ripping out his spine through his ravaged throat.

I don't want *my dear Father* to worry I'm coming for him.

I want him to *know* it.

Because he lacked the benefit of the Mingle, his wounds will scar him all his immortal life.

One day, perhaps the pain in my shoulders and arms will heal. But the wounds hidden within my heart will scar me forever.

Lig and Dessy have each sworn on their honor they will make him return, and they've promised to watch over Pretosia. Joss says I should trust them and Six agrees, but trust was never something I gave easily. Now, not at all.

Enemies do not betray you. Betrayal is reserved for family and friends.

Meanwhile, my people bake in the sun, awaiting release from their cryopod prisons. We are manually dragging away the damaged pods, stacking them the way Lig directed.

Six works beside me with as much fervor as if these honored dead were his own people. The work is backbreaking, but the memorial we build will stand for all time.

When each pod is placed, I commit the name of the person within to my memory. Most are people I know. Each time, I call out their names to the universe. The saying goes, *no Ultra has a soul*, but the universe is eternal and a life force given to it must surely rest once released.

It is as close to faith as I can go.

Yesterday, I read the name of my senior lieutenant, who served me faithfully for the past hundred and fifty years. At my side, he helped lead my finest soldiers, trained to the utmost in the art of combat. *Soomus Bellum. We Are War.* The elite of the elite. None better.

I pressed one hand to his nameplate and the other to my heart, too overcome with grief to continue. I know not how long I stood there before Six spoke, concerned I was unwell. All I could do was shake my head. Go back to work.

Today I found the other members of the cadre. All fifty perma-dead. Dropped from a great height, their delivery unit burst open and spilled its contents onto the sandy floor, shattering the frozen occupants.

Gone. Forever.

I will not forget any of them. Forgetting is not within my power.

I understand now, in a way I never had before, why humans mourn when a loved one dies. The finality of loss is crushing. How do such weak creatures survive it?

Six stopped work and looked at me, questioning.

I grabbed him and held on. I felt his hesitation, but he didn't pull away and after a moment, he hugged me back. When I released him, he stared up at me.

Not trusting my voice, I tapped a fist over my heart.

My friend echoed the salute, and at my side, went back to team-lifting the pods.

That my entire battalion was in this unit was no accident.

The pilfering scabs who robbed us meant it as a sign: The rule of Ultras is over. On the contrary, this act, above all others, sealed the doom of mankind.

The Ultra people will endure. Mankind will not.

Whether hot or cold, vengeance is delicious. I am known for my patience. I am immortal. Waiting means nothing. Treachery will be repaid a hundredfold.

I will avenge my people.

~ Pietas

Bonus: the Forged in Fire lyrics

This is the full battle song Forged in Fire performed by
Pietas.

Sung slowly in a minor key

Cast out upon a barren world, all hope of home forsaken now.
The rage of war has here begun. The vanquished cry as victors rise.
An Ultra's life is borne in grief.

*Raise high the shield. Cast out all fear. Our honor's choice will be
revealed.*
No dead to mourn. No debt to pay. The battle's won upon the field.
An Ultra's fate is built by strife.

There is no hearth. There is no home. No child to rock.
No love to lose. No peace to gain. The endless war becomes our own.
An Ultra's will is set in stone.

*We can't forget. We won't forgive. We must return. We shall
avenge.*
We never quit. We do not sway. Our enemies--we will repay.
An Ultra's heart is forged in fire. An Ultra's heart is forged in fire.
An Ultra's heart is forged in fire.

Don't forget to pick up Endure, Illustrated Quotes of Pietas!
https://kayelleallen.com/bro

Bringer of Chaos: the Origin of Pietas
Book 1 of the Bringer of Chaos series

Bringer of Chaos: the Origin of Pietas is shelved on Goodreads as Military Sci Fi, Sci Fi, Soldiers, Bad Boys, Adventure, Angst, and 6-Stars.

One reviewer wrote, "Watching Pietas and Six grapple through this deep dilemma was nothing short of beautiful for me. If these adversaries can navigate the chasm of hatred, distrust and male ego between them, maybe there's hope for our own fractured world. I called this a bromance, but it is much more. I highly recommend you read and find out why."

Why should Pietas end the war with humans?

His people are winning, yet they insist on peace talks. The Ultra people want to grant humans a seat on the Council. Pietas ap Lorectic, Chancellor of the High Council, War Leader and First Conqueror, disagrees. What's best for mortals is oppression, control, and if necessary, elimination.

Pietas seethes with rage at the idea of **human equality**. Humans might have created Ultras, but the creation has far surpassed the creator. Humans die. Ultras are reborn, no matter how grievous the injury. **They have no equals**.

His people permit him no choice. He must attend these insipid peace talks on Enderium Six and what's worse, be polite. To humans.

When a human special ops warrior is killed in battle, he's resurrected in a secret process and inducted into the Ghost Corps. He's given enough strength to perma-kill immortal Ultras. Ghosts are the most hated and feared of warriors.

When the ghost entraps and captures Pietas at the peace talks, **the two begin a long journey toward Sempervia**, an isolated and forgotten world. Once there, Pietas is marooned and the ghost abandoned alongside him. The two must either fight to perma-death, or join forces to survive. As Pietas comes to trust the human, an unlikely and awkward friendship begins.

Until he discovers how ghosts are resurrected...

The End -- or is it?

Thank you for taking time to read Bringer of Chaos: Forged in Fire. If you enjoyed it, please consider telling your friends or posting a short review. Word of mouth is an author's best friend and much appreciated.

Where else you can find Pietas

Pietas will be back in Bringer of Chaos: Watch Your Six
He has a fan page on Facebook
https://www.facebook.com/lordpietas/
He has his own board on Pinterest
https://www.pinterest.com/kayelleallen/bringer-of-chaos-pietas/

Download and print a Pietas and Six bookmark

Download a printable PDF bookmark from Bringer of Chaos. For Page Sizing and Handling, select "shrink oversized pages". (original art by Jamin Allen)
https://kayelleallen.com/media/boc-bookmark-double.pdf

Download Free Books

Join the Romance Lives Forever Reader Group
http://kayelleallen.com/bro/

Connect with Kayelle Allen

Kayelle Allen is a best selling American author. Her unstoppable heroes and heroines include contemporary every day folk, role-playing immortal gamers, futuristic covert agents, and warriors who purr. She writes Science Fiction, Science Fiction Romance, Mainstream Fantasy, Contemporary Romance, Gay Romance, and non-fiction. She likes to attend Science Fiction conventions, and has been a speaker at DragonCon, and Gaylaxicon. She holds an honorary lifetime membership to OutlantaCon, an Atlanta Scifi convention. Kayelle is the founder of the author-mentoring group Marketing for Romance Writers, and manages the successful Romance Lives Forever blog. Kayelle is married, has three grown children, and five grandchildren. She is a US Navy Veteran.

Have a question? Want to know more about something or someone in the book? Found an error or typo? Pop an email to Kayelle at author@kayelleallen.com
Website/blog https://kayelleallen.com
Twitter https://twitter.com/kayelleallen
Facebook https://facebook.com/kayelleallen.author
G+ https://plus.google.com/+KayelleAllen
Goodreads https://goodreads.com/KayelleAllen
Romance Lives Forever Reader Group
https://kayelleallen.com/bro

Cover and Copyright

Cover art, cover design, and book layout by Kayelle Allen
Courtesy of Depositphotos.com
Original art by Jamin Allen of Nimajination Studios
https://www.youtube.com/user/Nimajinationstudios/about
Story Editor: Patricia S Cook
Editor: Barb Caffrey

Disclaimers

Before You Say Good-bye...

When you close this book, you will have the opportunity to
review it, or share your thoughts on Facebook and Twitter. If
you believe the book has value and is worth sharing, would
you take a few seconds to let your friends know about it? If it
turns out they like it, they'll be grateful to you. As will I.